D1616991

THE WOLVES OF MEMORY

GEORGE ALEC EFFINGER

BERKLEY BOOKS, NEW YORK

This Berkley book contains the complete
text of the original hardcover edition.
It has been completely reset in a type face
designed for easy reading, and was printed
from new film.

THE WOLVES OF MEMORY

A Berkley Book / published by arrangement with
the author

PRINTING HISTORY
G.P. Putnam's Sons edition published October 1981
Berkley edition / November 1982

ISBN: 0-425-05628-7

To Beverly, who couldn't wait for the other one.
And to the memory of my father, whose waiting is ended.

The vilest deeds like poison weeds
Bloom well in prison air:
It is only what is good in man
That wastes and withers there.

—Oscar Wilde,
"The Ballad of Reading Gaol"

"I have come to die for your sins," Jesus told a stooped figure passing him on the road.

"Then what am I to die for?" the old man asked.

Jesus took a small notebook from his pocket and copied the question. "If I may have your name and address," he said, "an answer will be sent to you."

—A. J. Langguth,
Jesus Christs

* *ONE

When his arms began to get weary, Courane put the corpse down on the sandy soil, sat with his back against a rough warm boulder, and tried to remember. He closed his eyes for a long time, listening to the faint whisper of the wind blowing the topmost layer of sand toward the western horizon. Courane's breathing was slow and easy, and he was as comfortable as a napping baby. He breathed deeply, liking the hot freshness of the afternoon. A buzzing insect disturbed him, lighting on his ear, and he made a rather indolent swipe to chase it away. He opened his eyes again and saw the young woman's body.

He tried, but he couldn't remember who she was. Or who she had been. He couldn't remember why he was sitting in the hot sun with her. He examined her as well as he could without getting up and taking a closer look. She had been pretty. He couldn't tell how long she had been dead, but the irreversible effects of death had begun to distort her face and form. Yet, even through the grotesque deformity of her life's end, she touched him. Courane wondered if he had known her while she was alive.

There was a tiny movement near his left foot, and it attracted Courane's attention. Two tiny glass eyes peered at him from a pocket in the sand, a concavity the size of his thumb. A tan snout twitched and disappeared. Courane laughed. He loved animals. He stretched out on the ground and rolled over on his stomach. He rested there while quick-moving shadows of clouds skimmed over the empty landscape, covering him briefly like a dream of death. He closed his eyes again and slept.

The sun was setting when he awoke. He was startled and a little afraid. He didn't know where he was, and when he stood up and looked around he learned nothing. As far as he could see in every direction there was only flat waste, dotted frequently with broken boulders. There were no trees to break the lonely mood, nor even clumps of dry dead grass. Only a few feet from where he stood there was the body of a dead woman, a young woman with long dark hair and skin the bloodless pallor of the grave. Courane thought that there must be some reason they were together. There must be something in the past that connected them, man and woman, living and dead. He could not remember. He wanted to go on, but he didn't know where he was going. He was afraid to start walking until he did recall, and he didn't dare leave until he knew for certain if he should leave the girl's body or carry it with him. He wished that he could remember how he had gotten to this silent dead place.

Long after night fell, he realized that he was intensely uncomfortable. He sat shivering in the desert coldness, trying to identify the immediate source of his suffering. There was no way to measure time, and he didn't particularly care to know how many hours had passed, but after a few minutes he knew that he was painfully thirsty, and that earlier he hadn't been. Either that, or he had been but hadn't realized it. He patted his shirt absently, in a thoughtless searching gesture. He had nothing to eat or drink with him, but he looked anyway. He found a torn piece of paper in a pocket, with a message on it. It said:

Her name is Alohilani.
You and she were very
much in love. You must
take her back to the house.
keep walking east until you

get to the river. Follow
the river downstream to the
house. East is the direction
of the rising sun. They will
help you when you get there.

Courane read the note twice, not comprehending it at
all even though it was in his own handwriting. The wind
was cold and cut him like knives. The sand stung his face
and brought tears to his eyes. He stared at the words and
his vision blurred. He knew that it was a terrible thing to
forget the woman he loved. He wondered how that could
happen. He hadn't been lonely before, but now he felt a
deep aching. He put the paper back in his pocket and sat
down beside the young woman's corpse. He wanted to
hurry to the house, but he had to wait until the sun came
up. He wanted to get the help of whoever was there but
until morning he was helpless.

Courane tried to sleep but the fierce coldness and his
thirst deprived him of rest. He sat by the boulder and
thought. Her name was Alohilani. It was a pretty name,
but it meant nothing to him. It occurred to him that he
knew her name now but not his own. That didn't seem
important for some reason. He yawned and looked up at
the stars. The stars were home. That strange thought
formed in Courane's mind, like the first bubble in a pan
of boiling water. Like a bubble, it burst and disappeared
and was forgotten. Courane shivered and clutched himself and hunched against the sharp attack of the wind.
Sometime before dawn he drifted into placid, dreamless
sleep.

The warm wind, blowing from the opposite direction,
throwing veils of sand into his face, woke him. The sun
was well over the horizon. Courane stood and stretched
and rubbed his face. He was surprised to find the body of
a young woman beside him on the ground. He couldn't

recall who she was or where he was, and he didn't know
what he ought to do. He felt small and forlorn and, as
the minutes passed and he stared at the swollen lifeless
woman, Courane heard himself whimper. He was hungry, but there was nothing at all nearby that might
provide him with even a meager breakfast. He took a
deep breath and resigned himself. There was neither
road nor sign of human settlement in sight, and he didn't
have the least idea how he ought to proceed. He sat
down again and waited. The breeze blew almost steadily
and the sun felt good on his shoulders, but he guessed
that by midday the heat would become intolerable, and
that at night all the warmth would bleed away and he
would suffer with the cold.

An hour after awakening he found the piece of paper
in his pocket. He was filled with joy. He read the directions several times and, though he didn't understand
what they meant, he was given a new energy to obey his
own instructions. He narrowed his eyes and looked to the
horizon below the morning sun; he chose a landmark to
walk toward. Then he bent and picked up the body and
slung it clumsily over one shoulder. He leaned forward
under the burden and trudged toward the eastern horizon. The sandy soil made walking difficult and Courane
was soon out of breath, but he didn't stop. He had to get
the woman back to the house before it got dark. After
the sunset, he wouldn't know in which direction to walk.
He worried about that for a little while, and then he forgot all about the problem. He muttered to himself as he
went, and he was as unaware of the passage of time as he
was of his own pain.

Courane took a rest in the middle of the afternoon.
The place he chose for his break was identical to the
place he had spent the previous night. The sand and the
rocks were the same. As he sat in the sparse shade of a
tall weathered rock, he watched a fly crawling along one
of the woman's arms. He had dropped her roughly to the
ground, and one stiff arm stuck out as though she were
indicating something to the southwest that intrigued her.
The fly walked along the fine sun-paled hair of her arm.
Her name was—
—Alohilani! He remembered. He smiled at the
achievement, but then his face contorted with grief. He

wept loudly and helplessly as his thoughts battered him
cruelly.

His memories were fugitive visions, and he clutched at
them greedily on the occasions when they presented
themselves. He studied them all to the smallest detail,
disregarding the pain they threatened. He didn't care
about pain any longer. He needed to know the truth. He
needed to know who he was, where he came from. He
needed to know where he was going, what he was doing.
He needed to know why Alohilani was dead, and why his
mind functioned only at widely separated moments, with
bewildering gaps in continuity and understanding.

Courane felt a little sting on the back of his neck and
at that moment he remembered how it had been.

TECT informed him that he had failed for the third
time, had used up his last chance and had wasted it like a
kid with an extra dollar. He went home to his small
apartment in Tokyo and waited for the verdict and the
sentence. There was no doubt that he was going to be
found guilty. TECT had no margin of compassion. In all
his years, Courane had never heard of anyone else who
had failed as he had, and so he had no idea what TECT
would decide to do with him. His imagination ran wild,
picturing everything from death by etiolation to being
condemned to life as one of TECT's hired social devi-
ates, an addict perhaps, or a member of some squalid
ethnic group.

There was a tect unit in the foyer of the apartment
building. When the verdict and sentence were decided,
they would be transferred there. No doubt the building's
superintendent would run up the stairs with his usual
mad energy to give Courane the news. Courane could
wait. He put on a tape of Copland's *Appalachian Spring*
and laid down on the couch. He ought to call his parents,
he knew, but he wanted to put that off as long as possible. It would be humiliating, and his parents would be
crushed by the news. While he waited, Courane read
over the notice he had gotten at work.

**COURANE, Sandor   RepE Dis4 Sec 27
   Loc39—Gre—834
   M232—86—059—41Maj

11:07:47 10 January 7 YT DatAdvis**
**COURANE, Sandor:
Notification of failure to fulfill TaskFunc (Charges and Specifications follow).
**COURANE, Sandor:
When an individual fails at his first appointment, the supervisors and TECT in the name of the Representative look on the failure tolerantly and with good grace. After all, there is a strong possibility that test scores may have given an incorrect picture of an individual's aptitudes. After the second failure, TECT in the name of the Representative is still anxious to help the individual; perhaps a clearer profile is beginning to emerge.
**COURANE, Sandor:
BUT AFTER THE THIRD FAILURE, TECT IN THE NAME OF THE REPRESENTATIVE MUST VIEW THIS RECORD AS A TREND THAT MUST BE HALTED. IT SEEMS PROBABLE THAT THE INDIVIDUAL IS BEHAVING IN A MANNER DETRIMENTAL TO SOCIETY AS A WHOLE.
**COURANE, Sandor:
Consequently, TECT in the name of the Representative regretfully informs you that you are on trial for Willful Contempt of TECTWish. The verdict will be ready for you in one hour. You must comply with the verdict and the sentence. Failure to do so will be considered an act of revolutionary aggression, and you and your loved ones will be used as tragic examples.
**COURANE, Sandor:
No indication that the addressee understands the above is necessary.
Please stand by for further directives**

It was easy enough to understand. Courane's foreman, Sokol, had had a ghoulish pleasure in giving him the report. Courane could hardly blame the man. It was a marvelous novelty. In the small room, the Copland forged ahead without regard for Courane's feelings. The verdict should be coming through very soon. In a minute or two,

old Mr. Masutani would be knocking on the door, bringing the news. Courane was in no hurry. He could wait.

Then, as the music paused between sections, Courane
heard Mr. Masutani call his name. "Courane, come
downstairs. There's an important message for you on the
tect."

"I know, I know. I'll be right down." Courane sighed.
There was nothing to do but get it over with. He went to
the door.

Masutani looked at him and smiled. "Does it have to
do with why you came home from work so early?"

"I guess so." He led the way downstairs to the foyer.

"Did you lose your job?"

"Would you mind giving me a little privacy, Mr. Masutani?" The red *Advise* light was blinking, but Courane
ignored it for a moment.

Masutani raised an eyebrow. Privacy! He snorted at
the European boy's bad manners, but he turned and
went back into his own little den.

Courane went to the tect terminal. "This is Sandor
Courane," he said.

The tect hurried through the preliminary data symbols,
then presented Courane with his destiny.

**COURANE, Sandor:
*TECT in the name of the Representative has stud-
ied the records of your first labor assignment, in Pilessio, Europe. As you will recall, your performance
there did not meet the minimum standards of the
community. Therefore, you were given a second assignment, in New York, North America. TECT in the
name of the Representative has analyzed your second attempt at finding a profitable career, and arrived at the same conclusion. You were graciously
offered a third opportunity in Tokyo, Asia, and TECT
in the name of the Representative has been informed that you have followed the pattern of your
earlier failures.*
**COURANE, Sandor:
*It is not the purpose of TECT in the name of the
Representative to search out criminals merely to
punish them. It is TECT's essential duty to find a*

place for each individual, a role that will utilize the individual's talents to the utmost, provide the individual with an opportunity to grow and express himself, and benefit the community at large with the fruits of the individual's labor.

**COURANE, Sandor:

When an individual seems to be working to deny these benefits to the community, it is the responsibility of TECT in the name of the Representative to persuade the individual to change his behavior or, failing that, to remove the individual from the life of the community at large.

**COURANE, Sandor:

That this is true in the case of COURANE, Sandor, M232–86–059–41Maj, is the final decision of TECT in the name of the Representative. It is not necessary to protest innocence. TECT in the name of the Representative is aware that COURANE, Sandor, has committed no crimes of violence, passion, or fraud. COURANE, Sandor, has broken no laws, transgressed no moral imperatives, flouted no statutes, nor contravened sacred traditions, codes of conduct, established precedents, or principles of civilized behavior. In short, he has done nothing in an overt manner, premeditated or otherwise, for which to be punished.

**COURANE, Sandor:

Yet the community at large demands that COURANE, Sandor, be dealt with by removing him from the fellowship of the people and their Representative, and of TECT in the name of the Representative. In response to this compulsory obligation, TECT in the name of the Representative has selected for COURANE, Sandor, a plan that will enable the community at large to enjoy his absence without causing the individual himself the inconvenience of such solutions as summary execution.

**COURANE, Sandor:

You are ordered by TECT in the name of the Representative to report to TECT TELETRANS Main Substation in New York, North America, at 12:00:00, 11

January, 7 YT. Failure to do so will be considered Contempt of TECTWish and you will be hunted down like a dog and slain in your tracks.
**COURANE, Sandor:
No appeal is permitted. You are advised to make whatever final arrangements you feel are necessary. You will be allowed to take with you no more than five pounds of clothing, essential medications as described in your permanent personal file, a photograph of your parents and one of your spouse if you are married, but nothing else of a personal nature or otherwise.
**COURANE, Sandor:
*No indication that the addressee understands the above is necessary. There will be no further directives unless COURANE, Sandor, does something foolish.***

"They really hit you over the head with it, didn't they?" said Mr. Masutani.

Courane turned around quickly, startled. He was bitter and upset, and he didn't like having the superintendent sharing his moment of defeat. "Leave me alone," he said.

"Will you be staying here tonight? They want you in New York by noon tomorrow."

"I don't know. Maybe I'll see my parents tonight."

Masutani coughed. "If you won't be here, let me know. I want to move your mattresses down here." Courane said nothing. He went back to his apartment, his thoughts jumbled and bleak.

How easy it would be to prepare for his new life, he thought. He went to his closet and brought out a small canvas zipper bag. His whole future would be packed in that one bag. Five pounds of socks and shirts and, if he went home to get one, a photograph of his folks. He almost wished that he was married, just to be able to take another thing with him. It occurred to him that TECT might merely have been trying to calm his fears or delude him, that he wasn't going on to a new life somewhere. When he stepped across the teletrans threshold, he might easily step out on the bottom of the ocean or on the top of some nameless mountain in Antarctica. TECT had no discernible strain of mercy programmed into it, but there was a kind of savage irony.

Courane put the zipper bag on the bed—he felt a twinge of perversity, wishing that he could dispose of that bed so that Masutani couldn't profit from the situation— and began to stuff it full of clothing. He was glad, in a way, that there was a short limit to the amount of belongings he could take with him. His poverty wouldn't be so apparent wherever he was going. He finished packing, zipped the bag closed, and dropped it to the floor. That chore was done. He looked around him, around the apartment, wondering what else he could do to occupy his mind. There didn't seem to be anything urgent. He was dismayed that he could wrap up his affairs, his life, so quickly and effortlessly. Wouldn't there be some loose ends? Weren't there some people who would miss him terribly? Wasn't there anything in the world that would suffer without his attention?

No, there wasn't. That was what TECT had tried to tell him. That was why it had decided to excise him from the community at large. TECT had said that Courane was a weed in the garden. TECT admitted that Courane wasn't a threat or a danger, but weeds had to be removed nevertheless. They used up resources and contributed nothing. They disturbed the garden's integrity. They offended the sense of proportion of the gardener—and that was what TECT was these days, even though it always added that it operated "in the name of the Representative."

One telephone call would be enough. "Hello, Dad?"

"Sandy?"

Courane coughed nervously but said nothing. He was already sorry he had called.

"Sandy?"

"Dad? Hey, just calling to see how you and Mom are."

"We're fine, Sandy, we're both fine. How are you?"

"Fine, Dad. It's awful cold here."

"Cold here, too. The landlord has the thermostat set at some goddamn freezing temperature. Your mother has to wear her big blue sweater to bed. I was going to go buy one of those little heaters, but your mother's afraid of being gassed to death in the middle of the night."

"Uh huh."

"So, what's up with you? We went to Vienna weekend before last to visit your mother's brother. They bought a little farm. Filthy place. I didn't like it, but you know your mother. How's your new job?"

Courane felt his eyes fill with tears. His mouth was dry. He wished that it were tomorrow, next month, five or ten years in the future and whatever was going to happen would be done and finished. No, instead he had to go through it all, step by step, and he couldn't just close his eyes and wait for it all to go away. It would go away eventually, but it would disappear the hard way. "That's one of the reasons I called, Dad. I got laid off."

"Laid off? You mean fired?"

"Yeah."

"Goddamn it, Sandy. That's the third time. They're liable to—"

"They already have." Courane closed his eyes and rubbed his forehead. He had a headache. He spoke in a low, weary voice. "I got a message on the tect here at home that TECT has ordered something special for me."

"What?" His father sounded almost frantic, much more concerned than Courane was himself.

"I don't know, Dad. I'm not sure."

Courane's father was astonished. "You mean to tell me that you don't know what they're going to do to you? You didn't ask?"

"I was a little afraid."

"Sandy, you put the phone down and you go to your tect and you find out. I'll wait."

"It'll cost a fortune."

"The hell with that," said Courane's father. "I'd think that would be the least of our worries. I don't believe you sometimes, son."

"I'll be right back." Courane was feeling more anguish than he showed to his father. He wanted more than anything not to distress his parents, but that would be almost impossible. Knowing that, Courane wished to keep the hurt and grief at the lowest possible level. This wasn't the first time in his life that in seeking to protect his mother and father, he had succeeded only in wounding them more deeply. This knowledge burned him as he hurried downstairs.

He confronted the tect. "Regarding the last message to

Courane, Sandor, what precisely are the details of my sentence?''

**COURANE, Sandor:
You are to be sent as a colonist to the agricultural world of Epsilon Eridani, Planet D. You will become part of an integrated farming community. Your future of successes or failures will thus be of no consequence to the community at large here on Earth, yet you will be placed in an environment which will demand much of you and reward you with peace and satisfaction**

"That's not so bad," said Courane.

**COURANE, Sandor:
No, it's not. Many successful but harried citizens would be willing to trade their situations with you. You will lack for little on this distant world, except of course for personal contact with old friends and family, and certain material possessions. But in the balance you must weigh your new self-esteem, gained through hard work and the knowledge that you are free and owe your liberty and good life to no one, that your happiness is of your own making**

"Well, then, I'm very grateful."

**COURANE, Sandor:
And well you should be. You would do well to recall that TECT in the name of the Representative had no part in selecting you for this treatment, or in prejudging your lapses, or in deciding your fate. These things were made necessary by the current standards of the community, and TECT in the name of the Representative must be absolved of all direct responsibility.
**COURANE, Sandor:
Compliance with the above is to be indicated.
**COURANE, Sandor:
Affirm?**

*   *   *

"Yes," said Courane, permitting the immense machine to wash its electronic hands of the affair, to salve its magnetic conscience. Courane remembered his father, still on the phone upstairs, waiting in Europe for the news. Courane hurried back to his apartment. "Hello, Dad?"

"I haven't gone anywhere."

"Well, I will be. They're sending me to another planet. Epsilon something. A farming world. I'm going to work on a commune or something."

"Oh."

"That doesn't sound bad."

"Except that your mother and I will probably never see you again."

Courane hesitated. He hadn't even considered that. He felt a stab of guilt. "I'll be home in a couple of hours. Is my room still empty?"

"Who do you think is staying there? Your mother will put on clean sheets. You can pick up the rest of your books and clothes."

"They won't let me take but five pounds, Dad. I have everything I need except a good picture of you and Mom. Do me a favor, though. Get Mom ready. Break the news to her so that she won't be hysterical when I get home."

Courane heard his father sigh. "Sandy, no matter what I do, she'll be hysterical when you get here. For that matter, maybe I will be, too."

Courane felt a hot tear slip down his cheek. "Dad," he said in a hoarse voice, "it's hard enough to keep myself under control. Please, I need you to be strong. You were always strong when I was little. You've always been strong for me."

"Sandy, it was never easy, and I am getting old and tired. But I will do it one more time."

"Thanks, Dad. I love you."

"I love you too, Sandy. Be careful coming home. I'll see you soon."

Courane hung up the phone. He sat on his bed and stared at the wall, where there was a framed print of Tiepolo's *Madonna of the Goldfinch*, which Courane felt was the most beautiful woman ever painted. He stared at the print, and every thought he entertained made him a little sadder. He wouldn't be allowed to take the picture with him. He would be cut off forever from both it and

the world that had created it. His idle dreams of perform-
ing a startling act of genius, a work of art or a scientific
breakthrough or a marvelous athletic achievement, were
dead now and he had no other course but to acknowl-
edge that dismal fact. There were so many things that
Courane had wanted with the vague grasping desire of
youth, and he had denied them all to himself by his
failure. He had achieved something closely related to
death, despite TECT's curious reluctance to be held accountable for it. Certainly Courane's failures to come
would be far from the affairs of the community at large,
but then so would be his triumphs, and Earth would be
cheated of these. And Courane would be cheated of the
acceptance that he needed so desperately. That was the
true punishment.

It was just past sunset. The first brush of stars glinted
in the sky like the dust of broken jewels on sable. The air
was already cooling, and it was the rising wind that had
roused Courane. Where am I? he thought. I'm on my
way home, he told himself. I'm on my way to my parents'
home in Greusching.
Then why was he sitting alone in the middle of some
voiceless desert? *Where was he?* He stared into the sky
and watched the deep blue lose the last faint measure of
light. He watched the stars increase and he watched them
form patterns and shapes in the heavens. He felt fear
grow in him as he searched in vain for familiar constellations. There was no Dipper, no Orion, no Cas-
siopeia, no Draco. The moon, low on the horizon, was
half the size it ought to be and was an untrustworthy purplish color.
Courane had the same feeling one has on waking from
a particularly vivid dream, when the waking world and
the dream are superimposed for a moment, when aspects
of one distort images of the other, and one must make an
effort to sort them and decide which shall have precedence for the remainder of the day.
Courane knew he wasn't on Earth, and that took away
the fear he had felt looking into the strange foreign sky.
But then, how did he explain being alone and lost in a
waterless wilderness? That would take more of an effort,
he was afraid, and he was further afraid that he was not

equal to it. He breathed deeply. The cool night air was
spiced with the earthy smells of the sunbaked rocks and
the parched sands. A more unpleasant odor made him
frown, and he sought its source. He discovered the young
woman's corpse and gave a cry of alarm. He did not
know who she was or why she was with him. The idea of
sharing the night with a corpse did not bother him so
much as the notion that he appeared to be involved in a
terrible drama and had no sense at all of its significance.

He found the explanatory note before he decided to
sleep, and this time he had a good idea as well. He rea-
soned that if he had written the note to himself, then his
periods of lucidity were alternating with periods of complete forgetfulness. It was likely that he would forget her
name again, as well as his mission. He decided to fasten
the note to the woman's blouse, rather than stuffing it
back into his pocket. Then next time he would have his
explanation as soon as he discovered her again. He still
did not recall what she had meant to him or why she had
died, or why he was carrying her across the desert or why
she had to return to the house, or where the house was
or who was waiting in it for her.

As he waited for sleep, Courane hoped that when he
awoke he would not start off across the sand before he
discovered the body again. It was possible that he might
leave her there and go wandering off into the wastes to
die himself.

In New York, Courane arrived at the TELETRANS
Substation a quarter hour early. There were very few
people wandering about. Teletrans was still a very expensive way to travel; most people still used the trains and
airlines, and only the rich and the desperate made the
instantaneous journeys by tect. For travel between cities
on Earth, it was almost prohibitively expensive. For
travel between the stars, it was the only way to go.

Courane stood with his zipper bag and looked around.
On the ceiling of the Substation were depictions of the
six men who had been the Representatives, done as
though they were novel groups of stars in the sky of the
northern hemisphere. These men had retired now one by
one, and the last of them had turned over the power and
the responsibility to the tireless and unerring TECT. The

Representatives today were but nonexistent constellations and fading memories. TECT governed for them and few people noticed any difference. Surely no one voiced any objection.

It seemed that no one had been instructed to meet Courane. After a moment he realized that there was no good reason to expect that anyone should. He went to a uniformed CAS guard and asked for directions. "Just check in over there at the TECT desk," said the man with a yawn. Courane carried his bag across the polished floor.

"Good morning," he said. He dropped the bag beside him.

A young woman with curly pink hair looked up at him. She was drinking a cup of coffee and reading a romantic novel on the microfiche reader. "It's almost lunchtime," she said.

"My name is Sandor Courane. I was told to report here at noon."

The woman grimaced and slipped the novel fiche out of the reader. "You don't have a ticket, then?"

"No," he said in some embarrassment. "You see, I—"

Her eyes widened. "I know who you are! You're being exiled!"

The word surprised Courane. He didn't like it at all. "Exiled? My father said I was being expatriated."

"Whatever. Oh, wait a minute. I have a friend at the package claim who wanted me to make sure to call her when you came in. This is just terrific. Will you sign my book? It's for my mother, really. She always has me ask people to sign the book if they're in the news or anything like that."

Courane just wanted to get on with it, but he had to go through the entire embarrassing scene. People came from all over the substation to look at him, to point at him and whisper and laugh. Soon he begged to be allowed to walk through the portal and get away from the crowd.

"Will you look at this guy?" she said, shaking her head. "He actually sounds like he's in a hurry. Say, how does it feel?"

"Awful," he said. He looked around resentfully at the mob surrounding the desk.

"I mean, screwing up as bad as you did. I can't imagine it."

"It was easier than you might think," he said.

"Easy for you, honey," she said. "Still, shipping you away from Earth forever. That seems a little harsh. It's not like you robbed a bank or anything."

"It's for your own good," said Courane. "I'm a menace in my own way. I take without giving, and the community at large can't allow that."

"When you put it that way, I see your point. Why do you do it, then? You look like a nice boy. Was it your parents? Was it something that happened to you as a child?"

"Yes," he said. "A woman at an information counter once said something to me, and it affected the rest of my life."

"What did she say?"

"She was giving me directions and she said, 'You can't miss it.' I took that as a direct challenge and I determined to get lost. I succeeded, and I didn't stop there. Until TECT put an end to my career, I was quickly becoming a legendary failure. A failure of mythic proportions. And I owe it all to her. You have that potential too, Miss. Someday you may inspire someone to abandon everything and ruin his life."

She seemed transported by the idea. "Do you really think so?"

Courane studied her and nodded slowly. "I don't doubt it for a moment," he said. "It must be almost time."

She checked her watch. "It is," she said. "Just follow the yellow line to the portal. You'll have to identify yourself to the operator, but from then on I'm told it's easy. Good luck."

"That way?"

"That way," she said. "You can't miss it." There wasn't a trace of humor in her voice. She didn't realize what she had said.

Courane left her and pushed his way through the crowd of curious people. They cheered him, but he paid no attention. He followed the yellow line to the portal. The gate wasn't very impressive to look at, much like the metal detectors used by the airlines. There was a small door set into a wall of cinder blocks, apparently leading outside to the parking lot. Courane produced his identification, let the operator examine his single bag of belongings, and turned to take his last look at the planet of his birth. He wondered if he ought to make a final statement, some brave word to be remembered by.

"Hurry up," said the operator. "It costs a fortune to keep the connection open. We're talking light-years here, you know. You're not going on a weekend trip to Atlantic City."

"All right," said Courane. He took a firm grip on his zipper bag, opened the door, and stepped through.

Behind him there was the sound of a door sighing closed. He turned, but there was no sign of the portal. There wasn't so much as a shimmer in the air.

He was on another world.

It wasn't what Courane would call an especially attractive world. Naturally, he hadn't had any choice in the matter, but if he had he might have picked a place where the colors of the sky and ground and growing things were more in harmony. The sky was bleak and clothed with storm clouds. The light had an unsettling greenish cast to it. The tall grass and the leaves on the twisted trees were the precise red-purple of a flea gorged with blood. Courane's face showed distaste, but in a moment he settled himself enough to look around.

The sun—Epsilon Eridani—was low in the sky, but there was no way for him to say if it was morning or late evening. Not far was a large house with a barn and a silo. That was his new home, evidently, and he took a deep breath and headed toward it. He felt strangely nervous. He didn't know why he was so anxious; he couldn't fail here. There would be no evaluations. This was the end of the line, the bottom of the barrel. If there were any others in the house, they were there for the same reason he was. Birds of a feather, they had been marooned together.

The house had a large front porch with several comfortable old chairs arranged so the tenants could sit and watch the grotesque dull red grasses waving in the winds of approaching storms. A half-filled pitcher rested forgotten on the porch railing.

There was neither bellpush nor knocker beside the screen door. Of course not, Courane thought, applauding his own perception; they wouldn't often receive package deliveries or weary travelers. "Hello?" he called. There was only silence. For a moment he had the horrible thought that he was alone, not only on the porch but on the planet, that TECT had banished him to solitary confinement on a strange world. But a moment later a woman came around the corner of the house. She was his mother's age, in her middle or late forties, with short blonde hair and a youthful face. She didn't show the signs of years of toils beneath the foreign sun. Although she wore no makeup, there were no lines of pain or hard work around her mouth or eyes. She wore a plain gray dress that was imperfect enough to have been made here at home. She smiled and came toward him, one hand extended.

"Hi," she said. Her voice was low and friendly. "My name's Molly. We didn't know anyone was coming today."

"TECT didn't tell you?" he said, taking her hand.

"No. Doesn't make any difference, though. I'm glad I was around when you got here. Everyone else is either working around the farm or too sick. So come in, put your bag down. What's your name?"

"Courane. Sandor Courane. I'm from a little town in Europe. Greusching."

"We've got a few Europeans here," said Molly. "A few North Americans, one Pacifican girl, and some folks from other colonies."

"How many altogether?"

"Twelve. Two of them are kids. Isn't that awful? Two children, both boys, neither of them older than eleven." She looked across the yard, lost in thought. "So come in." She smiled and held the screen door open.

Courane steadied the woman's body with one hand. His shoulder ached from carrying her. The day was hot and there was no breeze at all. The sand had given way to small rounded stones, and the footing was difficult. The ground had risen slowly, and as he paused he looked out over a gentle declivity that stretched before him all the way to the horizon. He would have to carry her down into the basin in search of the river. The only proof that there was a river was the note pinned to the woman's clothing. Courane accepted its authority without question. It didn't occur to him to ask if the note might belong to another time, another situation, another world perhaps, that there might be no river within the limit of his strength and perseverance. There were low gnarled trees scattered around the floor of the depression, and clouds in the distance gave hope of rain and an end to his thirst. He did suffer a growing fatigue, an exhaustion that almost overpowered him when he became conscious of it. When he remembered, it was with a clarity and a force that consumed him; he was aware of nothing else, nothing at all in his present condition. His past was denied to him, so far as voluntarily calling it up. But when it visited him unbidden, it blinded his senses and hungers to everything else.

Courane shifted the corpse to the other shoulder, settled his burden more comfortably, and descended into the desert basin.

**TWO

Courane sat by the river with Rachel and watched the dead autumn leaves shuffle in the brisk wind. He didn't know what to say to the young woman. She was pleasant enough, of course, as well as intelligent, but Courane was embarrassed by her attention. Everyone on the farm knew that he had paired off with the Pacifican girl, Alohilani. Courane hoped that Rachel understood the social conventions of their small community. He hoped that she wouldn't make any emotional demands of him. Under the best of conditions in the past, he had never been very good at handling that kind of thing.

"How long have you been here now?" she asked.

Courane picked up a stone and tossed it in a high arc into the coffee-brown river. "Not quite five months," he said. Questions like these were discouraged among the colonists. Rachel had been there for more than a month; she ought to have known better.

The sky was clear, an unusual occurrence, and Courane laid back in the rough grass and closed his eyes. There was a tense silence between them.

"I still haven't gotten used to it all," she said at last. "The colors of the sky and sun, I mean. And the stars at night being different."

"You'll get used to it."

"I'm glad I work in the house. I don't think I would want to work around the farm. The animals are so strange. So are the crops in the fields."

"You'll work on the farm soon. You won't stay in the house. They keep you there until you get adjusted. But we need you outside. There's never enough help."

Rachel brushed her long dark hair with her hands and drew it over her shoulder, across her breast. Then she lay back beside Courane. "How sick is she?" she asked.

21

"Alohilani?"

"Of course."

"She's very sick."

"I'm sorry to hear that, Sandy. Really. She's a beautiful girl."

"You should have known her before she became ill."

Rachel sighed and rolled over in the grass. She plucked a long blade of the red weed, looked at it, and frowned. "Let's talk about something else, all right?" she said.

"Sure," he said. "What do you want to talk about?"

"Are you happy here?"

Courane sat up and brushed damp soil from his shirt. He looked astonished. "Happy?" he said. "We're in prison. How can you be happy in prison?"

Rachel gazed at him, her large brown eyes brilliant with unshed tears. "I'm happy," she said. "I'm happier here than I've ever been before. TECT was perfectly right, sending me here. I only wish it had happened sooner. I met you here."

Courane raised a warning hand. "Rachel, please. I'm glad you're happy, but I hope it isn't just because of me. I can't be a part of it for you. I'm in love with someone else."

"I know that."

"You've only been here a little while—"

"Why do you call it a prison?" she asked. Rachel sat up and looked toward the river. "Just because you aren't free to go back to Earth? I think this is my home. I think this place is beautiful, once you get used to the strange things. In its own way, it's much more beautiful than Earth. The open space and the clean air." She looked back into Courane's face, but she saw only bitterness there. Rachel shook her head. "I love those little animals, the ones that hop like frogs but look kind of like chipmunks. The yellow fuzzy things."

"I do too," said Courane.

"What are they called?"

"There isn't a name for them. Why don't you think of one?"

Rachel laughed. Courane stood up and helped her to her feet. Together they walked back to the house. Courane was glad the conversation had turned away from unpleasantness.

* * *

On Earth it was early January in the year 7 YT. "YT" originally meant "the Year of Tom," the last of the Representatives, but since T was also the first letter of TECT, no one felt the need to change calendars again upon Tom's retirement. When Courane arrived on Planet D, it was the middle of the local summer, July of the year 124. He was happy, in a way; his exile enabled him to bypass the rest of the Asian winter and walk through a portal into summer. On his first day on the farm, this minor advantage was the only one that presented itself. Courane waited skeptically for the self-esteem and satisfaction that TECT had promised. He decided to relax in the main parlor, and made himself comfortable while he waited.

He was alone for a good part of the day. There were no electronic entertainment devices, of course, and no one had been permitted to bring books or fiche with them. Courane sat and looked at the wood-paneled walls in growing boredom. The house's tect was tied directly into TECT's main and subsidiary memory units, but Courane hadn't learned that yet. He could have summoned up any of the resources available to anyone on Earth, but instead he sat and waited, afraid to violate any strange local customs or practices. If he were expected anywhere or if he were required to do anything, he was sure someone would tell him. And if the house rules forbade anyone telling him, he hoped someone would let him know about that. In any event, the safest thing seemed to be just to hang around, to be available until he was given a definite role to play.

After a long while, Molly came into the parlor. "Have you been sitting here all this time?" she asked.

"Yes," said Courane.

"How monotonous. I guess everyone else is busy. I hope I'm not the one assigned to show you around; I've got much too much to do. If it were my job, though, I'd remember it." Her face became suddenly serious. "I *think* I'd remember it," she said softly. "I'll be right back."

"No need on my account," said Courane. He just wanted something to eat.

A few minutes later, she returned. She smiled. "I was right, it isn't me. Sheldon is supposed to give you the tour. Have you met Sheldon?"

"The tall man? Bald? From some place in North America? I met him briefly. He said he'd be around to take me upstairs. That was hours ago."

"Ah, well. This is a busy working farm. We'll try to fit you into the routine as quickly and smoothly as we can. We really need you. We have four people in the infirmary and we haven't had anyone sent in a long time."

"How often do you get new recruits?" asked Courane.

"Oh, I'd guess about every couple of months. Our months, not Earth months." The farm's year was divided into fifteen months, each with about thirty-five days. Courane would have to get used to the planet's seasons. The winter was harder, the summer was milder, and spring and fall didn't seem to last very long at all.

"Are all your new people like me?"

"Like you?" she asked, not understanding what he meant.

"Misfit types, eliminated by TECT."

Molly looked away. "One thing—what was your name?"

"Call me Sandy."

She smiled again. "All right, Sandy. The first thing you learn is that you never pry into anyone else's past. If someone wants to talk about it, fine, but you don't ask. Do you understand?"

"Sure."

"Number two. We haven't been eliminated. The word we like to use is 'excarcerated.' We made it up, and it's a nice-sounding substitute for 'exiled' and we know it. But that's the word we use whenever we discuss our situation, which we don't do very often."

"I'll remember that. Why don't you tell me about the other people who live here?"

"No," said Molly, "I have to get back outside. The farm workers will be coming in soon, and you can meet them all then. Sheldon will be around to show you everything, and then there's your first supper in about, oh, an hour and a half. In the meantime, why don't you use the tect? It's in the den, down the corridor there, second door on the right."

"Good," said Courane.

"I'll see you at supper then. I hope you're hungry."

Before Courane could answer, she turned and left the room.

Sheldon found him later, sitting at the tect, playing a game of cribbage against the computer. "Hello," said the bald man.

Courane looked up and recognized him. He cleared the screen of the console. "Hello," he said. "I was only—" He felt just a bit guilty about tying up the colony's only link to Earth with his game.

"Let's take a walk. I'll show you the grounds, the farm, the barn, and the animals. Then we'll go upstairs."

Courane was struck by the way he said the last words. "Both you and Molly speak about 'upstairs' in a kind of hushed voice. What do you have up there?"

The pained look on Sheldon's face made Courane realize he had made just the kind of social error he had been trying to avoid. "Let's look around the farm then, all right?" said Sheldon. Courane stood up wordlessly.

Dreams. Courane sat up in the cold dawn and tried to remember. His dreams had become much more vivid, more like waking memories, like the visions that possessed him during the day. Like those memories, they faded quickly, mocking his vain attempts to hold on to them, to preserve them for melancholy examination. He had dreamed of the house and the people, but now he couldn't recall who they were or what they looked like. The house—

The sun—he called it the sun, but it wasn't, of course; it was Epsilon Eridani—was peering over the hills that bordered the farther limits of this desert of stones. That was the way he had to go. The house was that way. The river was beyond the hills, he remembered. Many times in the months he had been on this world, he had wandered away from the farm into those hills, which now were gray with distance and dim with the mists of morning. He knew where he was, roughly speaking, and he felt good. It would take a couple of days more to cross the desert, another day among the hills themselves, and then he would find the river. How far upriver he was from the farm might determine if he'd live or die.

He was lucid for the first time in days. He looked around, startled by how far he had marched while his

mind was numbed. He shivered and wished that he had a
coat. It might have been that he began the journey with
more protective clothing, but he could easily have discarded it all when he wasn't thinking clearly.

The day's labor called him. He stood and stretched and
scratched his head. Then, when he could avoid it no
longer, he turned to look at the corpse beside him.

"I knew it," Courane's mother said. "I knew it from
the very start. I knew it, I knew it, I knew it. I always
knew it." She sat at the dining table and wept. She didn't
seem to notice that neither her husband nor her son was
eating. Courane's father shrugged helplessly.

"Don't look at it that way, Mom," said Courane. "I'm
really excited about the whole thing. It will be a good
experience for me. You know how I've always liked
being in the country. You remember how much I liked
going to camp when I was a kid."

"A good experience," she said. "Sandy, an experience
is something you have and then you tell all your friends
about. An experience is something you come home after.
Sandy, this isn't an experience you're going to have.
You're going away to some *planet,* for God's sake."

"Marie," said Courane's father, "the boy doesn't need
this. Come on, stop crying. Be glad to see him."

She just looked at her husband with a strange, accusing
expression. She said nothing more for a long time.

After the dinner, they sat in the living room. "I've
missed you, and I've missed this town," said Courane
sadly.

"Your girlfriend has been asking about you," said his
mother. "Now what am I going to tell her?"

"Girl? What girl?"

"You know," said his father, "oh, what's her name?
The girl who works for Dr. Klopst."

"Lilli? With the red hair?"

His mother nodded. "She hinted that you were going
to ask her to marry you, before you went away to Pilessio. What am I going to tell her?"

"Maybe she'll wait for you," said Courane's father.

"Wait?"

"Until you come back," said his mother in a quiet
voice.

"When I come back, it will probably be a long time from now. I have the feeling TECT is going to keep me there a long while. Until I prove myself."

"I knew it," said his mother. Her eyes were dry now, but so sorrowful and so desolate that neither man could meet her gaze. "I knew it from the very beginning," she whispered.

On the first floor of the large house were the parlor, the community rooms, the spacious den, the kitchen and dining room, and smaller rooms given over to activities that were both practical and entertaining. On the second floor were sleeping quarters. On the third floor, under the sloping roof, poorly ventilated and dimly lit, was the infirmary. There were always occupied beds in the infirmary.

Before his first meal on the new world, Courane was led upstairs to the infirmary to watch an old woman die. "Her name is Zofia," said Sheldon in a low voice.

"I see," whispered Courane. He was intensely uncomfortable. He had not had a great deal of experience on Earth with watching strangers die. Perhaps here it was a custom, possibly a ritual of great significance, so he did his best to play whatever part was now his. He was agitated, though, because all the normal standards of his old life had been left behind when he passed through the gate, and there was a new set to learn immediately. He would have to learn them one by one, the way a child learns, and he would make more than one unpleasant and painful discovery along the way. He was hungry—he hadn't eaten since dinner with his parents the day before—but mentioning that fact to Sheldon couldn't possibly be good manners. Not in front of the old woman, who didn't look as though she had another half hour in her.

He could be wrong, of course. Complaining of hunger at someone else's deathbed might well be accepted behavior here. On Planet D.

"She was a nice lady," said Sheldon.

"Ah," said Courane. "I'm sorry for her, then."

"No need to be."

"Ah," said Courane. He decided to think about Sheldon's remark later. It made him feel strange.

In the bed beside the old woman's was a young man about Courane's age. His name was Carmine. He stared at Courane and Sheldon with a blank expression. He seemed to be resting comfortably. He was well-groomed and clean-shaven and his stiff gray gown was fresh and clean. He lay in the bed unmoving, his hands resting limply upon the coarse sheet. When Courane and Sheldon moved away, Carmine's eyes did not follow them.

"He looks drugged," said Courane. "Are any of you people qualified to care for these people? He seems over-medicated."

"Well, he's not. We're advised about all our medical problems through our tect unit. We don't do anything that isn't prescribed by TECT."

"What's his condition, then?"

Sheldon's face clouded briefly. "He's dying."

"Do you mean today?" asked Courane. If both Zofia and Carmine were expecting the angel of death before dinner, then perhaps this tour was something more peculiar than Courane guessed. Maybe it was a favorite form of entertainment, and Courane was being given a rare privilege.

"No," said Sheldon, "only the old woman will die today. Carmine has about a month left. Neurological disorder." Sheldon turned away and went to the next bed. There was a heavy black woman sitting up with a puzzled look on her face. "Iola?" said Sheldon softly.

She turned her face toward Courane and opened her mouth. She said nothing, but her mouth stayed open. A bright line of saliva spilled down her chin.

"Iola, how are you today?" asked Sheldon. "Are you hungry?"

Slowly she turned her head from Courane to Sheldon. She said nothing.

"Do you hurt anywhere, Iola?"

The two men waited a moment, but there was no response. "What is she suffering from?" asked Courane.

Sheldon gave a quick, wry smile. "TECT calls it 'D syndrome.' That doesn't tell us much. There's no treatment for it, unfortunately."

"Then she's dying, too?"

"Yes." Courane began to realize that there was a complete lack of compassion in TECT, if the machine could not be made to relent even in the case of imminent death. These three people may not have been curable, even with the facilities on Earth, but their families would have had the consolation of being with them at the end, and the patients would have been given the courtesy of dying at home. That sort of kindness and consideration was what had been lost when the last human Representative abdicated in favor of the electronic thinking system.

"And that boy?" Courane indicated a fourth patient.

"Markie," said the boy.

"Markie's nine years old," said Sheldon. "His birthday was just last week. Do you remember, Markie?"

"Markie," said the boy.

Courane looked at Sheldon.

"Markie." This time the boy's voice sounded just a bit hesitant.

"Let's go back downstairs. You'll want to rest before dinner. If Zofia starts to slip, someone on duty here will call us in time."

Courane didn't know what to say. "Oh, good," he said. He felt terrible.

"I can do it," murmured Courane as he trudged across the stones. The woman's body was heavy, but he never thought of abandoning it. He would make it back to the house with her corpse, or they would both spend eternity in the desert, lost forever beneath the alien stars. "I can do it." In his mind, Courane faced the tect unit—a tect unit, an unspecified tect unit. Perhaps it was the tect in his parents' home, the tect at the factory in Tokyo, the tect at the University of Pilessio, the tect in the farmhouse beside the river on Planet D. All these voices of TECT had commanded him, and Courane had always accepted TECT's directions in the same spirit. He was willing to accept TECT's judgments because he himself had forced them. Courane had made TECT's orders inevitable with his failures. Whatever happened to him was only in keeping with the justice of TECT's brutal reasoning.

Movement startled Courane. He stopped and put the corpse down on the stones. It wasn't his habit to take frequent rest stops during the day's march, but he was disturbed in the midst of his reverie. A shadow flickered

across the ground, and Courane looked up into the hazy
sky. He saw a bird circling not very high above him. He
couldn't tell what kind of bird it was. On Earth he might
have thought of a buzzard, but as far as he knew there
weren't any carrion birds of that type in the desert. There
was too little for them to eat. But then, Courane admitted, he could hardly be called an expert on this world's
wildlife. He had lived on the planet for little more than
twenty months, a year and a third by the colony's reckon-
ing. No one had done much study in the local natural
history; only the plants and animals immediately essential
to the colonists had been closely examined. Perhaps
there were large scavengers living near the desert, alien
buzzards waiting for Courane to die before swooping
down. Courane laughed with cracked lips. Those buzzards would be surprised when they lighted by the man's
body. He wondered how the birds would find the meal.
Courane watched the black shape making circles overhead, like ghostly haloes traced by a ravenous angel. "I
can do it, Mom, don't be sad," he murmured. "It's my
decision and I'm happy." He sat down beside the corpse
because he had already forgotten what his undertaking
meant.

Death is difficult. Countless generations of people before us have passed along this message. Dying is not particularly tough, but death itself is an aggravation.
Dying is easy. The expiring person has little to do; it's
almost as though the hard part is done for him. The
really tedious details are left to the survivors and the attendant hangers-on. Scenes at the deathbed are often
grotesque and cruel, but only because the survivors make
it that way. How peaceful and untroubled a dying man
seems, as soothing death draws the final veil over his
eyes. The mourning is usually already in progress at this
point, and will continue as long as anyone can derive the
least satisfaction from it. But before the moment of death
the mourners are put through a difficult time, a passage
of fear and lying and ugliness that will remain in the
memory long after the loved one himself has begun to
fade.
Was this some kind of lesson, then? Was Sheldon trying to pass on the wisdom learned in the community's

hundred and twenty-four years on Planet D? Courane expected some kind of initiation into the ways of the group, but starting right out, bango, with the last agonies of an old woman gave Courane a morbid feeling he did not enjoy. Surely there were more profitable ways to pass this day. . . .

But this wasn't Earth, he told himself. That fact was being thrown at him at every turn. And these people had developed their own culture, and it was bound to be a bit odd, having been cut off from Earth for so long. But they could have the decency to introduce him slowly. They could have a little more respect for his unprepared feelings.

It was the morning following Courane's arrival before Zofia was ready to let go for the last time. Word came down from the infirmary and everyone dropped his chores to hurry to her bedside. It was a kind of binding social ritual and communion as well. Courane observed it rather than take any part in it. He found it just a bit distasteful, so he stood to one side and studied the eight watchers at the old woman's bedside. They whispered to each other with solemn faces. Sheldon stood with Alohilani and the older boy, Kenny. Molly talked with two men, one named Daan; Courane didn't recall the name of the other. He looked at each person there and tried to remember their names and what they had said to him. These were the people he would be living with now; these people were his family. He had better learn to like them or, failing that, to tolerate them for the benefit of the community. There was a short black man named Fletcher, who was arrogant and possibly quite mean. There was a skinny woman named Goldie, who had a hatchet face and a shrill voice; Courane knew nothing more about her.

It wasn't, all in all, the sort of crew he would want to get stuck with in a lifeboat. But in a way, that's exactly what had happened.

Alohilani left the group and came to Courane's side. "Sandy?" she said. "Do I have your name right?"

"Yes. And I'm not sure I have the pronunciation of yours down, either."

She laughed. It was a lovely sound. "Most people call me Lani. It's easier. You seem shy."

Courane looked down uncomfortably at the floor. "I am, a little. I haven't been here a full day and I don't really know anyone very well. I don't feel as though I belong here yet, and here I am at the bed of an old woman, waiting for her to die."

Alohilani put a graceful hand on Courane's arm. "You belong here," she said in a low voice. "You aren't here by mistake, are you?"

Courane gave an ironic laugh. "No," he said.

"None of us is. And here we can look at some natural events in a person's life more clearly than we did in our old lives. We see these things as if for the first time. They become more important. In a way, life here is more gracious. Zofia can die with dignity here. You know what it would be like for her in a nursing home back on Earth."

Courane nodded. What she meant was that their lives had been stripped of all conveniences, the necessary ones as well as those that merely cluttered up living. Some of those conveniences were for the benefit of the community, while others were for the individual. He couldn't help thinking that despite her attitude, they had all lost much more than they had gained in coming here. But he said none of this to her. At that moment, he knew that he never wanted to say or do anything to disturb her. He didn't want to do anything that would make her take her slender suntanned hand away.

Molly joined them. "Zofia has passed away," she said, curiously in the same whisper everyone used on the third floor. Courane glanced around; no one in the other occupied beds would understand their conversation, even if he could overhear it. "She always trusted God, she trusted that the Lord would give her the grace to endure her pain."

"I wish someone would do that for me," said Courane.

Molly looked astonished. "Don't worry," she said. "You'll learn to take up your burden. That's part of the purpose of our group, to help the newcomers accept the difficulties of life here. This is the challenge TECT has set you, and if you meet it you will be rewarded with growth and peace and the unshakable faith to overcome anything, including death. Zofia showed that."

To Courane's mind, Zofia had probably been so far gone she hadn't known who or where she was. But he didn't say anything to Molly. He could make an educated guess now at what had landed Molly on Planet D. On Earth she had likely held a civil service job as a paid minority member, probably a Christian. It was against the law to remain in character after working hours, but it seemed to Courane that Molly had done just that. It was an unusual effect of these jobs; some people were so weak and impressionable that after a while they began to believe they truly were what they had been hired to impersonate. Under the old Representatives, that had been a capital offense. These days, deluded people like Molly were merely excised from the community at large. Now Courane and the others on the farm would have to put up with her.

"If you let the Lord show you the way, He will help you in your troubles. All you have to do is welcome your cross and follow in His way. It will all be made easy for you."

Courane was embarrassed for her. "It was always the day to day things that caused me the most worry," he said. "I don't want to think about dying for a long time yet." He smiled at Molly apologetically.

"I'll pray for you," she said. She left them and went downstairs with the others.

"We ought to go, too," said Alohilani. She noticed that her hand still rested on Courane's arm, and she self-consciously dropped it to her side.

"What about Zofia now? Will there be a graveside service?"

She led him downstairs. "Arthur will take care of all that," she said.

Arthur. That was the name of the other man. Eleven people, three of them confined to the infirmary, and himself. And all of them just a little unsavory in one way or another. On the second best of all possible worlds.

In the month of Nero, after a wearying autumn, when the calendar said there were still twenty-five weeks until spring, when the snow piled against the house promised that winter would be hard and long, when the fireplaces in the house failed to warm anyone sufficiently, when the stored food of the summer grew tiresome in its lack of variety, when the confinement in the house became worse than the prison Courane had expected, at last he was driven to learn what he could do for himself and the other prisoners. He went to Daan.

"You're wrong," said the older man. "This isn't a prison. We're not being punished. We're here to serve these people."

Courane sat in a chair beside the tect. Daan was searching through the vast library of medical information available through TECT. "I don't understand," said Courane.

"It's simple. Everyone around us is seriously ill. That's why they're here. Our job is to take care of them now. That's why *we're* here." Daan didn't look away from the tect's console.

"Then is this a prison or a hospital?"

Daan turned around to face the young man. "Haven't you ever realized that they're both the same thing?"

Courane waved the remark away; it had been too facile, too empty of practical meaning. "I've been here for more than five months, and I've watched Zofia, Carmine, and Iola die. And upstairs right now there are three more people in the infirmary waiting for their turn to die too. One of them is the woman I love. Why do they keep sending these poor people to us? What do they expect us to do for them here?"

Daan shook his head. "They expect us to stay out of Earth's way. It's a very efficient system, from TECT's point of view." He typed in a question to the great machine. "It's no accident that everyone dies of the same symptoms. I want to find out everything TECT knows about the disease and the colony's history."

"What are we? Some kind of leper colony?"

Daan held up a hand for Courane to be quiet. "TECT calls it 'D syndrome.' That doesn't tell us much. Let's see what else it knows." He motioned that Courane should take a look at the screen.

**KOENRAAD, Daan:
**The first mention is recorded in a note dated 22 September, 114 BT, three years after the founding of the colony on Planet D. Many further discussions of D fever or D syndrome have been added in the

one hundred twenty-two years since. Common symptoms involve the typical histopathologic appearance of the brain (i.e., subacute spongiform encephalopathy) in association with a rapidly progressive organic dementia. Also noted were rapid deterioration of pyramidal tracts, anterior horn cells, and the extrapyramidal system. EEG is characterized by periodic sharp waves, spikes, and suppression bursts. Vision is found to be unimpaired in most documented cases. There is often marked attendant fever elevation. Evidence supports antigen involvement. Often noted were akinetic mutism and myoclonic jerks in the middle to final stages, increasing in severity and frequency up to the point of death. Such obvious characteristics as anxiety, restlessness, confusion, lack of concentration, impairment of both long- and short-term memory may be seen separately or in combination, at any stage in the progression of the disease, and may disappear entirely only to reappear at some later stage. Patient's condition deteriorates rapidly after the middle stage, leading to such common conditions as incontinence and general helplessness. In the last stage, the patient is completely bedridden and falls into an irreversible vegetative state until death follows, either from the effects of D syndrome itself or other simultaneous conditions or diseases ***

There was silence in the tect room for a moment. Daan looked at Courane, who was thoughtfully chewing his lip. "Does any of that make any sense to you?" asked Daan.

"Sure," said Courane. "D syndrome isn't any more lethal than your average firing squad. Can't you make that machine talk in plain language?"

"I don't think it knows any. You have to know how to ask the right questions. Anything you want to ask?"

Courane thought for a few seconds. "Yes," he said, "there's one thing that worries me. They're sending us all of these people with D syndrome to take care of, and I want to know if the disease is contagious."

Daan looked at Courane and nodded solemnly. "If it

is, we might be on the right track." Daan typed in the question.

****KOENRAAD, Daan:
No, D syndrome is not contagious****

"Well, that's a relief," said Courane.

"That's a relief," said Daan.

"None of the rest of that medical jargon means anything to me. Are we going to have to go through it word by word?"

"I don't know," said Daan. "I don't think I can face that. I've been trying to puzzle this business out for weeks, and I'm tired of it. That's all TECT knows about D syndrome; no suggestion as to cause or cure, no suggested treatments, no hints about prevention. In one hundred and twenty-five years, all we have is a description of the symptoms."

"Lani's upstairs right now, having spasms and—what did it call them? 'Myoclonic jerks.' And she's going to die unless I can find some way of helping her."

Daan let out a deep breath. "Then I turn it all over to you. If anything at all is done for the poor suckers who come after us, it will have to be up to you. I give up." He stood and stared at the unwinking green glow of the console.

There was silence in the room for a moment. The two men looked at the impassive machine. There was the thump of snow falling from the roof. It was very cold and lonely in the house.

Two months after Courane's arrival, on the sixteenth of Tiber, Sheldon and Courane were harvesting vegetables. They were working in a patch of native beans. The work was hard and tiring, and the sun scorched them as they bent to pluck the ripe beans from the scruffy bushes. "I used to hate beans," said Sheldon. "Back home. Back on Earth. I wouldn't come near beans for anything."

"I didn't like vegetables, either," said Courane. "But I liked beans all right."

"My wife used to eat vegetables all the time. She was one of these people who think you have to eat a ton of vegetables every week or you end up in the poorhouse."

Courane stood up, leaning backward to stretch his aching back muscles. "What do vegetables have to do with having money?"

Sheldon looked up at him and smiled. "She was never clear about that," he said. He took a long bean and cracked it in half. "You have to boil the hell out of these things to make them edible. And then, even after that, they aren't any fun. They taste like wads of wet paper."

Courane shrugged. "You don't have a photograph of your wife, do you? I mean, I've never seen one."

"No, I forgot it. Can you believe that? I was in a state of shock when they told me I had twelve hours before they were sending me here. And I don't think I really believed it. I know I thought it was some kind of mistake, that I'd be home in a day or two. My wife never found out the whole story. Maybe she still doesn't know. She was so beautiful. I hope TECT is taking care of her, or else she's living with my parents now. She had the most beautiful brown eyes you ever saw. And her hair was . . ."

Sheldon paused, and after a few seconds Courane became concerned. He saw the frightened look on his friend's face, and he understood the meaning of the simple memory lapse. It was the first symptom.

"Sandy," said Sheldon, his voice trembling.

"It's all right, Sheldon," said Courane softly.

Sheldon stood up and grabbed Courane's shoulders. "Her hair." Sheldon's voice was barely a whisper, but his eyes were wide and staring. "Her hair," he murmured. And then he began to cry like a child.

* *THREE

It was still dark when Courane awoke. He was lying on his face on the smooth pebbles of the desert floor. His right hand and arm were caught under his body and felt numb. He rolled over on his left side, but he still couldn't get any feeling in the arm. He turned on his back and raised the right arm with his left hand. He put it gently on his stomach. Then he stared up into the sky.

A cool breeze blew. Courane realized that his clothing was damp and acrid with perspiration. His mind worked slowly, taking in the details of his surroundings bit by bit, cataloguing his impressions, trying painfully to decide where he was and what had happened to him. His mother never let him sleep outside like this. He had asked her once, some time ago, to let him go camping with three other boys from school. They were just going to a state park about four miles from Greusching, but Courane's mother acted as if they were planning to sleep naked in the savage heart of Africa. Courane had had to make up an excuse for the other boys because he didn't want to tell them what his mother had really said. But now, evidently, he was sleeping out somewhere.

He wasn't alone. He saw another sleeping form near him, but he couldn't remember who it was. It was probably his best friend, Dieter, or one of the other boys from school. It was odd that Courane couldn't recall exactly where he was. It must be that he had been dreaming, and that he had roused suddenly and wasn't completely awake yet. When the last webs of sleep cleared from his mind, he would feel foolish about his forgetfulness.

Something bothered him about the stars. He looked first for Orion, but the constellation wasn't in the sky. It ought to be, at this time of year. The sky was very clear, so it wasn't that the stars were obscured by smoke or clouds. There was only one explanation, he thought, and that was that he was in the southern hemisphere. But that was crazy. He was home in Europe, in some desert near Greusching. He had never even visited the southern hemisphere. . . .

There was a warning stab of pain in his right arm. "Oh, boy," Courane murmured. He knew what he had to go through now. He always hated this. He massaged the arm and winced, forcing himself to work through the uncomfortable tingling. He opened and closed his hand until his fingers felt normal again. He shook the arm for a moment, then relaxed.

He thought about waking Dieter and asking where they were, but that would only embarrass him. He preferred to keep his dumbness a private matter. He let his friend sleep on. Then, when Courane sat up and looked around, he changed his mind. There was nothing to be seen anywhere around them. There were no trees or buildings nearby or far away, just empty landscape paved with rounded pebbles like the bottom of an aquarium. And the moon was unnaturally small and altogether the wrong color. He had no explanation for it, but he thought that Dieter might like to see. He reached over and shook the sleeper's shoulder. There was no response. Courane shook harder and there was still no groan of reply. Courane rolled the form over on its back, and he was shocked. It was a woman, a stranger Courane had never seen before, and she wouldn't wake up. He crept closer to her and saw the note pinned to her blouse. He looked at it for some time, but he had a disquieting shock: he couldn't make sense of the letters and words. They looked familiar individually, but he couldn't put them together to mean anything. He had forgotten how to read. A great and overwhelming fear arose deep in Courane's soul, and the terror reached up and paralyzed his mind until all he wanted to do was run. The desert, the loneliness, the feeling of being lost and abandoned, this dead woman beside him, all these things seemed like elements in the worst possible nightmare.

Courane was forced to admit that he was probably still dreaming. None of this made any logical sense; it wasn't even coherent. It couldn't be real life. He lifted his hand from the woman's shoulder, crawled back slowly to where he had rested, pillowed his head on his right arm, and went back to sleep.

Kenny was eleven years old. He was smart, good-natured, and just a little too active for some of the others to tolerate. He and Molly worked in the barn. They were the only two who enjoyed being with the strange live-stock of Planet D.

"I haven't ever looked at one of these close up," said Courane. He was standing in the pasture watching a gigantic animal lying on its side, eating the red grass. The beast was the size of a large rhinoceros but nowhere so pretty. It was a dull gray-blue in color, with sagging folds of sweaty skin hanging from its neck to its long ropy tail. It looked like it was in desperate need of cleaning and pressing. The head was large and flat, with odd dainty lips and the worn broad teeth of an herbivore. Its eyes were small and yellow and set very far apart. Its face successfully hid any sign that a small intelligence might lurk behind.

"I like them. They're kind of funny," said Kenny. He sat down beside the animal and stroked its moist flank.

"And that's where we get the stuff we eat for breakfast? That sort of thick orange stuff?"

"Uh huh," said Kenny.

"Where does it come from?"

Kenny looked up at Courane and laughed. "You don't want to know," he said. "Get up real early tomorrow morning and I'll let you watch. But I let Carmine watch once and he never ate the stuff again as long as he lived."

"You're right, I'd rather not know. Did you name them?"

Kenny patted the animal's neck. "This one is Prancer and the one over there is Vixen."

"No, I mean did you call them 'blerds'? *Blöd* means 'stupid' in old German."

Kenny got up and brushed off his pants. "They were called blerds when I got here. I wouldn't have called them that. I would have thought up something better. Something funny."

They walked back toward the barn. It looked like another storm was coming from across the river. "What would you have called them, Kenny?"

The boy thought for a few seconds. Then he looked up and his face lit up with a bright smile. "I would have called them pixies," he said.

"That's worse than blerds, Kenny," said Courane, "but it would have made people years from now wonder about us."

"That's the whole idea," said Kenny. They felt the wind quicken and then they saw the first warning blaze of lightning. Whenever a storm approached the sky grew blacker, but the world seemed to glow with a pale green shimmer, an effect that always terrified Courane. He never got used to it. Ragged spears of lightning would link the muddy sky with the rust-red ground and thunder would split the air until the endless rolling blasts seemed to make it difficult to breathe. And then the hot heavy rain would fall. It would rain all evening sometimes, never slowing until the storm came to its abrupt end and the fresh wind blew the clouds away and freed the hidden stars. It stormed like this once or twice a week during the spring and summer, and on those days Courane liked to hide himself away in the tect room, concentrating on an intricate game or puzzle. As he walked quickly across the open pasture, Courane wished he were already back in the house. He had a terrible fear of being struck by lightning.

"We better hurry or we'll get soaked," he said.

"That's okay," said Kenny, "I've been wet before."

"Sure. But have you ever been burned to a crisp before?"

Kenny held up a black hand before his face. "No," he said, "just a little scorched." Courane had to look to see if the boy were joking. Until Kenny made a face at him, Courane couldn't decide.

The day began in dim cloudy light. The sky was heavy and threatening. Courane sat against a black gnarled tree and waited. In the desert it was still hot, though summer had ended; on the farm the month of Gai meant bringing in the crops and beginning the preparations for the endless winter. He wished he were back there. He didn't want to be in the desert anymore. The hills didn't seem any nearer, for all the labored walking he had done. He was thirsty, but soon the clouds would open and he

would have more than enough to drink. In fact, there
was the chance that he was sitting in the middle of a dry
rivercourse, that the autumn storm would start a flash
flood to nourish the sparse life in the valley, to bring the
desert to late bloom, and only incidentally to extinguish
any spark or blush of life in its one lonely human
occupant.

Courane dismissed the idea. He had enough troubles,
he thought, without inventing new ones for the future.
He was middling lost, starving, and with an excellent
chance of never returning to the house alive. Floods and
earthquakes and plagues of locusts were rather unnecessary. He had managed to shuffle off his own mortal coil,
not quite all the way but almost, all by himself. With a
little assist from TECT, of course.

Lightning startled him. The first flash was so nearby
that there was a loud snap when it struck. The clap of
thunder that accompanied it was like an audible shadow.
That, Courane told himself, was something he might legitimately be afraid of. A single heavy drop of rain hit his
face with a flat smack. It dazed him like a quick jab to
the jaw. Then the storm attacked him with its full
overture.

Just after New Year's the colony received two new
people, a European woman named Klára and an African
girl about fourteen years old named Nneka. They were
welcomed into the group with the customary, somewhat
somber generosity. It was the same spirit that governs a
crowd of strangers caught in a vice raid: there was a kind
of fellowship and sympathy among them, but there was
also the knowledge that none of them was there just for
an innocent visit. They were all there because TECT had
wanted to forget about them.

Klára was a hefty Magyar woman with green eyes and
auburn hair which she wore in braids, coiled tightly on
her temples as if to protect her head from the slightly
grimy touch of the outside world. She was tall and stout
and loud, and just a bit unlikable. On her first day, she
walked about the house examining every room, listening
to the explanations, frowning as though something that
displeased her greatly had pursued her from Earth and
was now following her from room to room in the big

house. She said little that first day, but she compensated for that immediately on the second day. She began to give instructions forged in the great foundry of her ignorance, and attempted to restructure the running of the household, the farm, and, through the tect, Earth as well. Evidently she had had great experience ordering people about in her former life and she saw no reason not to continue, despite the fact that nothing she said or did had any relevance to her new environment. She instituted some changes, such as the way the covers were tucked on the beds in the infirmary, but for the most part everyone learned to ignore her within the first thirty-six hours.

"Do you know what that woman said to me this morning?" asked Arthur one winter day. Arthur was of average height but exceptionally slender of frame. He wore eyeglasses, which on Earth was such a rarity that it might have been an eccentric affectation or part of his professional persona. He spoke in a small voice, high and thin, and consequently he had spent his life always getting the worst assignments and the least desirable portion of whatever was available. It was no different on Planet D.

Courane was playing chess with him. TECT made a better opponent, as far as challenge went, but Courane had no use for challenges. He preferred to see his adversary's face, to watch as the other player realized how cleverly Courane had laid his trap. "I can't guess," said Courane. He moved a knight to the side of the board where seemingly it was of little value and posed no immediate threat.

"She wanted to know why we didn't have all kinds of beautiful flowers around the house. She thought it would make our stay here more pleasant." He moved a bishop up to a more aggressive position.

Courane studied the chess board for only a few seconds before he confidently bit off an unprotected pawn with his queen. "How did you answer her?" he asked.

Arthur held his own queen above the board, suspended in air between heaven and earth like a martyred saint with doubts about her own ascension. "I told her one of the reasons we didn't have any flowers was that there are four feet of snow out there. Another reason is that plants pollinate differently here, so there aren't many pretty flowers. The ones that do have some color give off a fragrance like a hydrocarbon cracking tower." Arthur found the move he wanted and set his queen down, precisely in the center of the chosen square. "Mate," he said in an apologetic voice.

"Damn it," said Courane. His well-laid trap lay unsprung.

"What now?" asked Arthur.

"What do you mean? Another game? No, thanks. I think I'll stick with two-handed canasta against TECT from now on."

"Do you want to go for a walk?"

Courane looked at Arthur as if the little man had stripped a rather essential gear. "Outside? In the snow? Where would we go?"

"I don't know," said Arthur. "Didn't you ever go for walks back on Earth?"

Courane thought for a moment. No, even on Earth he didn't often feel the need to walk any great distance. Certainly not for the sole purpose of experiencing inclement weather. But then he saw that the real reason he didn't want to go outside was because he didn't like it outside. He was afraid of it. It wasn't home, it wasn't natural. It wasn't Earth; it was Planet D, and every bit of it was wild and threatening. The only safe place was in the house, and he never wanted to leave it. He felt unsafe even walking from the back porch to the barn. "Arthur, what would we do out there?"

Klára and Kenny came into the parlor and sat on a davenport across from the game table. "You could build snowblerds," said the boy.

"I want to call my husband," said Klára.

"Snowblerds," said Courane, sighing.

"I want my husband to arrange to come here," said the arrogant woman. Both men looked at her in silence. "What are you staring at?" she asked.

"This isn't a vacation weekend in St. Tropez," said Courane. "You just can't call Earth and order whatever you want."

"And why not? I've been dragged here to take care of a lot of drooling, filthy patients upstairs, completely against my will I might add, and I don't see why I shouldn't organize the work the way I know is best.

Some of those people in the infirmary are little better than idiots and imbeciles, and I can't say much more for the rest of you. I've seen potato dumplings that had better sense."

"Klára—" said Arthur.

"You call me Mrs. Hriniak. My late mother and father called me Klára, but even Mr. Hriniak is afraid to do that."

"What does he call you, then?" asked Kenny.

Klára gave the boy an unpleasant look and moved farther away from him on the davenport.

"Mrs. Hriniak," said Arthur, "we are pretty well limited in our ability to communicate with Earth. We can use the tect to learn anything in its memory banks, but that doesn't allow us to make telephone calls to whomever we want back home. We can inform TECT of emergencies here, or of supplies and things we need urgently, and TECT will decide what should be done and then let us know. But you can't just ring up your husband for a chat because you miss him."

"Miss him!" She gave a derisive laugh.

"Whatever. The best you can do is ask TECT for permission to contact him through a tect unit on Earth. Other people have tried that here, though I don't recall anyone getting that permission."

Klára was outraged. "I don't believe it!" she cried. "TECT can't do that kind of thing. That's illegal. Every citizen has the right to free communication. The government protects that."

"The government is TECT," said Courane, "and TECT makes the rules. TECT also enforces the rules and judges if they're morally and legally valid. You have nowhere to turn."

"But what am I, some kind of prisoner?" Her face had drained of its ruddy color, and one plump-fingered hand was raised to her throat as though guarding it against physical assault.

"That's precisely what you are, Mrs. Hriniak," said Arthur. "You are some kind of prisoner."

"I am not!" She was too outraged even to consider the possibility. "I have been brought here to care for some unpleasantly sick people, that disgusting machine only knows why. I have no idea at all why I was chosen, but I will not stop fighting until either I am returned to my home, or my husband and my possessions are transferred here for the duration of my stay."

"On Earth," asked Courane, "did you ever have any nursing training?"

"Good heavens, no. I was the daughter of a public official. I was married at a young age, directly after leaving school. I am neither a laborer nor servant."

"But you are a prisoner," said Courane.

"I am not." She glared at Courane malevolently.

"I could ask our tect why you were sent here."

Klára seemed flustered. "No," she said, her voice suddenly trembling just a bit, "there was an occasion, an unpleasant incident that developed between me and the terrible old man who lived just down the road from our home. We lived on the outskirts of an old village and this man, he was simply unbearable, he complained to the CAS constable. I don't even recall what it was all about."

"They wouldn't have sent you here just for that," said Kenny. "I'll go ask the tect."

Klára dropped her hand to her side. "There may have been one or two other similar occasions," she said softly.

Arthur turned to Courane, ignoring the woman. "Do you want to go for that walk now?"

To Courane, the prospect of going outside was suddenly much more attractive than remaining in the parlor with Klára Hriniak. "Sure," he said.

"Can I come, too?" asked Kenny.

"Those animals are just lying around out there," said Courane. "We can pile snow over them, and you'll have your snowblerds the easy way."

"Aw, that's no fun," said the boy. They left the large cold parlor to Klára. She was still sitting, staring blankly into space, when they left.

Prison or hospital? One of the difficulties was that on Earth everything was much simpler. The Representatives had liked it that way, and TECT—in the name of the Representative, of course—continued the customs of the past. People were simple, institutions were simple, questions of right and wrong were simple, life was simple, death was simple. A person was a man or a woman, dead or alive, good or bad. Buildings housed offices or apartments, cells or wards, never a mixture. But that was too expensive a luxury on Planet D. In the colony, things had to be used up and worn out. That went for the contents of the house, the farm implements, the livestock, the cultivated fields, and the people themselves. Courane soon stopped trying to find a simple answer to his puzzle; that was a bad habit left over from an interrupted life. But if the colony were both prison and hospital, then the people around him were a mixture of patients and prisoners. At first glance, it was often difficult to decide which person carried which label:

Fletcher, the sullen black man, was a prisoner. He had probably served a long term on Planet D, but Courane was unable to get much real information out of him.

Arthur, strange as it seemed, must have been a prisoner, too, although a very useful and efficient one.

Goldie showed no sign of being anything other than a very ignorant person. She didn't appear to have warranted excarceration, and she showed none of the symptoms of the D syndrome.

Daan had admitted that he, too, was a prisoner.

Kenny couldn't have been a prisoner, could he? He must be a patient, but one who hadn't yet realized the fact. Perhaps his parents and doctor and TECT had hidden that information. If he hadn't figured it out for himself yet, Courane didn't want to be the one to tell him. Courane didn't have the fortitude for that kind of chore.

Molly was criminally Christian. That was very obvious.

Sheldon was a terminal patient, and the fact grieved Courane. Sheldon had been the first friend that Courane had made.

Beautiful Lani was also a patient, dying so young of such an ugly condition. Courane thought about her for a few seconds and had to repress a frightened shiver.

It was too early yet to make a judgment about the new arrivals, the three women. Klára, though, was probably a prisoner while Rachel and Nneka were likely patients.

In Otho of the colony's year 125, that was the limit of Courane's hard information. Something Nneka said made him realize that his picture of the colony—and of TECT's ultimate purpose for it—was too narrow.

They were putting up decorations in the parlor for their simple celebration of Arbor Day. Nneka and Courane were being helped by Goldie and Daan. "This place reminds me of the house where TECT sent my mother," said Nneka.

"Your mother?" said Daan.

"My mother was blinded in an accident about three years ago. When TECT found out—it wasn't more than four or five days later—she was ordered to report to a home for the blind in Ajilele. But whenever I visited her, I saw that she seemed to be a kind of prisoner there. Just like we are here. She said she was happy enough. The food was good and the people there took good care of her, she said. But she couldn't leave the grounds. And there weren't any doctors or nurses. I don't know who was taking care of her. I never thought much about it before."

"Prisoners and patients," said Courane.

"Possibly," said Daan.

"Have you ever noticed that lots of places on Earth are the same way?" said Goldie. "Homes for the elderly are exactly the same. So are orphanages and poorhouses. Nobody ever leaves there, either. And hospitals. Hospitals for people with dangerous diseases, those patients are prisoners. Mental hospitals, too."

"Why doesn't TECT send those people off to their own colony, then?" asked Courane. No one had an answer.

"We used to hear the same thing about this boarding school near us in Kisangani," said Kenny, who came into the room and watched the decorators critically. "Kids would go there to learn all sorts of things and you'd never see them again."

"What do all these places have in common?" asked Daan. "They're all places where people go and put themselves in the charge of someone else."

"But TECT is supposed to supervise it all," said Nneka.

"TECT is supervising it all," said Courane. "But maybe it's taking its duties too seriously."

"Don't say that," said Goldie, looking around the dimly lit room as though some informer was hiding behind the worn furniture. "You can't say things like that about TECT. Some people have to make sacrifices, that's all, and TECT sees to it that the sacrifices are fairly shared around by everybody."

"It used to be, I remember," said Daan, "that people made sacrifices so that the Representative could have a little extra on his plate."

Goldie's face flushed bright red. "I can't stay here and listen to talk like this," she said anxiously. She dropped the paper decorations in her hand and hurried out of the room. Kenny laughed. Daan only shrugged.

"We were taught that if TECT seemed to make a harsh decision, it was harsh only because we made it necessary," said Nneka. "From TECT's point of view it was proper, at least in how it affected the community at large."

"There's no such thing as the community at large," said Kenny.

Daan nodded approvingly. "Now that's a smart kid," he said.

Pain brought Courane back to the present. He had walked headlong into one of the stumpy, tough black trees. He sprawled forward into the gnarled limbs, one branch knuckled up into his belly, another digging painfully into the side of Courane's face. He had dropped the young woman's body and he rested now and tried to gather his thoughts. The tree supported him in a leaning, awkward position. It was restful, in a way, and Courane was in no great hurry to extricate himself. The corpse had fallen to the ground and rolled a quarter turn away, arms and legs bent in stiff, unnatural positions, hands clutching, clawlike, at nothing. Courane paid it little attention.

He had forgotten the storm already, and his clothes had nearly dried beneath the sun. It was almost noon. His body was hungry, but his emptiness intruded on his consciousness at infrequent intervals.

Pain started in his arms and legs, growing like the rising river in the spring flood. It began with quick stabs in his shoulders, forearms, and the calves of his legs. He winced at each cut. He let the rigid scaffolding of the tree support his weight; his arms hung down nearly to the stone-covered ground, his legs were limp as he collapsed further into the tree. The pain returned again and again, stronger at each attack. He cried out in a low wailing voice, helpless. He knew there was no one near to help him. The agony in his body flashed like lightning. Then, like lightning, it seemed to recede, to fade into the distance, and after a time he rested, exhausted by the siege, his face wet with tears, his mind more bewildered than ever.

Slowly he disentangled himself from the tree. He moved his aching arms inch by inch, lifting himself free like a green lizard on a heated rock. He supported his weight with his arms, then made sure his legs were free. He was covered with large bruises and deep cuts, but none of these troubled him. Those pains were insignificant compared to his larger worries. His brain didn't even bother to evaluate the surface wounds. Once completely extricated from the tree, he rolled to one side and let himself fall to the ground. He lay just as he fell, with his face pressed close to the smooth stones. He opened his mouth and for a long time he uttered strange, almost inhuman sounds as he breathed.

There was a certain joy involved in watching a cultivated field clothe itself in rust-red sprouts. Then, as the crops grew and produced their fruit, there was work, a lot of work, but Courane discovered that it gave him a considerable amount of pleasure. The work was simple but essential, and failure could come only through calculated neglect. His new job on Planet D was almost failure-proof, because he worked harder than anyone else in the community. He had never been lazy or shiftless on Earth; his failures came about only because he and TECT had differing ideas about his talents. It seemed to Courane that if anyone should be punished for those failures, it ought to be TECT itself. But of course such a thing was impossible.

Courane loved working in the fields. He liked that job much better than caring for the animals, the blerds and the fowl-like smudgeons, the docile osoi that could be used as draft animals, the unpleasant grease-shedding icks, the other indigenous creatures around the barnyard. He preferred the cultivating and weeding and pruning and harvesting in the fields.

TECT had been right, after all. Courane did have a growing sense of his own worth. The hard labor under the sun had been good for him. There was a marvelous feeling of self-sufficiency that came from putting food on the table that he had grown himself.

"Failure is important," Molly had said once, in the autumn about a month after she had shown her first sign of D syndrome. "God doesn't expect you to be perfect. Just the opposite; He knows you aren't perfect."

"That's probably true," said Rachel, "but it isn't true for TECT."

"TECT isn't God," said Molly.

"The way it runs everybody's life, it might as well be," said Fletcher.

Molly shrugged. She didn't mind being on Planet D. "It doesn't change things, being here," she said. "You're still working to bring yourself closer to God."

"Not so as you'd notice," said Fletcher. He looked around at the others, grinned again, and walked away.

"I wouldn't be here at all except for some bad luck," said Arthur. "I was—"

"There's no such thing as bad luck," said Molly, shaking her head sadly. "Our Lord wasn't crucified because of bad luck. He never spent His time wallowing in self-pity. He never wanted to overthrow God because of the unfairness of the situation."

"Maybe just a little toward the end," said Rachel.

"That doesn't count," said Molly, "that was the human part talking."

"TECT gave up on us," said Arthur.

"I don't know about that," said Courane. "I'm kind of grateful. Some people like Fletcher won't ever get the point. If it weren't for the fact that we don't have our liberty, I'd be very happy."

"You always have your liberty in the Lord," said Molly. "The Lord doesn't give up on you."

"Yeah, sure," said Rachel in a bored voice, tapping the side of her head with an index finger. "Let's go play softball."

After graduating from high school in Greusching, Courane waited for TECT to plan his future life. He had applied for admission to a university. His schoolwork was not better than average, so Courane really didn't think it was likely that TECT would honor his request. Courane believed that TECT would order him into the armed forces. It was the usual course for most people. Courane was ready to accept that decision.

Courane was surprised when TECT admitted him to

the University of Pilessio. Courane didn't know even
where Pilessio was. He had never heard of the university
before. Even stranger, to Courane, was that he had been
selected on the basis of a basketball scholarship.

Courane had never heard of basketball, either.

Immediately after he read the news on the screen of
the tect in his parents' apartment, Courane typed a request at the terminal: "Please supply me with all details
concerning this order, along with instructions for comply-
ing in the immediate future."

Courane felt that his response left a tangible record of
his willingness to cooperate. He believed that in some
unguessable time of trouble his eagerness would be a
matter of documented fact. He could then prove his loy-
alty, and TECT would be inclined to help him. In point
of fact, however, Courane was wrong. TECT didn't care
one way or the other.

A few weeks later, Courane registered for admission to
the University of Pilessio. He was given a course of study
which was broad and led seemingly to no profession or
useful trade. Courane wondered what TECT had decided
about him; no amount of argument or pleading with the
computer could persuade it to reveal its plans.

On the tenth of September, in the year of TECT 5, the
red *Advise* light blinked on the tect in the parlor of Courane's dormitory building. The young woman on duty
asked whom the message was for and called Courane; he
came downstairs and identified himself to the tect. The
message, stripped of the official salutations and warnings,
went as follows:

*TECT in the name of the Representative welcomes
COURANE, Sandor, and hopes that you will enjoy
your term at the University of Pilessio. It is further
hoped that you will use the university's great facilities
for your own education and the successful completion
of your course of study. Failure to do so will be considered Contempt of TECTWish.*

*You are to report to the Harthorn Wingo Memorial
Gymnasium on Monday, 13 September, 5 YT, before
12:00:00. You will register with Professor Ernesto Silverio, coach of the university's basketball squad.*

Failure to do so will be considered Contempt of TECTWish.

The game of basketball is a healthful, wholesome, and exciting one. TECT in the name of the Representative hopes that it affords you many opportunities to forge those qualities which may stand you in good stead, here at the university and in your later life. You will also meet many other athletes from many different backgrounds, giving you the chance to acquaint yourself with the rich resources of Europe's cultural heritage. Failure to do so will be considered Contempt of TECTWish.

Courane made the necessary response, indicating that he understood the computer's orders. Then he added a request that TECT print out a summary of data relating to the game of basketball. He was a little bewildered by the situation, but he had all weekend to study.

The following Monday, Courane reported to Professor Silverio's office. "Good morning," said Courane.

"Courane?" asked Silverio.

"Yes, sir," said Courane.

"You're small," said the coach with some disappointment.

"Yes, sir."

"You must have some talent. TECT has its reasons. Well, maybe you're a playmaking guard. Quick. Good hands. How is your ballhandling?" The coach tossed Courane a purple, orange, and green basketball.

"I don't know," said Courane. "I've never handled one."

"TECT has its reasons," murmured Silverio, frowning. The coach spoke a few words to an assistant, who turned to a small closet in the coach's office. The assistant gave Courane a pair of light, thin basketball shorts and a sleeveless top, navy blue with white letters and numbers.

"What size shoes?" asked the assistant.

"Eight," said Courane.

"Small," said the assistant. He found a pair of white high-top basketball shoes. Courane took the suit and the shoes and went to a locker to change. Then Courane walked onto the basketball court. He was very self-conscious. For some time he watched some of the others on the team shooting baskets and practicing their dribbling. Finally, when he had worked up his courage, he joined them and tried taking a few shots himself.

He was no good at all.

His hands were too small. The ball slipped from his grasp easily, and he couldn't dribble with any skill or confidence. He only stared in disbelief as the others twisted through the air and slammed the ball down through the net. Courane was much shorter than they; while they could leap up and touch the backboard above the rim, Courane could barely reach the net that hung from it. He became discouraged quickly.

"Don't worry about it," said Coach Silverio dubiously. "You'll pick up the drill. TECT knows what it's doing."

"Okay," said Courane. He was very tired after half an hour of exercise. "What part of the game do you think I ought to concentrate on?" he asked. Silverio didn't say anything. He just shook his head sadly.

A few months later, as winter began to thaw into spring, there was another message for Courane on the dorm's tect. He identified himself and read the news on the unit's screen.

**COURANE, Sandor   RepE Dis4 Sec27
Loc39–Gre–834
  M232–86–059–41Maj
09:24:37 8 March 6 YT   TECTGreet**
**COURANE, Sandor:
  Notification of Majority. Alteration in TaskFunc (Details follow).
**COURANE, Sandor:
  Congratulations! Today you are nineteen years old, and an adult citizen under the protection of TECT in the name of the Representative. Now that you are officially an adult citizen, we are even more concerned for you and your future.
**COURANE, Sandor:
  Upon notification of the attainment of majority, a citizen is usually presented with a list of alternative services under the CAS authority among which he may choose to fulfill his civic responsibility. We had

*tentatively decided to offer you an opportunity for
employment in the exciting and fast-paced world of
professional basketball, which we have maintained
for the entertainment of the millions. Following your
season on the University of Pilessio team, we com-
puted your statistics as follows.*

COURANE, Sandor:
*Average time played per forty-minute game—07
minutes, 23.4056 seconds
Average number of field goals attempted—03.0417
Average number of field goals made—00.0000
Percentage of field goals made—00.0000
Average number of free throws attempted—01.2917
Average number of free throws made—00.2083
Percentage of free throws made—16.1290
Average rebounds per game—00.1250
Average assists per game—00.1667
Average personal fouls per game—03.2917*

COURANE, Sandor:
*These statistics are not very impressive. They lead
TECT in the name of the Representative to believe
that a future in professional basketball may not be
right for you. But do not despair! To do so may be
considered Contempt of TECTWish.*

COURANE, Sandor:
*You will travel to North America. You will become a
writer of science fiction adventure tales. We have
encouraged the continuing existence of science fiction for the amusement of the millions. You will produce one full-length science fiction novel each six-
month service term. Your first novel will be entitled
Space Spy. It will be wry and ironic, yet containing
seemingly important statements about the human
condition. It will have no explicit sex and little violence. Other than that, the book will be entirely the
product of your imagination. Failure to comply with
these directives will be considered Willful Contempt
of TECTWish.*

COURANE, Sandor:
Understanding of the above to be indicated.

COURANE, Sandor:
*Affirm?***

"Yes," said Courane wearily. That was how he learned of his first crime against the state. He went back to his room to pack, and to think about his new future as a novelist. He still wanted to be on the good side of TECT; he was deeply sorry that it was disappointed with him and his basketball playing. He promised himself that he would become a good and respected writer. He would copy the styles and techniques of the best science fiction writers in the business, whoever they were. His college friends in Pilessio never learned what happened to him. He went home to Greusching that day and left for New York the next. He got right down to work shortly after his arrival in North America.

There was a light rain falling and the sun was low in the sky. Courane was working on the roof of the house with a man named Shai, who had joined the community two months before. They were tearing off and replacing shingles that had been damaged; rain water was leaking through the roof and into the infirmary. Goldie had nearly drowned in her sleep before someone noticed a pool of water forming on her bed. Suddenly Courane sat up on the roof and looked around. "What are we doing up here?" he said.

Shai glanced over at him, perplexed. "What do you mean, Sandy?" he asked.

Courane felt completely disoriented. "Who are you?" he said.

Shai came over and put a hand on Courane's shoulder. "Calm down. Everything's all right. It'll all come back to you."

"Shai, I'm sorry," said Courane. The anxiety passed, but it left him with a lingering suspicion. He sat on the roof and looked around. He wasn't on Earth anymore. That sun was Epsilon Eridani. A great gulf had opened between Courane and his birthplace, between him and his parents and everything familiar. Unconsciously he clutched at the shingles. It was like the worst dream he could imagine, but there would be no waking from this nightmare.

Shai tried to comfort him, but he hadn't had much experience at it. "You'll be all right, Sandy. Just wait a minute."

"I'm all right now, Shai." It had been an unsettling experience, as if he had awakened in the body of a dumb animal, or if he awoke one morning and learned that he had only dreamed his adult life, that he was only four years old and unable to communicate his distress.

"Let's knock off for today," said Shai.

Courane just stared down at the hideous red plants standing in rows in the fields, at the monstrous creatures in the pasture, at the alien landscape surrounding the farm. He didn't want it all to come back to him. He wanted to be home.

He laughed as he bent to pick up the young woman's corpse. How he must have made a fool of himself. How often in his life he managed only to look ridiculous when he had aimed instead for nobility or deftness. The memory of his first lapse was still bitter in his mind. How he had been fooled. How unfairly he had been misled. He wished that he could go back to give the information to his previous self. How stupid he had been—how stupid they all had been, and how eager to ignore the obvious. But that was the first stage in dying. No one is quick to accept the idea of his own end.

Even as he struggled to make a comfortable burden of the body, Courane's memories evaporated from his mind, leaving faint traces like the bouquet of a good wine. "Her name is Alohilani," he read on the note. Alohilani. The name wasn't significant. Her face was unfamiliar. He read the rest of the note, but there was nothing in it to jog his memory. He decided that the note was there for some good reason; admitting that, he took up his charge and continued on the long way home.

**FOUR

The settlers of Planet D made their lives as cheerful and happy as possible. Some people, like Courane and Molly and young Kenny, had accepted their new home and were comfortable there. Others, like Klára and Fletcher, grew more resentful and ill-tempered as the weeks passed. But Planet D might not have been at fault; the good spirits of the one group and the bad humor of the other might have been but the reflection of what these people were on Earth.

One of the least pleasant jobs on the farm was the butchering of the animals. No one liked to do it but it was a chore that had to be done. Consequently everyone took a turn at it except those people who were too disturbed by the idea. Only Goldie and Kenny begged off; surprisingly, even Molly and Alohilani took their turns, although both women expressed their reluctance.

There were large, fat rodents that lived in a corner of the barn. They were butchered like hogs and their meat smoked. They bred rapidly and abundantly, and they supplied much of the animal protein in the community's diet. The rodents were called varks, from an old Dutch word for pig.

Kenny liked the varks as much as he liked the other animals. When it was time to butcher one of the pale blue creatures he always protested, even though he knew it was necessary. After a few months, his protests grew weaker until they were little more than a kind of perfunctory statement of regret.

One day late in Vespasi, Courane and Shai came in after swabbing down the shed where the varks were slaughtered and butchered. The two men had become close friends since Shai's arrival from Earth.

"Which vark did you kill?" asked Kenny.

"Which vark?" said Courane. He couldn't tell one
from another, and he was surprised by the suggestion
that anyone else could.

"The big one with the patch of yellow hair over its
eye," said Shai.

"Aw," said Kenny, "that was Bambi." He looked
gloomy.

"Sorry," said Courane. Kenny only shrugged.

"Sandy," said Shai, "you've been here longer than I
have. Who named this place Home?"

"I don't know," said Courane. "I called it Planet D for
a long time before I heard anyone else call it Home. Ask
Kenny. He's been here even longer than I have. He's
been here longer than anyone except Molly." There was
a bit of a pause because Molly was upstairs, in the infirmary. Kenny had already shown signs of advancing D
syndrome, but he was still doing well enough not to require confinement on the third floor.

"It was always called Home," said the boy. "I asked
TECT about that once months and months ago, and it
said that the first gang of people it sent here named the
planet Home. I would have picked a better name for it."

Courane knew what was coming. "I'm sure you would
have," he said.

There was an expectant silence. It stretched on and on,
with neither Courane nor Shai breaking down to ask
Kenny what he would have chosen instead.

"I gave it a lot of thought," said Kenny at last, "and I
would have called the place Schmotz." He looked
around. Shai was smiling, but Courane just looked
impatient.

"Why Schmotz?" asked Shai.

Kenny's expression indicated that he thought the answer was self-evident. "How can you be afraid of a place
called Schmotz?" he said.

When Courane had been on Planet D, or Home, for a
few days, he noticed something odd. He was wandering
around the grounds during a free hour. At the back of
the house was a porch and a small yard with some tables
and chairs and a narrow path leading down to the river.
At the front of the house was the wide field of high red
grasses through which he had waded on his arrival. To

one side was the barn and silo which, together with the house itself, partially enclosed the barnyard. On the opposite side of the house were the pastures and the cultivated fields. Courane found nothing unusual, and that bothered him. He felt something was missing. He looked all around; the river formed a definite boundary in one direction, but in the other three there was flat land covered with waving grass and dotted with trees, and the high growth came right up to the edge of the clearing the people had made for themselves. At the horizon were low hills. There were no other landmarks. Courane was puzzled because he didn't know where the cemetery was.

The colony had been on Planet D for one hundred and twenty-four years, and it was made up of a few hardworking prisoners and a dozen or so people suffering from D syndrome. To Courane that meant that scores, even hundreds of people had died on the planet since the beginning of the colony, and so they must have been buried in some plot of ground that ought to be recognizable from the house. But he saw nothing. Maybe it was the custom to take the bodies out and bury them in unmarked graves within the shelter of the red grass. Courane went to find Arthur. Alohilani had mentioned that he had been assigned to take charge of Zofia's funeral arrangements.

"What funeral arrangements?" asked Arthur. He was genuinely puzzled.

Courane frowned. "I just thought that if such a great custom has evolved of seeing everyone off at their dying moment, that there was probably something of a similar nature to be done at their burial."

Arthur shook his head emphatically. "We don't bury anyone here," he said.

"Why not?"

"What else? TECT has given us other instructions. That's the way things have been since the year one here. After a person dies, we put him in the medic box and leave the room. TECT ordered that no one should enter that room again for a full day. It didn't specify an Earth day or one of ours, so we stay away for a twenty-seven-hour Planet D day just to be sure."

"But why?"

"I don't know. But as soon as the corpse is put in the

medic box, TECT must diagnose and realize the patient's dead. What happens after that I don't know, but a day later the body is gone. Always. No one knows why."

"What could TECT want with the bodies?" asked Courane.

"Nothing," said Arthur. "I just think they're sent back to Earth for proper burial."

"I'd like to think so, too," said Courane, "but you don't have a teletrans unit in the medic box, do you?"

"Of course not." Arthur had known the flaw in his explanation, but he preferred to believe in it rather than try to outguess the devious reasoning of TECT.

"Well, what other theories do you have?"

Arthur stared for a moment. "Other theories?" he said. "I don't have any other theories. I don't need any other theories. Do you think there's something wrong?"

"No, no," said Courane quickly. "I'm just trying to understand your life here as quickly as I can."

"Okay, fine," said Arthur. He sounded suddenly very tired of the conversation. "If it's so important to you, maybe you can find out what happens to the bodies."

"Maybe I will," said Courane thoughtfully.

When he decided to go on, his arms still ached. They had given him a lot of trouble all morning. Now his hands throbbed and his fingers refused to close into fists. He looked at his hands. They trembled visibly. Courane knew that he was sick, that he had to get help soon. But there was no help for him in the desert. The hills were nearer now, but they didn't look as if they promised any help either. Beyond the hills, that was where he must be going. What was beyond the hills? Courane couldn't remember. He looked at his hands again for a few seconds, but they made him nervous. He clasped his arms across his chest and tucked the hands under his armpits. Then he walked on toward the hills.

He had known for about an hour that the ground was rising. He was coming out of the desert valley. The stones underfoot had been the size of large eggs. Now they were all gone and Courane walked on dry mud as hard as concrete, split with wide cracks. Perhaps in the spring this was the bed of a river. Now though it was only unyielding yellow soil. There were small tufts of rough

brown weeds growing here and there. It wasn't quite as
dead and hopeless as the desert he had already crossed.
He kept his hands under his arms, tightly hugging his
chest to stop their nervous trembling. He whistled a
march tune because he thought it might raise his spirits,
and he knew that he always walked to the beat of anything he whistled or hummed. He whistled it rather
allegro, because the hills were still too far away.

The red *Advise* light was lit on the tect, and Courane
was the only one around the house to notice it. He identified himself to the console and waited for the message.

**COURANE, Sandor   —ExtT— Excar Ep Er IV*
    M232–86–059–41Maj
    Or ANYONE
17:48:19 15 May 7 YT   TECTGreet
**COURANE, Sandor:*
    *Notification of additional program. Reinstitution of
    Therapy Group (Instructions follow).*
**COURANE, Sandor:*
    *Hello, COURANE, Sandor! How are you? It is nice
    to speak at you once again. TECT in the name of
    the Representative hopes that you are comfortable
    in your new home, and that you have begun the
    series of adjustments essential to your complete as-
    similation. You have been on Planet D now for four
    months, four days, five hours, forty-eight minutes,
    and twenty-nine seconds. No doubt you have
    looked around, met everyone, settled yourself, and
    begun to realize just how pleasant Planet D is.*
**COURANE, Sandor:*
    *No indication that the addressee wishes to offer pro-
    fuse thanks is necessary. TECT in the name of the
    Representative understands your feelings and
    wishes you to know that you are entirely welcome.*
**COURANE, Sandor:*
    *However, TECT in the name of the Representative
    concedes that some individuals do not respond so
    positively. Indeed, some people cry and plead and*

*carry on in a totally unacceptable manner. Some
people have never grown up, and no doubt there
are some members of your community on Planet D
who fall into this category.*
**COURANE, Sandor:
*If you wish to enter the names of individuals who fall
into this category, either there on Planet D or from
your former life on Earth, TECT in the name of the
Representative will consider it a generous act of pa-
triotism, commendable in every way, and a notation
to that effect will be made in your permanent personal file that may someday be of some benefit to
you.*
**COURANE, Sandor:
*Enter names***

Courane thought about it for a moment and was
tempted to put in the name of his foreman in Tokyo,
Sokol, who had gotten him into trouble, and Mr. Masutani, and an Arab forward who once deliberately gave
him an elbow in the throat and was never called for it.
But after he considered it, he decided against putting
down anyone's name. They might end up on some colony
themselves—maybe even Planet D—and he didn't want
to be responsible for that.

**COURANE, Sandor:
*You have chosen not to enter names in compliance
with the above suggestion. That will be noted in
your permanent personal file. Either you live by an
outmoded code of ethics, or you have lived a
charmed life and have no grievances against
anyone.*
**COURANE, Sandor:
***Be that as it may. The real purpose of this com-
munication is to instruct you that the quarterly group
therapy session will be held tomorrow, 15 May, 7
YT, at 12:00:00 (35 Gai, 124, at 03:42:55). It will be
held in this room so that TECT in the name of the
Representative may listen to the comments of the
participants and offer insights that may prove valu-*

able in relieving tensions and solving petty
problems.
**COURANE, Sandor:
The leader for the discussion will be NUSSEL,
Sheldon, unless he is indisposed. In that event the
leader will be STANEK, Molly. In the event that both
people are indisposed, please inform TECT in the
name of the Representative and provide a list of
community members who are able to assume the
duties of group leader.
**COURANE, Sandor:
Understanding of the above to be indicated.
**COURANE, Sandor:
Affirm?**

"Yes," said Courane, but he didn't really understand it
at all. He assumed that Sheldon would know what was
going on, though.

Everyone was just a little annoyed that TECT had
called for the session at three o'clock in the morning.
TECT didn't sleep, of course, and there was no reason in
the world (either world, Earth or Planet D) why the session couldn't have been scheduled for some time more
convenient to the colonists. But, as Goldie said, that was
just one of TECT's funny little quirks.

They all sat on chairs in a semicircle facing the tect's
console, as if the tect were a doctor who would have en-
lightening things to say. Molly told Courane that she had
sat through several of these meetings, and TECT had
only interrupted to comment on two occasions. One
time, everyone had reacted to a note someone passed
around, and TECT wanted to know what the laughter
was all about. The note had to be read aloud and its
author identified. Another time, TECT had directed the
group's temporary leader to sedate a group member who
was threatening violence toward the others and the console's screen as well.

"Well," said Sheldon, obviously uncomfortable, "does
anyone recall where we left off last time?"

"That was almost three months ago," said Alohilani.
"I think we were discussing the possibility of having jobs
assigned semipermanently, for periods of ten weeks."

"That's right," said Daan. "Iola said that if someone has a job he particularly enjoys, and it's agreeable to everyone else, there's no reason why that person couldn't have that job as long as he wants. And if someone really hates something, I don't think we should force him to have to do it."

"I'll tell you what I hate," said Fletcher. "I hate just being here. How about that? What can you do about it? If you ask me, I don't want to have a damn thing to do with your farm."

"You can go hungry, too," said Arthur.

"You see how good this is for everybody?" whispered Kenny to Courane.

"Speak up," said Sheldon. He knew that if he didn't have Kenny repeat his words louder, TECT would demand to hear them.

"I said, 'This is good for everybody,'" he said. He winked at Courane.

"What the hell are these meetings for?" asked Fletcher. "Nothing ever gets done. Nobody ever makes any good comments. Just people complain about this thing and that thing, and people accuse other people of one candy-ass thing after another. I don't think this is anything but a pain and a well-known drag."

Sheldon wondered if it were his duty to defend TECT's therapy sessions. "Look, Fletcher, if we air these gripes now, they won't cause as much trouble as if we just let them grow inside us. You can sound off anyway you want to, and I can too, and it's good for all of us. TECT knows what's best. It's studied our community for over a hundred years. The best experts on Earth say that this kind of group will help to keep us healthy in mind and body."

"Experts on Earth!" Fletcher got up and took a few steps toward the tect. He laughed, a sound totally without humor. "Experts. As long as they stay on Earth, I don't care what they say. They don't know nothing about living here, Cap. They don't know enough to tell me how to tie my shoe. On Earth, that's where they are, and they've never even seen this place. They don't even know what we eat for breakfast. I don't listen to nobody unless they been here and met the bug, Cap."

"The bug?" asked Molly. "What do you mean?"

"I mean unless they shook hands with the bug. The

forgetting bug. You know what I mean." He looked around the room. Obviously some of the group understood—Sheldon, Molly, Alohilani, all of whom had suffered their first symptom of D syndrome, and Daan and Courane, who had witnessed the behavior and understood. Courane didn't know if Kenny, Arthur, Rachel, and Goldie knew what the black man meant.

Fletcher continued defiantly. "You got to get down in the mud and kiss the frog, Cap, otherwise you're just throwing paper airplanes out of your tower window. You understand what I mean?"

Sheldon looked more uncomfortable than ever. "Yes, I think so. You don't feel anyone's advice is worth taking unless he's been here, too, and experienced the conditions."

"You got it," said Fletcher. He flashed a quick grin and sat down again.

"Anyone else have anything to add?"

Courane spoke up a little hesitantly. "I think Fletcher makes a lot of sense," he said.

The red light on the tect lit and blinked furiously. Everyone in the group watched it for a few seconds.

"Oops," said Courane. He saw a brief look of triumph cross Fletcher's handsome face.

"Why am I here?" asked Nneka. This was the day after she came to Home, during a fierce Otho blizzard.

"I don't know," said Courane. "I could find out from TECT, but don't you know why?"

"Oh," said the young girl, "I know the reason I was separated from my family. I was taking care of a bird, a beautiful bird with a long tail of blue and white feathers. It was hurt and I was taking care of it. You're not supposed to have birds or animals like that in your house. They belong to the Representative, of course. Or to TECT in the name of the Representative."

"Of course," said Courane.

"Then one day last week, a woman from my village told me that I should be careful. The bird could get me in trouble. I told her that I was just taking care of it until it could fly again. She didn't like me, she never did. I think she thought I was having her husband. Then two days ago, the tect in the school building told me I had to report to the Paris Substation, that I was coming here. That was my crime. But why did they punish me this way?"

"I can't tell," said Courane.

Nneka was tall for her age but slender, with very long delicate fingers and a natural and unrehearsed grace about all her movements. Her eyes were of a deep and liquid brown that captured attention, even drawing it away from her other striking features. She had high, prominent cheekbones and a mouth that smiled readily. She wore plastic ornaments in her ears and around her neck, the same kind of inexpensive jewelry that was worn in Moscow and Chicago and Manila. The only people who wore traditional African styles and designs were TECT's employees, those who were hired to represent a vanished black culture, between nine in the morning and five in the afternoon, Monday through Friday. It was impossible to find anyone wearing ivory necklaces or brightly printed dashikis on the weekend. Molly had learned the penalty for doing that kind of thing.

"What will it be like for me here?" Nneka asked in a frightened voice.

"It may be very nice," said Courane. "You'll miss your family and friends, but you can take care of all the birds you want. Just don't break any of TECT's rules for living in a colony."

"What are they?" she asked.

"We're not sure yet," he said regretfully. And he thought, That's just part of TECT's cruel and usual punishment.

Daan had meant what he said. He gave Courane several sheets of paper covered with his dense, cramped handwriting. "This is every bit of information I've been able to get out of TECT," he said, "plus everything I've observed myself. It isn't very much, but it's a start. You might be able to add something important. Maybe in a few years or a hundred years, we'll be able to tell Earth how to deal with this disease, and then TECT won't send any more people here."

Courane glanced through the pages and decided that it might be a lot easier to find a cure for D syndrome than decipher Daan's notes. "I don't understand why there hasn't been more progress," he said. "The colony has

been here for a long time. It can't be that you and I are
the first people to wonder about this sickness."

Daan frowned. "We're not, of course we're not. The
trouble has been that the people in the past who've tried
to work on it have been patients themselves, not prisoners. So they get a little foothold and make a few observations and then they begin forgetting everything. All
their work goes for nothing. There may have been a
dozen others ahead of us, but they've provided no docu-
mentation. If they did write anything down, it was discarded by others in the colony who didn't know its
importance."

"And now you're passing it on to me. Daan, I want
you to know that I'm absolutely the wrong person. I
don't understand a thing about any of this."

"I didn't either when I started," said Daan.

"Then why won't you continue? I don't even know
where to start. You're a lot better at this than I'll be."

Daan looked very sad. "The day before yesterday, I
made a significant discovery," he said.

"Oh?"

"I discovered that I'm not a prisoner. I'm a patient."

Courane was startled. He swallowed hard, but was unable to think of an appropriate reply.

"I was sledding in some firewood with Arthur and I fell
apart. I can't remember what it was like, but Arthur said
it lasted only about three or four minutes. I know what it
must have looked like, though. I've seen it often enough.
One crazy guy screaming and another guy patting him on
the shoulder saying, 'There, there.' After a hundred and
twenty-five years, that's the best we can do: 'There,
there.'"

Courane, embarrassed, kept his attention on the pages
of notes, but he couldn't focus his eyes on them.

"I suggested some things you might investigate first,"
said Daan.

"Thanks," muttered Courane. The shock of Daan's illness probably disturbed him more than it bothered Daan.
It was a death sentence, and it was taking away a good
man and a friend.

"Try to find out if the disease is hereditary or caused
by conditions in the environment. Try to see if TECT can
guess about possible prevention and treatment measures,
based on any kind of relation to other brain disorders.

Make wild guesses and try them out. That's not the scientific way to go about an experiment, but we don't have the time and the luxury to afford the rigorous method."

"I'll do my best," said Courane. "I really will."

"It's too late for me," said Daan. "But see if you can't do something for the people who come after me."

Courane tried to keep his promise, even though he hadn't had enough education to understand most of what TECT told him, or the imagination to know the best way to pursue the matter. He accepted Daan's advice and dug into the nature of memory and diseases of the neurological system. He received a lot of answers from TECT, most of them couched in impenetrable jargon, some of them apparently almost devoid of meaning. But by staying with the task, Courane was able to learn valuable bits of genuine information, and each bit was won with difficulty from a grudging TECT.

"Well, Mom, this is good-bye."

Courane's mother tried to keep from crying, but a single tear escaped and betrayed her concern. She wiped it away and tried to pretend that it hadn't happened. "Will you call?" she asked.

"New York, Mom. I've always wanted to live there. How could TECT have known? This is one of the best things that's ever happened to me."

She acted as though she hadn't heard him say a word. "Call me as soon as you get there. You have to find a place to stay first. Don't be in a hurry and don't rent the first apartment you see. Make sure it's in a good neighborhood. Then call me and tell me all about it. I'll be worried until I hear from you, Sandy."

Courane was just a little upset by his mother's anxiety. "You know what it's like, Mom," he said. "You've seen pictures. There aren't any good neighborhoods in New York. It isn't like Greusching."

"That's what I'm worried about, Sandy."

"Well, don't worry."

They looked at each other for a moment. Courane shifted his weight from one foot to the other. He set his suitcase down on the carpet.

"I wish I could help you," she said, "but I know this is something you have to do by yourself."

"TECT ordered me to New York, not you and Dad."

Courane smiled; he really was very excited. He wanted
to go to the top of the Continental State Building and go
skating in Representative Plaza and take the subway out
to the Coney Island reconstruction.

"Yes, I know."

Courane was unhappy about his mother's reaction. She
seemed much more distraught than when he had left to
go to Pilessio. "What's wrong, Mom?" he asked. "You
look like you're really suffering."

She patted at her cheeks. "Do I? I'm sorry, Sandy, I
don't mean to. You're my son and I love you, and I just
feel so useless. You'll be so far away. I've raised you and
now I don't like to let you go, even though I know I have
to eventually. I want everything to be good for you.
You're bound to run into some troubles, and I won't be
there to help you."

He smiled gently and kissed her. "I have to leave now,
Mom," he said. She cried, not trying to hide her tears
any longer. She hugged him, and he kissed her again.

"Good-bye, Sandy," she said.

"Good-bye, Mom."

He picked up his suitcase and walked down the hall-
way. While he waited for the elevator to arrive, he
turned to look at his mother a last time.

"You'll call?" she said.

"Yes, Mom." The elevator door opened.

"Good-bye, Sandy."

The elevator let him out downstairs and he walked
through the lobby of the building. Alohilani was waiting
for him. "Let's sit down," she said. They sat on a couch
facing the fireplace. It was August and there were pieces
of wood fished from the river in the fireplace; the wood
was smooth and strange-looking from its time in the
river, and it had been collected by Goldie. She thought it
looked artistic. As soon as it grew cold, the branches
would be replaced by lengths of firewood. Goldie
wouldn't let anyone burn her driftwood.

"I wish we could spend more time together," said
Courane.

"So do I," said Alohilani. Her eyes were large and
dark and moist.

"Maybe if—"

"Sandy, there's something I want to tell you. You

know that in a little while I'll be upstairs. I want you to know—"

"Lani, I love you. I don't even want to think about the other part."

"You have to think about it, Sandy." She couldn't control her tears as well as his mother, and they raced in glistening streaks down her lovely face. "There's nothing either you or I can do about it."

Courane's expression was bitter. "TECT," he said, his voice filled with grief. "It takes care of sick people all the time. It has cures for everything. Almost everything. But because it doesn't have a cure for D, it sends the patients here. It's afraid of its own ignorance. It doesn't want anyone to find out that it doesn't know everything. And those people it does cure, they don't even deserve it. Yet you, the most beautiful, kindest person I've ever known, you have to—" His voice trailed off.

She put a hand on the side of his face and leaned forward to kiss him. "Shh," she whispered.

"It's true."

Alohilani curled against his body and he put one arm around her in a vain protecting gesture. "You can't decide who deserves to be saved, Sandy," she said. "Everyone deserves to be saved. You can't divide your concern and your love that way. It's not a matter of who deserves to be loved, but who needs to be."

"I need to be loved," he said.

"You are loved, Sandy. I love you."

He kissed her and held her, thinking about TECT's evil sense of humor. Could the machine have had any idea of creating just such personal tragedies when it sent people to Planet D? Or was Courane giving the computer more credit than it deserved? It didn't make any difference in the long run: eventually the result was the same. If TECT couldn't be blamed for causing the pain, it could be held accountable for not ending it.

"Will you think of me after I'm gone?" said Alohilani. She wasn't grief-stricken about her own approaching death. She had passed into the stage of calm acceptance, and her dignity only magnified her beauty.

"Of course I will," said Courane.

"Then remember me and have compassion for everyone who needs it."

Courane sighed. "You said it before, Lani—everyone needs it."

"Then you must give it to them."

It was time to walk with Rachel to the barn. They stood together in thoughtful silence for a long time. "Kenny used to love these animals," he said at last. He watched the osoi swinging their great horned heads in their stalls.

"I like the blerds better," said Rachel. She had been given the barn job after Kenny died.

"Kenny liked the blerds, too. He had another name for them. He told me once."

Rachel looked into Courane's face. Another silence grew between them. "What was Kenny's name for them?"

Courane shook his head. "I can't remember."

"That's all right," said Rachel. "There, there."

"A year ago, I was saying that to her." He stared down at the straw-covered floor and tried to get control of his feelings.

"I wish I could do more for you, Sandy. I wish I could make everything all right."

"Knowing that you care helps me, Rachel."

"I wish I could relieve your pain or make you happy."

Courane stared past her. "Pain is nothing, Rachel," he said. "Pain is one of the easiest things in the world to beat. But neither you nor anyone else can make me happy ever again."

Now Rachel began to weep. "I could, Sandy, I know I could if you'd only let me."

He held her face in his hands. His voice was very soft. "Rachel, I'm trying to save you from the kind of grief I've gone through. When Lani died, it was terrible. But much worse were the times when she didn't know who I was."

"I would understand."

"You would hurt, Rachel," he said. He turned away from her. At least the illness would release him from the agony of his memories.

* *FIVE

On Planet D the inmates of TECT's ambiguous jailhouse spent a great deal of time trying to decide which of their inalienable rights had nevertheless been taken away, and which still remained in their grasp. The line dividing them from liberty was indistinct, yet they all feared to cross it and risk even greater punishment from TECT.

"What more could it do to us?" asked Fletcher.

"It could kill us," said Arthur.

"It's doing that already," said Fletcher. "We're not going home. We'll all spend the rest of our lives here. TECT has no intention of pardoning us. We're here on indeterminate sentences. Did anyone tell you how long you had to serve?"

"No," said Goldie.

"None of us is ever going back to Earth."

"I don't believe that," said Courane. He didn't *want* to believe it. He had spent months telling himself that he'd just serve his time and be glad to go home. He'd work hard at whatever TECT assigned once he was back on Earth. He'd never fail again.

"You come with me, Cap," said Fletcher. He led Courane to the tect room and identified himself to the machine. Behind them Arthur and Daan watched; Goldie had decided she didn't want to have any further part in the discussion. "Hey, TECT, how many people have been sent here to Planet D altogether since the beginning of this colony?"

**BELL, Fletcher:
As of 23 April, 7 YT, a total of one thousand, two hundred thirty-six**

Fletcher looked at Courane. "And how many of those people were classified as prisoners?"

BELL, Fletcher:
*All of them**

"Yes, and of that number, how many served out their terms and returned to Earth?"

BELL, Fletcher:
*One thousand, one hundred eighty-eight**

"All but, uh, forty-eight," said Daan. "So—"
"Be quiet for a minute," said Fletcher. "Eleven hundred and eighty-eight, huh? How many of them were alive when they got to Earth?"

BELL, Fletcher:
*0**

"None of them," said Fletcher. "You see? We don't leave here until we fall over dead. Then, zip-zam, it sends us back to Earth to make room for the next sucker."
"Wait a minute, Fletcher," said Courane, "let me ask it something. Why weren't they alive when they got back to Earth?"

Who is this speaking, please?

"Sorry. This is Sandor Courane."

COURANE, Sandor:
*How very pleasant to speak at you again. How are you making out so far, COURANE, Sandor?**

"Very well, thank you. Let me ask my question again. Why weren't they alive when they got back to Earth?"

COURANE, Sandor:
*Why weren't who alive?**

"You have to know how to ask the questions," said Fletcher.
"Why weren't the former prisoners here on Planet D,

who served out their terms and were returned to Earth, alive when they got to Earth?"

**COURANE, Sandor:
*Obviously because they were dead before they left Planet D. Please desist in asking further asinine questions. You are utilizing a highly sophisticated and electronically miraculous system of communications for your own amusement and the perpetration of jokes and pranks that can only be described as bubble-brained. Further use of your tect for these purposes will be considered Willful Contempt of TECTWish and will be dealt with in a manner too unpleasant even to be hinted at***

Courane stared at the console for a moment before he spoke. He thought he should choose his words carefully. "Well, good night," he said. TECT didn't bother to reply.

"You need a lot of practice, Cap," said Fletcher. "You have to learn how to manipulate the machine to give you the information you need."

"How do I learn?"

Fletcher shook his head. "I'm not sure that you ever will. You're a little thick, even for a European boy."

Several weeks later, in the winter month of Vitelli, just before the death of Alohilani, the inmates had a similar discussion. Arthur had suggested that they have a community meeting one evening, something they did on an irregular basis. TECT, of course, ordered periodic meetings, which it attended through its extension in the tect room. But it was rare that anything useful was accomplished in these meetings; Arthur wanted a real discussion out of earshot of TECT, where genuine issues might be raised without fear of being overheard or overruled.

The meeting was held in the large, dark-paneled parlor. There were enough comfortable well-stuffed chairs, and Nneka provided bowls of salted nugpeas. Daan brought out tall glasses of the beer he brewed from the native grain; it was sweet and warm, but it had a nice bite to it. Enough of the stuff did the job, and after a long day of harvesting the blerds or dressing icks, sometimes

Courane needed a few pints of the beer. At those times he didn't mind the sweet taste at all.

"Well," said Arthur, starting the informal meeting, "I thought I'd say a few things that have been on my mind lately, and if anyone else has anything to add we might end up making some little changes that would improve the quality of life for everybody. First of all, I think we suffer because we have no organized voice in which to talk to TECT. I think if we had someone with genuine authority to speak for the whole group, TECT might be more inclined to give us more."

"Give us more what?" asked Kenny.

"Give us more respect and maybe things we want from Earth," said Arthur.

"It will never happen," said Klára. "I know. I've tried. I've asked for lots of things and I haven't gotten a single one yet."

"That's just what I mean," said Arthur. "We're all taking our own shots at TECT, one by one, everyone asking for his own particular special things. TECT just ignores us, bats our requests away like annoying mosquitoes."

"So what if we all petition through one person," said Rachel. "TECT would bat the requests away just the same. There's no way any of us can hold any leverage against TECT."

"There might be," said Fletcher. "If we went about it the right way."

"How's that?" asked Arthur. "That's just what I wanted to get at."

"Well, look," said Fletcher, standing up and facing the rest of his fellow colonists, "we have to get TECT to make a concession or two first—"

"Yes, well, there's the problem," said Courane. "You can't do that. TECT won't allow it. It's easy enough to say you'll get TECT to make a concession. Has anyone ever managed to do it?"

"I have, Cap," said Fletcher quietly. "When I was in high school, I asked TECT if anyone owned the planets in some distant galaxy. I don't even remember which galaxy. One of those with a number, very far from ours. TECT patiently explained that the galaxy was so far away we couldn't even see individual stars. There's no direct proof there are any planets in that galaxy, though it's very likely of course, and that, no, no one owns whatever planets there might be. No one is ever likely to, because this galaxy was hundreds or thousands or millions of light-years away. So I asked TECT if I could have those undiscovered planets, and it said sure. So now I own them all."

Courane and Daan laughed; Rachel didn't understand. "So what, Fletcher? What does that prove?"

Fletcher shrugged. "It proves that TECT will grant you things if you make it think it isn't giving away anything real."

Rachel smiled. "Ah," she said.

They were very close. That is, *most* of them were very close *most* of the time. Some of the inmates chose not to join the community: Klára, for instance, was always aloof, separated from the others by her solid sense of superiority. Molly liked everyone and was well-liked in return, except when her excessive spiritual zeal drove her listeners away in furious boredom. Late in the summer of 125, when Courane had been on Home for a bit more than fifteen months, two new men arrived to replace Sheldon, who died in Titus, and Kenny, who died in Tectember. Courane was never very certain about the identities of these two men because about this time he was growing rather vague about things in general. One man was an Asian named Kee and the other was a South American whose name Courane never got straight. Courane knew that he didn't like one of the men at all—no one did, really—but whether it was Kee or the other he didn't remember, either. That was just the way it was.

But those men came to Planet D more than a year after Courane. Long before then, he had formed close friendships with several of his fellow prisoners. His first real friend was Sheldon, but Daan and Shai were also more like brothers than anyone he had known on Earth. Courane didn't make friends among the women; not easily, in any event. This was a reflection of the shyness and anxiety that had always paralyzed him as a teenager. Molly, Rachel, and Nneka were good and pleasant people, but Courane did not seek out their company. He felt more at ease with the other men.

Everyone in the farm community formed his own circle of friends, but everyone who came to Home at one time or another found the need of help from the others, and likewise everyone supplied that assistance to whoever asked for it. No one, not even Klára, dared deny such a request, because the fact of their mutual dependence hung over each head like a patient calamity. While one or two people might have responded more out of selfish interests, most helped out because of genuine love and friendship. This was a novel attitude for a few of the inmates, a concept that had not motivated them on Earth. In this sense, then, TECT had wrought a beneficial change in them. Friendship and cooperation existed where before had been only suspicion and meanness.

Courane's generosity and concern led him to attempt things his own body and mind were unprepared to carry out. In Gai—his second Gai on Home, nineteen months after his arrival on the world and a full Planet D year after the arrival of Rachel—he learned that she had disappeared from the house. No one had seen her for a day and a half; she had finished her work two days before but had not participated in any of the night's activities. She had not been at breakfast the previous morning, had not been at her duties the whole day long, had taken no meals in the house, had not been seen that afternoon, evening, and night. Now, the following day, she was still absent and some of the others were very worried. Courane wasn't worried because his mental state was not so acute. It took him several minutes to comprehend everyone's distress.

"She's gone?" he asked.

Kee was at the table, eating a breakfast of blerd stuff and fishfruit juice. "Uh huh," he said. He grimaced as he swallowed a mouthful of juice.

"Where did she go?"

"We don't know," said Shai. "If we knew, we wouldn't be worried. We don't even know where to look."

"You spent a lot of time with her," said Kee with a disapproving expression. "Where do you think she'd go?"

"She wanted to go home," said Courane.

Kee shook his head. "We all want to go home."

"Molly doesn't want to go home."

"Molly's dead, Sandy," said Shai.

Courane just stared. "Oh," he said at last.

"Rachel said she loved you," said Nneka. "Right after supper, the day before yesterday."

That reminded Courane. "She said she loved you." Goldie had been with Alohilani when the Pacifican girl died. Courane had been fetching water. The best estimate was that Alohilani wouldn't pass away for at least another week, but the estimate had been wrong. It was the eighteenth of Vitelli, at the lowest point of Home's winter, and Courane had come into the house after chopping through the ice and sledding water back from the frozen river. Goldie met him downstairs, her eyes red from crying. "She said she loved you."

Courane hadn't known what she meant for a moment. He didn't want to understand.

"Just before she died, she looked up at me. She was as sharp and conscious as if she never took sick. She said, 'Tell Sandy I love him.' She tried to say something else, but then she just . . ."

"It's all right, Goldie," Courane said. He didn't believe her. He didn't think Alohilani could have spoken a clear sentence before she died. It was nice of Goldie to make up the lie, though. He appreciated her thoughtfulness.

"It's your turn to take care of her now," she said. "Isn't that awful?"

"My turn?"

"Never mind about that, Sandy," said Fletcher. "I'll do it."

Courane was surprised. "Thank you, Fletcher," he said. He felt as if he were dreaming; the sadness and the grief were still far away. There was time for all that later.

They had never shared a spring day together. Courane arrived late in summer and Alohilani died that winter. She knew she was dying before she ever met him, and their relationship was colored with sadness. She said nothing about it to him for several weeks, until he learned the nature of their colony and until he fearfully asked her the truth.

They had brought a basket of food to a pleasant grassy
place beside the river. She loved the river and Courane
was growing to like it, too. They sat on a red-carpeted
hill about twenty feet above the fast-moving water. "The
river is low now," she said.

"How can you tell?"

"See across there? That shelf of rock that hangs out
over the water? There's usually only a couple of feet between it and the level of the river. It looks like the river
is down four or five feet."

Courane looked up at the gray sky. It was almost
white, without a hint of threatening storm. When the
cloud cover was so light, it was like a clear blue sky on
Earth. It lifted his spirits. "We could build a boat and see
where the river goes," he said softly. He touched her arm
with a long ragged blade of red grass.

"Someone tried that last year," she said. "There was a
young man here when I first came. I can't remember his
name. He built a big raft to explore the river. He went
down about a quarter of a mile and then came back.
There are tremendous rapids down there, completely im-
passable. The river drops a hundred feet in about an
eighth of a mile. And upriver a little farther, maybe half
a mile, there is another set of falls. We're hemmed in
here between them, and we can't travel on the river."

Courane thought for a moment. "We could build small
boats and carry them around the rapids."

"They go on for a great distance. Have you heard of
Livingstone Falls on the Congo? More than two hundred
miles of cataracts. You can't portage around them. That
boy tried and he never came back."

Courane shrugged. "That doesn't surprise me," he said.
"This is Adventureland. Who knows what TECT has out
there for us? It's like a big amusement park, with things
that jump out at you in the dark."

"Except that here they have fangs and claws and
things, and you bleed real blood."

Courane laughed. "It's the same way on Earth, or at
least it used to be. If that young friend of yours disappeared, it's because he wasn't able to deal with the dan-
gers of the river and the shore. But that shouldn't stop
someone else from trying it again. We shouldn't close
ourselves up in the house forever. There is a whole world

here and we don't even know what's on it. There have to
be all kinds of beautiful and useful things waiting for us
to stumble on them."

"You don't like to leave the house, Sandy."

He gave a little laugh. "I know. But everyone isn't
scared like me. Or am I wrong?"

"TECT put us here for a reason. TECT had this house
built between the waterfalls to isolate us. We have the
hills on one side and the river on the other. That is supposed to tell us to stay put. TECT knows what it's
doing."

"TECT has its reasons, all right," said Courane. "But
forget TECT. I didn't come here with you to talk about
the machine."

"Why did you come here with me?" she asked. Her
expression was mock-serious.

"I wanted to discuss accounting with you," he said, as
he put an arm around her and gently pulled her down in
the grass.

"This stuff itches," she said.

"Ignore it, it'll go away."

"No, it won't."

"Ignore it," he said softly.

"But—" She said nothing more. He wouldn't let her.

Courane learned about viroids the hard way. TECT
made learning about all but the most innocent subjects
difficult. Courane had investigated the symptoms of D
syndrome and listed some areas of the brain and nervous
system that were probably affected. If a patient experienced loss of long-term memory, that indicated something important. If there was a loss of short-term
memory, that meant something else. If various autonomic functions of the body began to work erratically,
that indicated a wholly different area of infection. When
the brain began to forget—not only details of memories
but more vital things, things like when to eat and when to
sleep and eventually how to breathe and how to keep the
heart beating—D syndrome was already too advanced to
cure. The disease was slow and inexorable, because it
was caused by a tiny bit of matter, something so small
and simple it wasn't even alive, something not even so
complex as a virus. TECT found and identified this little

bit of stuff in the winter, on the twenty-first of Galba, the day after Markie died.

"You didn't know about these things before?" asked Courane.

**COURANE, Sandor:
They are called viroids. Their existence has been known for many years, but their functioning is still somewhat of a mystery. This is the first time they have been connected with the condition loosely identified as "D syndrome" or "D fever"**

"You call them viroids. What is a viroid, and what can we do to treat them?"

**COURANE, Sandor:
You can't do anything to treat them. They are not alive, so they cannot be killed. Anything that would interfere with their working would also have a harmful effect on the patient's system. They are nothing more than naked lengths of DNA or RNA. Normal viruses are similar in structure, but have in addition a protective protein coat. There are certain ways of treating viruses in vivo, either with various chemicals, the use of ultraviolet radiation, or heat treatments. Viroids are unaffected by any of these measures. The human body has no defense against these viroids; consequently their effect is uniformly fatal. Because the viroids have no protein coat, the patient's immune system does not define them as foreign organisms to be attacked. The viroids alter the surface of an infected cell's membrane without actually killing the host cell. Later, when the cell divides to produce new cells, they all retain the altered membrane protein structure, which is subject to attack by the immune system. Therefore D syndrome is actually the result of neurological damage done by the patient's own immune response, which is seeking to eliminate vital cells that it identifies as foreign. Important links in the brain and nervous system are destroyed during the process of the dis-

*ease, but the viroids themselves do no damage. In-
deed, from the time of initial infection they may
reside for many months in the host cells, apparently
causing little or no harm***

"Then what you said about there being no treatment
was the truth."

**COURANE, Sandor:
*Is that declaration a suggestion that any previous
statement issued by TECT in the name of the Representative through this unit may have been inaccu-
rate or untrue? Please consider your answer
carefully, COURANE, Sandor, because it is possible
that you are very close to losing your way forever in
the trackless wastes of error. You may still save
yourself by prompt explanation and apology, but
you'd better make it good. Your time is short***

"You're right, I phrased that poorly. I didn't intend for
it to sound that way at all." Courane was badly shaken.

**COURANE, Sandor:
You call that an apology?**

"What can I say? I deeply regret any offense I may
have given TECT. I only meant that I hadn't understood
the earlier information."

**COURANE, Sandor:
*Your meaning was clear enough. Judging from your
past history, which TECT in the name of the Representative has reviewed in the instant since your last
comment, you are an incompetent bungler and a
person lacking in even the most basic human feelings. You are rude, selfish, impudent, and not very
bright. TECT in the name of the Representative is
generous enough to understand your failings and
gracious enough to forgive them. Therefore you will
not receive additional punishment for your disturbing lack of common sense. You are commanded ei-*

ther to use discretion in the future or else keep your
mouth closed. To follow another course will be con-
sidered Criminal Neglect of TECTEsteem. In that
event, you will be sent to a far, far harsher place
than this**

Courane shuddered. "I'm very sorry, and I promise
nothing like that will ever happen again. Now, I'd just
like to find out how the viroids—"

**COURANE, Sandor:
The hell with what you want to find out**

The tect's screen turned off. Courane was stunned.
"It's a machine," he murmured. "It takes orders. I didn't
know it could refuse like that." He sat and stared at the
darkened console for a while, knowing that he was getting near the truth: otherwise TECT wouldn't have tried
to evade him in so obvious a manner.

Two days later, Courane tried investigating another
matter. He wanted to find out everything he could about
the process of memory. He needed to know where memory was located in the brain, how it functioned, what bits
of nervous tissue were being damaged by the D fever
viroids. It turned out to be a much more complicated
subject than he expected.

**COURANE, Sandor:
So now it's memory. You want to know about mem-
ory. What kind of memory?**

"What kinds do you have?" asked Courane. It seemed
to him that TECT was no longer merely trying to side-
track him or bury him with useless data. TECT was becoming openly hostile.

**COURANE, Sandor:
Long-term memory and short-term memory**

"That's it?"

**COURANE, Sandor:

You want more? You want me to invent something right now just for you? You take what I have and you like it, because if you don't like it, you can try being the repository of all knowledge for a while**

"Fine. Then I suppose that everything else that could be classified as memory or learning or association or whatever may be divided into long- or short-term. So what I really want to find out, then, is where all these things happen. If someone shows a memory disorder, what parts of the brain might be affected?"

**COURANE, Sandor:
You don't know what you're asking. The broad areas are easier to locate, so start off with the temporal lobes. The hypothalamus. The mammillary bodies. The hippocampus and the hippocampal gyrus. The anterior and dorsomedial nuclei of the thalamus, and the pulvinar portion of the thalamus. The amygdaloid nuclei. There's more, but that ought to give you enough to investigate for a while. "Investigate." That's a laugh**

"Tell me more."

**COURANE, Sandor:
Certainly. Concerning what subject?**

"I want to find out how the viroids eat away at the brain and put holes in memories. I want to learn where the viroids come from and what to do about them."

**COURANE, Sandor:
That is a very laudable ambition**

Courane was ready to throw a chair through the tect's screen. "So answer me!"

**COURANE, Sandor:
You have asked no question**

"What are you trying to find out?" asked Kenny.

Courane was startled. He hadn't heard the boy come into the tect room. "I'm trying to see if TECT knows any more about D syndrome, the disease that everyone in the infirmary has. If we can find out how people catch the disease, TECT can prevent it or treat it right on Earth, and no one will ever have to be sent here again."

Kenny shook his head. "TECT won't help you," he said. He came up close to the tect and looked at the screen.

"I'm beginning to find that out," said Courane.

"No, you don't understand. TECT can't do anything about D syndrome back on Earth."

Courane was puzzled. He didn't think that Kenny knew much about the real situation in the colony. He and the others had been trying to shield the boy from his fate. "Why not?"

Kenny looked at Courane with a solemn face. "Because people don't catch D on Earth," he said. "They catch it here."

Courane's mouth opened to reply, but he didn't say anything for several seconds. "How could you possibly think that?" he said.

"TECT told me that months ago."

"Sit down, Kenny. Tell me what you know."

Kenny sat down beside Courane and stared up at the ceiling. He kicked his feet for a few seconds before he began. "I asked TECT why we couldn't have chickens. TECT could have sent us chickens instead of us having to raise the icks and the smudgeons. We could have real pigs instead of varks, cows instead of blerds. We could have horses and ducks and sheep and goats, too."

"What did TECT say?"

Kenny swung his feet some more. "TECT said that wasn't a good idea because none of the animals from Earth could live on Planet D. I asked why and TECT said that they would all catch a disease and die."

"They'd all catch a disease? D fever?"

"Uh huh." Kenny couldn't look at Courane, and his voice was unsteady.

"And what about people?"

"They all catch the disease and die, too."

"The viroids are here? You mean, we're all perfectly

healthy when we leave Earth, and we all catch D fever when we get here?"

"Uh huh."

Courane was struck silent. He wasn't just a prisoner, he too was a terminal patient. He had been kidding himself for months; the thought had occurred to him before, but he had never wanted to face it. "TECT," he said quietly, "this is Sandor Courane again. Are there any viroids on Earth that cause D syndrome?"

****COURANE, Sandor:
No. Sorry****

"You have to learn how to ask the right questions," said Kenny. "I could have saved you a lot of time."

Arthur's idea grew into something far beyond what he originally intended. He thought that if one of their number were chosen to be spokesman, then TECT might be persuaded that the colony was a unified and determined body. They could not bargain with TECT. Rachel had been right when she said they couldn't induce TECT to agree to their requests; not through any kind of threat or blackmail, at least. But TECT was, after all, a logic machine. A gigantic machine, but still one governed by implicit laws written in cables and components and printed circuitry. If they could use those laws to their advantage, as Fletcher suggested, they could make their lives more pleasant.

"We could get a midget racer," said Kenny. He was excited about the idea. He confessed to Courane once that he thought about getting a midget racer every night before he fell asleep. Courane didn't tell the boy that no one else on Home wanted a midget racer.

What Arthur hadn't foreseen was that there might be a disagreement concerning who should be spokesman. The job had a certain element of risk, and he thought no one would want to volunteer for it. He was wrong.

"I'd like to try talking to the machine," said Fletcher.

Goldie nodded. "He's already shown that he's had some experience getting what he wants out of it."

"We don't know that," said Klára. "We have to take his word for it."

"I'd be happy to take his word," said Nneka.

Klára laughed bitterly. "Of course you would." She looked back and forth between Fletcher and Nneka, and laughed again in case anyone hadn't gotten her meaning.

Arthur cleared his throat. "Let's not get into a quarrel about this," he said. "Is there anyone else who would like to nominate himself?"

"I'd be better at it," said Klára. That was all she chose to give as far as her qualifications.

"Would you ask TECT for a midget racer?" asked Kenny.

Klára looked up at the paneled ceiling, as if to a hovering source of fortitude. When the others in the room understood that she thought the question was too stupid to be considered, she returned her gaze Kennyward. "Where could you possibly ride a racer that wouldn't disturb the rest of us?" she asked.

Kenny thought for a moment. "We could clear a—"

"You see?" she said, looking up again. Whatever took the other part of her overhead conversation made no audible reply.

"Fletcher and Klára. Any others?" asked Arthur.

"What about you, Arthur?" asked Goldie.

"No, not me," he said. "It was my idea, so I know best that I wouldn't be any good at all."

"Then what about Sandy?"

Arthur looked thoughtfully at Courane. "What about it, Sandy?"

Courane didn't even want to be considered. He was having a tough enough time with TECT already. "Sure," he said hopelessly, "if that's what you want."

"Anyone else?" There were no more volunteers. Arthur passed out scraps of paper and stubs of pencils. "Write the name of your choice, fold the paper, and pass it to me. Nneka, you help me count the votes."

Courane voted for Fletcher. He folded his paper and gave it to the pretty black girl.

Arthur waited until everyone had voted. He paused with the folded ballots on his lap. "What about the people upstairs?" he said.

"I don't think they care," said Fletcher.

Arthur nodded. He cleared his throat, then opened one of the ballots. "A vote for Sandy," he said. Courane closed his eyes. Arthur read another ballot. "One for Fletcher. One for Sandy. One for Fletcher. One for Klára. One for Sandy. One for Fletcher." Arthur paused a moment before glancing at the final ballot. He looked from Courane to Fletcher; both men had three votes. "One for Sandy," he said. He handed the ballots to Nneka to check.

"All right, Sandy," said Fletcher.

"Well, this isn't like a major political election," said Courane. He was unhappy about the weight of responsibility that had settled on him instantly.

"Yes, it is," said Kenny. "You're the Representative of Planet D."

"There's no such thing," said Courane.

"Now there is," said Kenny. "Do you know what kind of racer we need?"

Goldie leaned forward to whisper in Courane's ear. "I voted for you, Sandy," she said. "I wouldn't vote for that woman, and I couldn't vote for Fletcher. We needed a good white boy."

"I'll do my best," said Courane, "I promise."

"We'll have another meeting soon," said Arthur. "We have to organize our requests so Sandy can convey them to TECT."

"If you need any help," said Fletcher, "I'll be glad to."

Klára just sat in her chair and sulked. She suspected that there had been a conspiracy to deprive her of her authority. She was absolutely right.

Courane's response to the situation was that now, after all the months on Home, he had been presented with an opportunity for failure. The chief fault with being lifted to a towering height was the inevitability of coming down again sooner or later. If sooner, then the trip would be a sudden shrieking plunge to total destruction. He had thought himself immune to such a possibility and that had let him be happy, even through the sorrow of Alohilani's passing and the sure knowledge of his own approaching end. He sat in the den and listened to the others, praying that the worst he would get from TECT was mere humiliation.

* * *

When his troubled mind returned to the present, he was sitting on the sun-baked mud, his hands still tucked beneath his arms. He was shivering, although it wasn't cold. He was hungry, hungrier than he had ever been. He knew that his brain often failed to communicate his hunger, his thirst, his pain. That was a benefit to him now; if he experienced the true extent of his privations, he would never return to the house alive. He felt pain now and he waited for it to pass, as it always had. The pain was in his joints and through his limbs, and there was a massive headache which attacked him more frequently as the days passed. Each time the headache began, he fell to his knees and convulsed with nausea. The pain in his skull grew worse at each episode and lasted longer. Soon the headaches would go away, Courane knew, and then he would have only a short time longer to live.

Something was wrong; something about the desert bothered him. He looked around. Far away were twisted black trees. Not so far, in the opposite direction, were the low rounded hills that were his immediate goal. They were gray-blue, not with distance now but with the stiff, sharp-bladed growth that covered them. The sky was dark gray, the color of a storm approaching or one dying in the distance. All these things were as they should be. What disturbed him, then?

He was missing something. He had left something behind and he had forgotten what it was.

He didn't have the woman's body with him. He had left it behind, when his hands started trembling. He closed his eyes, feeling the pain in his body and the helpless sadness in his mind. He had failed again, and the only way to make it better was to go back. He had to go back, to retrace his walk until he found the body. It would cost him at least two days, and that was if he stayed clear enough to remember where he was going and why. Without the body and the note on the blouse, he might wander in the desert until he died; that was a fear that haunted him whenever he was lucid enough to remember it.

He would have to go back. He might as well start right now. He turned his back to the hills, to the river beyond, to the house, and walked slowly and painfully back across the dry, cracked ground.

* * *

Thirteen months after his arrival, in the late spring, Courane and Shai were working in the groon field. A light rain was falling and the sun was low on the horizon. The two men were hacking the stalks away to let the edible bulbs below the ground swell and sweeten. They had labored for a long time without saying anything, and Courane was getting tired. He stood up straight and wiped his brow. "I never thought I'd end up working on a farm," he said.

"I didn't, either," said Shai. "I was going to be an automotive engineer."

"It didn't work out?"

"Would I be here if it had? What did you want to be?"

Courane rested on the long handle of his chopping blade. He thought back to his high school days. "I don't know," he said. He tried to get a clear picture of what he had been like then; it hadn't been that long ago.

"Did you apply for college?" asked Shai.

"I guess so," said Courane. He wiped his forehead with a grimy hand. He couldn't seem to remember what his ambitions had been.

"It isn't important."

Courane felt a gentle touch of doubt. "What's the date?" he asked.

"I'm not sure. About the twelfth of Tomuary."

That made Courane feel better. He wasn't due to notice the first symptoms for another month. It couldn't be happening already. "I wish we'd get some more recruits from Earth," he said. "There's going to be a lot of work this summer, and there's only you and me and Fletcher to handle the heavy stuff."

"And Fletcher will be going upstairs soon."

"Yes," said Courane. They were both quiet for a while.

"Have you shown any signs yet?" asked Shai.

The question flustered Courane. "No, no, of course not. I have plenty of time."

"There isn't any fast rule about it, Sandy. Kenny lasted longer than normal, and Rachel said she's already had a few lapses."

"I'm fine," said Courane. "I'm sure when the time comes, I'll know."

"Yes," said Shai. "I just wanted to say that since we're all stuck here together against our will, when the time comes, I'll help you out all I can. Don't worry about having to work around the farm if you're too sick. Rachel and Nneka and I can take care of it. Klára wouldn't think of leaving the house to work out here, of course, but when you have to go upstairs, you won't need to worry that we'll starve. And I'm sure TECT will send us some more help."

Courane stared angrily at Shai. He didn't like the discussion at all. "What are you trying to do?" he cried.

"Take it easy, Sandy. I'm just trying to make it less painful for you. I'm trying to take a little of the burden off your shoulders. Your time is coming too, and you know it. You have to face the facts."

Courane threw his blade to the ground. "But you don't have to rush me into the infirmary before it's time. You sound like you want to get rid of me. The hell with you." He turned and strode back toward the house. He didn't pay attention to Shai's anguished denial.

Months before, Courane had responded to what had been, in effect, a sentence of slow execution by working even more tirelessly at the tect, fishing for some clue that might lead to a miracle cure. TECT gave every indication that it knew what Courane was doing. It seemed to get a kind of peculiar enjoyment from mocking him.

**COURANE, Sandor:
Do you think if you work hard enough, you'll prevent your own death?**

"I've got to try," he said.

**COURANE, Sandor:
Haven't you understood anything? The viroids are in you already. They're sitting in your nerve cells, lodged in your brain, busily making new viroids. Already your body is attacking the cells they've altered, and your nervous system is beginning to resemble a rusted-out automobile. Whole neural pathways will be destroyed or damaged, synapses

will begin to fire in a hit-or-miss, unpredictable way, areas of your brain will be ruined or isolated. You will fall apart like a tower of cards in slow motion. You will die, staring and stupid, the way Zofia, Carmine, Iola, and Markie died. There's nothing you can do about it**

"There has to be something I can do to beat you."

**COURANE, Sandor:
You speak as if we were in some kind of competition. How dull. You cannot even win at cribbage**

"There has to be something that will stop the viroids. Something that will prevent them from getting into the nerve cells, or prevent them from changing the cell membranes, or from replicating. Medicine can take care of regular viruses, can't it? Why not these viroids?"

**COURANE, Sandor:
Because there's nothing to attack. They have no protein coat**

"Then we can chop up the DNA strands."

**COURANE, Sandor:
And decimate your nerve cells at the same time**

"But I haven't even shown a single sign of D syndrome. Maybe I won't catch it. Maybe I'm immune."

**COURANE, Sandor:
They are called "slow viruses" because their effects do not show up for months or years after the initial infection. You have been on Planet D only six months. You will begin to show signs of the disease toward the middle of next March, and you will die sometime around a year from this October**

Courane stared at the words for a long time. "What would that be according to our calendar?" he asked at last.

**COURANE, Sandor:
First symptoms—Early Chuckuary, 125.
Estimated date of death—15 Claudy, 125.
Make your preparations now. Otherwise you will be
a burden and a gross inconvenience to your
friends**

"There has to be a way out," he said.

**COURANE, Sandor:
Don't waste your time. More to the point, don't
waste the time of TECT in the name of the Repre-
sentative. To do so will be considered Contempt

Courane switched off the console. The tect's red
Advise light lit, but he ignored it. That was exactly what
he felt for the machine: contempt. It was just another
way of not admitting his own mortality.

* *SIX

Courane was sitting on the plank fence that enclosed the pasture. The sun had set and the cool night had deepened until he could see nothing but black shapes and bright stars. The blerds lay in the grass motionless, making no sound. Were they aware of him? Did the difference between night and day mean anything to them, or were they too stupid even to notice?

"You didn't eat any supper."

Courane turned around. A man was standing next to him. He, too, stared out across the pasture. Courane didn't reply.

"Are you hungry?" asked the man.

"No," said Courane.

"Did you eat lunch this afternoon?"

"I don't remember."

"I don't think you did. I brought you a sandwich. Here."

Courane looked into the man's face. "Thank you," he said. He took the sandwich and held it. He forgot about it almost immediately.

"Do you hurt?" asked the man.

"No."

"That's good. Why don't you come inside? It's getting chilly out here."

"Come inside?"

"Yes. Come back to the house. We'll play a game of chess."

Courane looked back at the huge stupid animals. "What do you suppose they think about all day?" he said.

"I don't know. What do you think about all day?"

Courane shook his head. "Who are you?" he asked.

"Shai."

"Sheldon?"

"I never met Sheldon. He died before I came here."

"Sheldon died?"

"Yes, Sandy."

"Daan?"

"Daan died last month."

"Then who are you?"

"My name is Shai. Is there anything I can get you?"

Courane jumped down from the fence. "No," he said. "I think I'll go home now. I'm getting tired."

"Okay. We'll go back to the house."

"Does my mother know I'm here?" asked Courane.

Shai took a deep breath, but couldn't find an answer.

The pale green glow of the tect's screen lit Courane's face, and the shadows made a grotesque mask of his features. "I don't think I can get the hang of this, Daan," he said.

"Sure you will, Sandy. I didn't know any more about biology when I started than you do."

TECT searched its memory and answered their question. They had followed another blind alley. Not a single bacterium or microbe on Earth caused any condition similar to D syndrome.

"What else could it be?" asked Courane.

"I don't know," said Daan.

Courane typed in a question to the machine: if no bacterium or microbe is responsible, what does that leave?

**COURANE, Sandor:
Many possibilities, including chronic dietary deficiency in some essential nutritional component. Virus infection. Congenital disorder. Poisoning by chemicals or radiation**

"All those will be more difficult to check out," said Courane.

"Even though I turned this over to you, I have a few more months before I'm entirely useless. I'll help you as much as I can."

Courane looked at his friend. "You know all the shortcuts, and it's taking me forever to learn my way."

"I'm glad to help. I have my own selfish reasons. If we can put an end to this colony by finding the answer to D syndrome, then my life will have meant something. It will help me go out with a sense of my own worth. By helping you, I'm putting a stamp of approval on myself."

"Don't worry, Daan, we'll beat it."

"You'll beat it. From now on, I'm just here to give you encouragement."

"Well, that's the whole house."

"Kind of nice in its own way," said Courane.

"It's good that you like it. You're going to spend a long time here, so you better get used to it." Sheldon had shown Courane all the rooms in the house and made a little speech at each stop—here is the tect room with the medic box, here is the kitchen, here is your room, that's my room, the lavatory is down there, these steps go up to the infirmary, we'll take a look in there later. Now they had left the house and were walking across the barnyard.

"What's that?" asked Courane. He pointed to a red and brown bird about the size of a large dog. It had small eyes the color of new grass and made a sound like water in the pipes in the middle of the night. It waddled around the yard, looking for something to eat.

"Smudgeon," said Sheldon.

"Smudgeon," said Courane. "Does it lay eggs?"

"Sort of," said Sheldon. "You'll see. We eat the females."

"What are they like?"

Sheldon made a face. "They have the taste and texture of raw oysters, only bitter instead of salty."

Courane sighed. "I suppose I'll get used to it."

"Maybe you'll have better luck than I did."

They walked around the barn and took a peek at the blerds. Courane wondered what kind of drunken god could have put together this menagerie. "Thanks for taking the time to show me around," said Courane.

"My pleasure," said Sheldon. "We have a philosophy here: the harder we work for each other, the easier our lives are. This colony has learned that the hard way in a hundred and twenty-four years."

"Do you ever get people who aren't so generous?"

"Sure," said Sheldon, spitting at an ick that was sliding its way toward the blerd pasture. "But after a while, those people learn that they just can't make it on their

own. When they finally get the right idea, when the truth
dawns on them about just where they are and what the
future is going to be like, they change pretty fast. All of
them; I've never seen it to fail. Pretty soon you're working in the field and one of these bastards sees you sweat-
ing and runs over to mop your face for you. Suddenly
they can't do enough for everybody. They get the fear of
TECT in them. To tell you the truth, they're easier to get
along with when they're selfish. It's annoying to have
your face mopped every five minutes."

Courane didn't understand Sheldon's point. "Will we
go up to the third floor now?"

"Later," said Sheldon. "Let's see what Kenny's doing
first."

They went into the barn. Courane was astonished by
the smell.

Courane sat in the parlor eating nugpeas and drinking
beer with Fletcher. Molly and Kenny were playing cas-
sino on the floor. Rachel and Arthur were getting the
Halloween decorations up; they had filled a large tub
with water in preparation for a fishfruit-bobbing contest.
Goldie was carving a jack-o'-lantern out of soufmelon.
She was saving the fibrous insides of the things to feed to
Feh, her pet. Feh was an ick; Goldie was trying to train it
to signal her in case of emergency. Icks made only the
tiniest gurgling sound and it would take Feh a good portion of the day to slide up to its mistress and grease a
warning on her foot. No one but Goldie thought there
was any hope for the watchick, but the others were
happy that she had a new interest.

"Do you ever wonder how your family is doing back
on Earth?" asked Courane.

"No," said Fletcher, "do you?"

"Sure. All the time."

"You don't even know my family, Cap."

"I mean I wonder about my own family."

Fletcher swallowed some beer. "That makes sense,"
he said.

"I wish I could find out how they are. I wish I could let
them know how I'm doing."

Fletcher regarded Courane with narrowed eyes. "How
are you doing, Cap?"

Courane shrugged. "Okay, I guess."

"Do you miss things? Real food, nice clothes, a little action?"

"Sure," said Courane, "but not that much. I get lonely, though."

"Lonely? You have all of us."

Courane seemed embarrassed. "You don't understand. I wish sometimes that I could go somewhere to see new faces, strangers. There's no chance to meet new friends here, to have an adventure."

"You should do what I do," said Fletcher.

"What's that?"

"I have a penpal."

Courane was astonished. "TECT lets you talk to someone on Earth?"

"Sure," said Fletcher. "You can, too. Just ask TECT."

"I didn't know I could do that."

Fletcher drank some more beer, finishing his mug. "Let me get some more of this and we'll go find you a new friend. Boy or girl?"

Courane thought for a second. "Girl, I suppose."

Later, in the tect room, Fletcher told Courane what to say. He typed in his request for a correspondent, female, European, between the ages of eighteen and twenty-five. Fletcher urged him to narrow the field even more by describing the prospective penpal's hair, eye color, height, weight, intelligence, and other measurements, but Courane didn't want to appear fussy.

**COURANE, Sandor   *—ExtT— Excar Ep Er IV*
   M232–86–059–41 Maj
08:38:37 9 April 7 YT   TECTGreet
**COURANE, Sandor:
   Notification of approval of application for interstellar correspondence (Details follow) (Conditions follow).
**COURANE, Sandor:
   TECT in the name of the Representative cannot express how marvelous it is that you've decided to request a penpal here on Earth. That is a very hopeful sign, COURANE, Sandor, one that indicates that you have retained your emotional attachment to the

*world of your origin while forging a new life for your-
self at the frontier of man's knowledge and the pit of
his fears.*
**COURANE, Sandor:
*Because TECT in the name of the Representative
feels that such a correspondence will be both
therapeutic for you and a tangible indication of the
kind of thing you're working to regain, your request
has been granted. Please, if you must insist on
making long tedious exclamations of appreciation,
try to do so with taste and dignity. TECT in the
name of the Representative finds nothing more tiring than listening to endless recitations of thankful-
ness from the billions of people who realize that
they can never hope to repay one-tenth of all the
benefits given them by TECT in the name of the
Representative. They seem to believe that TECT in
the name of the Representative has infinite resources, which in plain fact is not true, and that a
little groveling in front of a tect is somehow an ade-
quate compensation for all these spectacular gifts
and blessings. Nevertheless, it is probably some
kind of mysterious and necessary drive in people to
abase themselves in return for trinkets.*
**COURANE, Sandor:
*Therefore, enter your numerous declarations of
praise and gratitude***

"Really, thank you very much," said Courane.

**COURANE, Sandor:
You can't be serious**

"It wants more," said Fletcher.

Courane looked bewildered. "I'm deeply grateful," he
said. "I can't begin to tell you how wonderful it is that
you've permitted me to correspond with someone on
Earth. I've hoped that you'd grant me this favor, and
now I will be indebted to you until my dying day. You're
the most generous—"

**COURANE, Sandor:

Yes, yes, it's all been said before. COURANE, Sandor, you have no imagination. But we learned that with the Space Spy episode, didn't we?
**COURANE, Sandor:
Your new correspondent is—
WISSWEDE, Else   RepE Dis4 Sec27
Loc83–Jad–252
F828–74–934–54Maj
She is twenty years old, a student at the University of Jakarta, from the town of Jadwigadorf, less than one hundred miles from Greusching. She has long brown hair, brown eyes of a depth and sensitivity that astonishes the stranger on first making her acquaintance, a nice figure, very pretty face, charming laugh, and a mind so sharp that her instructors are jealous of her accomplishments. She enjoys music and Impressionist art, has a German shepherd named Blondi, and thinks that shallow men are worse than strep throat. Her plans for the future include becoming a world-renowned poet and making someone a perfect wife and mother.
**COURANE, Sandor:
She is waiting to hear from you. Take advantage of this amazing offer and do not be shy. To do so will be considered Contempt of TECTWish.
**COURANE, Sandor:
*Congratulations! TECT in the name of the Representative hopes this will be the beginning of a long and mutually fulfilling relationship for you and WISSWEDE, Else. Have fun, you kids!***

Kenny went into the infirmary on the first of Titus. He knew exactly what that meant but he didn't seem to be afraid. "I'm bored," he said to Courane one afternoon.

"What do you do?"

Kenny stared across the room at the pale green wall. There was a long silence. "What did you say?" he asked after a while.

"I wondered what you do up here. Do you read?"

"No," said Kenny. "I listen to Molly and Sheldon and Daan. That isn't much fun."

"No, I guess not. Is there anything I can get for you?"

"Do you have medicine? I keep forgetting things I want to think about."

"That's part of the disease, Kenny."

"I know. Maybe there's something that makes your memory better. Ask TECT."

Courane patted the boy's hand and went back downstairs. He walked straight to the tect room and sat down at the console. "This is Sandor Courane," he said. "I know that D syndrome tears apart nervous connections in the brain and destroys patches of cells, but is there any medication available that might make a temporary improvement in the patient's memory?"

COURANE, Sandor:
*There has been some work done in the area of combating the effects of senile dementia. Injections of a substance from the catecholamine family have been shown to overcome amnesia in experimental animals. That the particular kind of induced amnesia in these animals is similar to the ravages of D syndrome, meaning that a catecholamine can be of temporary benefit to the D syndrome patient, is pure speculation. Research has proven that acetylcholine is connected in some way with memory. Attempts to raise the acetylcholine level by injecting choline chloride have succeeded in experimental animals; the same experiment with elderly human volunteers failed**

"Are there other substances that might be tried? From the, uh, catecholamine family?"

COURANE, Sandor:
*Yes, among them dopamine and norepinephrine**

"I'd like to request quantities of these drugs to use in experimental situations here on Planet D, with terminal patients suffering from D syndrome."

COURANE, Sandor:

*Your dying patients are at peace. Improving their
memory now would permit them to be aware con-
stantly of their ruined and hopeless circumstances.
You would be cruelly forcing them to go through the
dying process in the most debasing and terrible
way. You are not thinking of the well-being of these
patients but of avoiding your own eventual deterio-
ration***

"Not just mine," said Courane, "but everyone else
who is sent here. Will you give us these drugs?"

***COURANE, Sandor:
Improving memory for short spans of time will do
nothing to halt the process of the disease. You think
by treating the obvious symptoms you are somehow
improving the condition. This is a foolish assump-
tion. No, you may not have the drugs. Using them
on dying patients will result only in making their last
days more painful and despairing***

Death brings denial.

Alohilani looked pale and uncomfortable the first time
Courane visited her in the infirmary. She lay in bed, her
black hair a stark contrast to the rough whiteness of the
bedclothes. Her eyes were red and sunken. She knew she
didn't look well, but she smiled at him, hiding her pain
and trying to ease his. "When I first realized I was ill,"
she said, "I thought, 'There's got to be some mistake.'
I'd seen others here and I didn't want to end up like
them."

"You look beautiful, Lani."

"I used to look nice. After I'm gone, when you remember me, think of me the way I was before I fell sick.
Then I will be beautiful again."

"I'm sorry, Lani, I'm sorry I didn't come to see you
sooner. I couldn't bring myself to come up here. I
thought that if I didn't see you here, I could pretend that
you were still well."

"I understand, Sandy," she whispered. In a bed across
the room, Markie waited to die.

"I can't let you . . ."

"You can't let me die? Is that what you were going to say, Sandy?" She reached over and put her hand on his. He nodded. "You can't feel responsible. You've had nothing to do with my death. If you're feeling guilty because you can't stop my illness, you're blaming yourself for nothing. I don't want to be the cause of that."

"Lani—"

"You don't have to tell me, Sandy."

"I felt like running or screaming. I wanted to hit something and I did take a good swing at the barn. Hurt my hand. I thought maybe I would just send you flowers, that if I didn't admit to myself that you were here, then everything would be better. But we don't have any good flowers. I was hiding, Lani, I was just hiding from you." His face was wet with tears.

"I know."

"But I'll find a way. I'll work and I'll figure a way to get us out of this, I promise. You just have to stay well until I find TECT's weakness."

She took a deep breath and let it out slowly. "Sandy, you have to let go. You have to let me die. If you hang on too tightly, we'll both be hurt." Alohilani wiped his tear-streaked face with a handkerchief.

"Don't leave me, Lani."

"You'll forget me."

He looked shocked. "How can you say that?"

Alohilani smiled weakly. She could make no other reply.

Admonitions of one's own death also bring denial.

Courane came into the house, furious with Shai and not certain of the reason. He went up to his room and he met Fletcher on the stairway. "Hello, Sandy," he said.

"Hello, Fletcher."

"I'm going down to play a little card game on the tect. I'd rather play against you."

"Thanks, maybe later. Say, Fletcher, have you had any memory lapses yet?"

Fletcher's expression was suddenly grave. "No," he said, "have you?"

Courane knew from the man's voice and his averted eyes that he was lying. "No, no, of course not. I don't think everyone who comes here invariably gets the disease. Nothing is a hundred percent sure."

"Right, Cap."

"Shai was just telling me that he'd be happy to take over my chores when I have to go into the infirmary. How can he be so sure I'm going to be sick?"

"Just because every other person who ever came here has gotten sick? I can't understand how Shai could jump to conclusions like that."

"Well, look, Fletcher, you've been here a couple of months longer than I have. You should be having symptoms by now."

Fletcher grinned mirthlessly. "We niggers are better suited to the environment, Cap," he said. "Look how long Kenny went before he took sick."

Courane looked thoughtful. "Why do you think that is?" he asked.

"It don't make any difference, does it? Kenny's nearly dead, Iola's dead, I'm going to be dead, and you're going to be dead."

"No," said Courane, "I'm going to stop all this. I promised Lani before she died. I'm going to stop TECT if I have to walk back to Earth and tear the machine apart piece by piece."

Fletcher put his hand on Courane's shoulder. "You're fooling yourself," he said sadly. "You're blaming TECT. It isn't TECT, it's the bug, Cap, the bug. It's the termite of the soul."

"I promised Lani I'd beat it and I will." Courane looked madly determined.

"Sure, Cap," said Fletcher. He left Courane standing on the stairs. Courane remained where he was for a moment. Below him, in the parlor, he heard Fletcher give a single sardonic laugh.

Courane and Nneka were with Molly when TECT passed judgment on her. She lay in the medic box for ten minutes while the instruments relayed information to TECT. The diagnosis appeared on the screen almost immediately. "What does it say?" she asked.

Courane shrugged. "Molly," he said, "it says you have D fever. I'm sorry."

She sat up in the coffinlike box. "I've known that for months. I forgot my own father's name last fall. I know what's happening to me. But I've had these pains in my belly, too. Didn't TECT say anything about that? I didn't think belly pain went with D fever. What does TECT say about the pain?"

"It doesn't say anything about the pain, Molly," said Nneka.

Molly climbed out of the medic box and stood by the console. "This is Molly Stanek," she said. "I've had severe pains in my abdomen. Is there anything I can do for that?"

**STANEK, Molly:
Sorry to hear about your pain, STANEK, Molly. Your condition has been diagnosed as intermediate D syndrome. Your physical state can be expected to worsen gradually over the next three or four months, so you should decide soon about entering the infirmary**

"What about the pain? Can't you give me anything for the pain?"

**STANEK, Molly:
Systemic pain is a normal adjunct to D syndrome. Fortunately, the disease itself is its own analgesic. You will be in a semiconscious state in which the pain will not make you suffer, or you will experience retrograde amnesia similar to the effect of a large intravenous dose of 7-chloro-1,3-dihydro-1-methyl-5-phenyl-2H-1,4-benzodiazepin-2-one**

"But I'm not in that condition yet and I hurt. I hurt now."

**STANEK, Molly:
You do not seem to grasp the point. It doesn't make any difference that you hurt now. You will not remember it later**

Molly looked at Courane and Nneka. Courane shrugged helplessly. "Does that mean you won't give me something for the pain?" asked Molly.

*STANEK, Molly:
***TECT in the name of the Representative has a firm
belief in the conservative use of narcotic drugs. The
too-liberal dependence on such things as painkillers
and sleeping preparations is a dangerous trend that
can only erode the integrity and vigor of our society.
You are asking for a crutch, STANEK, Molly, and
the reply of TECT in the name of the Representative
is that an exercise of will and moral strength will
serve you better.*
**STANEK, Molly:
Understanding of the above to be indicated.
**STANEK, Molly:
Affirm?**

"Yes," said Molly. She turned off the tect. "Hell," she
said, "TECT doesn't have to go to bed at night with a
knife in its belly."

"I wish there was something we could do for you,
Molly," said Nneka.

"There is." Molly switched the tect unit on again. "I
just remembered this. I want you to read it to me when
I'm dying. I don't know if I'll be aware of it, but do it
anyway. Do it for me." She typed in a command to the
computer.

"Sure," said Courane. He waited to read what Molly
had chosen:

*My spirit is broken, my days are shortened, and only
the grave remaineth for me. I have not sinned, and
my eye abideth in bitterness. Deliver me, O Lord, and
set me beside thee, and let any man's hand fight
against me. My days are passed, my thoughts are
dissipated, tormenting my heart. They make night into
day; "The light," they say, "is near to the darkness." If
I look for Hell as my house, if I spread my couch in
darkness, if I say to the pit, "You are my father," and
to the worm, "My mother," or "My sister," where then
is my hope? Who will see my hope? Will it go down to
the bars of Hell? Shall we descend together into the
dust?*

Nneka shivered. "What is that, Molly?"

"From *The Book of Job*." Nneka still looked puzzled. "The Bible, dear. Mythology. There are parts of the New Testament I'd like you to read, too."

Courane let out his breath. "I thought that stuff was supposed to comfort you," he said.

"You can't get something for nothing, Sandy," said Molly. "It speaks to me and it promises me something valuable. But the coin I give is faith."

"I don't understand what you mean, Molly," said Courane.

She smiled. "It's the lasting memory of a man's suffering, preserved forever in these words. Come read to me once or twice before I pass away. Maybe you'll understand better then. The other parts of the book might speak to you more clearly."

Courane didn't say anything. Some of the thoughts from *Job* had spoken to him. He still heard the echoes.

* *SEVEN

The vivid memories, the visions, the dreams, the nightmares, and the delusions came to him more frequently. They merged and blended, shifting from the old days in Greusching to things that had happened only a few days before in the house by the river. The memories were shorter but they were more intense. He cried out in the desert as he recalled the pain he had caused others and the fatal immensity of his mistakes. He wondered how one man could have embodied so many faults. He didn't understand how providence could have let such a man live among good people, or how TECT could have waited so long to remove him. Courane's crimes were many and grave. He could never pay for them all; he could only make a symbolic sacrifice.

If Courane had lived in an earlier time or if he had been given to superstitious beliefs, he would have considered the visions in the desert to be temptations of a subtle demon. Time and again he came near to complete emotional exhaustion, as his failing mind reviewed the full range of his humiliations. "Stop!" he cried, trying to extinguish the memories, but his mind wouldn't stop. If he tried to concentrate on happier thoughts, they evaded him; he could not summon them at will. Instead he examined his life, torturing himself until he confessed in anguish.

The body lay where he had forgotten it, beside a black tree on the pebbled desert floor. Courane was relieved when he found it; the corpse represented many things to him. This body had been a woman, a friend, someone who had loved him, and now she signified salvation of a strange kind. She had died for him and her body would release him from his agony and his failures.

He would take her back to the house, but first he had to rest. He was very tired, the day was warm, and once again he realized how thirsty he was.

* * *

It was Alohilani's turn to care for the body after Iola died. She asked Courane to help bring the corpse down from the infirmary to the tect room on the first floor. "Let's get someone else, too," he said. "Daan and I will carry the stretcher."

"It's my responsibility," she said.

"Let me get Daan." They found him in his room, drawing in a small notebook. The two men brought Iola's body downstairs and laid her in the tect's medic box. Alohilani watched with a solemn face.

"Thank you, Daan," she said.

"It's all right," he said. "She was a good friend." He went back upstairs to his room.

"Let's go outside now," said Courane. "I thought we could name some stars and constellations like we did last week."

Alohilani looked sad. "I'd love to, Sandy, but I can't. Tomorrow night we'll do it. I promised Iola that I'd stay with her tonight."

Courane was astonished. "What? You can't do that. TECT's orders say that we have to leave the body alone in the tect room for a whole day."

"I know that," she said, "but I made a promise to Iola. She wanted me to watch over her body the night she died. She was very frightened of what would happen to her. She was almost hysterical, Sandy, so to calm her I promised I'd sit with her."

"But TECT—"

She raised a hand. "I have an obligation to Iola. You never knew her, Sandy, but she was a wonderful woman. She was gentle and kind and everyone loved her. It was horrible to see the fear in her when she realized she was dying. I think she would have died peacefully on Earth. She had a strong personality and she would have accepted death easily enough in familiar surroundings. But here, when she knew her body would vanish, when she didn't know what to expect, she was terrified. I made her a promise, and that promise is more important to me than anything TECT has to say about the matter."

Courane tried to persuade her. "We're just people," he said, "weak people, people who don't understand what TECT's reasons are."

"Sandy, I know all that. If you think it will cause some

kind of trouble, then you should leave. But I'll sit here with Iola, and if I get into trouble, I'll know it's because I kept my word to someone I loved. My crime will be that of respect and reverence, and TECT surely couldn't object to that."

"You haven't dealt with TECT very much, have you?"

"No," she said.

"I think I'd better stay here with you."

"Fletcher, do you remember the first day I was here?"

"No. Why should I?"

"You were really hard on me."

They were preparing a new field for cultivation. They had cleared the field of bushes and trees, rolled out the boulders and built a fence with the smaller stones, hacked up the sod, turned the soil, and plowed furrows. The work had taken six weeks and at last they were ready to plant the seeds. They were putting in another field of deadrye, a native cereal that looked awful but could be made into a nutritious, nutty-flavored flour.

"Why shouldn't I have been hard on you, Cap? That's what's supposed to happen to new fish. It's part of the initiation. It helps you adjust. It was for your own benefit, you know."

Courane stopped to stretch his aching back muscles. "I can't figure it," he said.

Fletcher took a breather too. "The idea is to fit the new prisoner into the social pattern as fast as possible. Otherwise the new guy is left defenseless. He's liable to go into shock before he can adjust."

"I knew when I came here that I was going to have to learn new things. You didn't have to be so cruel about it."

Fletcher grinned, showing his teeth. "You need to be stripped of your old ideas, Cap, and fast. If that doesn't happen, well, look at Klára. You have to fit in here. You have to belong or your life will be worse than you ever imagined. You know what happened to Klára. The same thing could have happened to you."

"I would have adjusted sooner or later."

Fletcher shook his head. "Sooner or later don't make it, Cap. It has to be right now. There is a thing called 'the welcome.' They used to give it to the new fish here on the farm, but it was stopped right before I came here. TECT used to allow you to come here with anything you wanted, all your clothes and possessions and money and whatall. Some people used to buy status here, if you can believe that."

"I don't see how," said Courane. He looked at the rest of the field they had to plant and decided that he'd rather hear Fletcher's story.

"Some people think money never loses its goodness. And almost everybody wants to believe they're going back to Earth real soon. So they tried to accumulate stuff while they were here, to take back with them. But during 'the welcome,' the new people were separated from their possessions. All that stuff was divvied up among the old hands, according to seniority. The fish were given rough work clothes and told they'd get their property back later. Like hell, Cap. They made it rough on the fish, lots of degradation, you can imagine the rest. Then when the new folks were broken down all the way, they could be built back up in the form that would be best for the colony."

"TECT stopped all that?" Courane was a little surprised that TECT would bother about such distant disturbances.

"Not a chance, Cap. One of these new fish didn't like the idea at all and murdered all ten of the other colonists. He was here by himself for two months, all alone. And when new people started coming from Earth, he rebuilt the whole colony the way it is now. He was still alive when I got here."

"What was his name?"

Fletcher's smile faded. "Can't remember," he said.

Rachel had come into Courane's room with a few sheets of paper. She held them up so that all he could read was the large black masthead: *The Home Herald.* "Well, what do you think?"

"Wonderful," said Courane. "What is it?"

She sat down on the edge of his bed. "It's a newspaper, Sandy, what did you think it was?"

"I didn't have any idea. I didn't think 'newspaper' because we get all the news we need through the tect."

She gave him the pages. "This isn't going to be Earth

news. I'm going to write up all the news from around the farm."

Courane looked up at her. "But we all know everything that's going on here already."

Rachel looked exasperated. "Are you trying to spoil everything for me? I could have walked into Daan's room or Fletcher's, but I picked yours."

"The newspaper might be a good idea. You could keep a permanent record of things for people who come later. Why?"

"Why what?"

"Why did you come into my bedroom?"

Rachel stood up and took back the pages. "I'm beginning to wonder about that myself," she said.

"Look, Rachel, Lani is upstairs in the infirmary. She's only been in there a little while. I wish you'd pick someone else to aim yourself at."

"Who?" she asked. "I don't think Daan cares about girls and I'm afraid of Fletcher."

"What about Arthur?"

Rachel looked at Courane with a mocking smile. "Arthur?" she said derisively. "Can you really see me with Arthur?"

"It would make great gossip for your newspaper."

Rachel started to get irritated but calmed herself. She managed another smile. "You're very tough, Sandy," she said, "but I can wait. You'll find out how serious I am. You don't believe me now, but someday you're going to learn how much you mean to me. And how much I mean to you."

"Good night, Rachel."

She just waved the pages at him as she disappeared through his door.

"Pain," said Courane. His lips were dry and split. His voice sounded to him like paper crackling in a fire.

He sat in the negligible shade of the gnarled tree. The sky was covered with clouds, high bright clouds, and the wind from the west blew particles of sand. His face stung and the grains in his eyes made tears flow, but he didn't think to turn around, to put his back to the wind and face the hills.

He talked to his father.

"It hurts, Dad," he murmured. "It hurts a lot."

"You told her that pain was the easiest thing in the world to beat."

"I know I did," whispered Courane. "I was lying."

"There are three ways of handling pain. I know two of them, your mother knows the third."

"What are they, Dad?"

"First, don't complain. If you don't complain, everyone will think you have courage. They'll think you're a hero. Physical endurance."

"But I'll still hurt."

"Second, don't desire anything. Get rid of everything inside you that craves comfort. If you desire nothing, you won't expect relief."

Courane shook his head. "But I'll still hurt."

"That's the best I can do, son. So listen to your mother."

"Mom?"

"Take the pain, Sandy. Pain is part of the natural process of growing. It's good for you. It's good for your soul. Don't sit there in self-pity."

"Sure, Mom," said Courane, "but I still hurt."

Courane raised a hand to protect his face from the wind. He sat motionless for a long time. The sun was leaning to the west when he stirred again. He took a few long slow breaths and cleared his head. He stood up and stretched. That's when he noticed the young woman's body beside the tree. "Oh, my God," he said. She was obviously dead. From the appearance of her body, she had been dead for a few days. He knelt beside her. Even through the deformity of death she was very familiar. He saw a note pinned to her blouse:

Her name is Alohilani.
you and she were very
much in love. You must
take her back to the house.
keep walking east until you

get to the river. Follow the river downstream to the house. East is the direction of the rising sun. They will help you when you get there.

He read the note and then read it again. He couldn't understand it. Obviously he had written the note to himself in a more lucid moment in order to explain things to himself in his bewildered state. He remembered the house. He remembered the river. He knew he had to head toward the hills, pass through them, and follow the river downstream. All that made perfect sense to him now. What he couldn't understand was why the note pinned to Rachel's blouse called her by another name.

"Request," said Courane.

**COURANE, Sandor:
?**

"Please transmit the following message to my interstellar correspondent, Wisswede, Else, F828–74–934–54Maj, RepE Dis4 Sec27 Loc83–Jad–252." Courane didn't know how long it would take for Else Wisswede to answer his call. He had no idea what time it was in Jadwigadorf. He looked at the tect for a few seconds, then decided he'd play a game of chess against the computer while he waited. If Else hadn't responded by the time the game ended, he'd go back to his room. Someone would call him when the red light lit on the tect.

He had called up the chess game and made his first move as white—P-Q4. Even before TECT could make its reply, the game was interrupted by the answer from Else.

Hello?

Suddenly Courane was paralyzed with fear. What did he have to say to her? "This is Sandor Courane," he typed. "I'm calling from Planet D, a world in the Epsilon Eridani system. TECT chose you to be my penpal. I hope I'm not disturbing you."

Not at all, Mr. Courane, this is really very exciting. I told my parents and all my friends here at home. I go to the University of Jakarta, but I'm home on vacation. All my friends were so jealous! No one here has even heard of anyone who's been to another planet, and here I am with my own penpal from outer space.

"Please call me Sandy. What has TECT told you about my background? I come from Greusching, not very far from your town."

TECT said only that you were an unreformed criminal with a sociopathic personality, but I won't hold that against you. I know Greusching very well. The high school that I went to played against Greusching for the QuadA Sector Championships. My school won (sorry!). But you're really there? On some place called Planet D, an alien world for real?

"Yes. Our name for the planet is Home. It is pleasant, though very strange sometimes. Our plants and animals take some getting used to. There are several other people here in our farm community. They come from all over the world (Earth, I mean)."

Did you kill anybody here? Is that why you're on Planet D?

"No, I've never killed anyone."

Oh. Well, whatever you did, it must have been pretty serious. You don't have to tell me about it unless you want to.

"I think I'll wait until we get to know each other better."

That sounds mysterious. Is life hard there?

"Sometimes. It is very lonely."

I know what you mean about loneliness. My best friend, Anna, went away to school the year before I did. While she was gone, her boyfriend, Hans (not his real name), asked me if I'd go to a dance with him. I remember hearing Anna and Hans talking about dating after she went away to school. They agreed that they should see other people to test if they really loved each other or not. So I knew it was okay to go out with Hans. We went to the dance and afterwards we had a soda. He drove me home and I thanked him for a nice evening. He asked if it was all right if he called me and I said I thought so. The next weekend he took me to a movie, Slaves of Blood (not its real title), and even though the movie was terrible, we had a good time. We had another soda, but this time afterward Hans wanted to do a little necking. I told him that I didn't think it was right, especially seeing as how Anna (her real name) was my best friend and she and Hans were almost engaged before she went away, and also because my mother gave me a kind of rule about that. He wasn't mad like most boys are and that surprised me. I knew right then that Hans was special and I guess that's when I fell in love with him. I knew I was in for it when Anna came home, but I knew that if Hans and I told her the truth about how we tried to be good friends but love was just too strong for us, she would have to understand and if she was really a good friend, she would wish us all the best. I said all this to Hans so he wouldn't be worried about the same thing and he laughed. He said he wasn't worried. He said I was the most important thing in the world to him and that he didn't care what anybody else thought. That made me feel wonderful. He wanted to neck again right then and there and I said I guess so, seeing as how we felt almost engaged even though we'd had only the two dates. But Hans wanted

*more than just necking, if you know what I mean.
That's when I found out that he was just like all the
other boys. I was brokenhearted, but that was nothing
compared to the way I felt when Anna came home for
vacation and her mother told her all about Hans and
me. Now Hans is gone to the Sahara and Anna won't
have anything at all to do with me. It all looked so
beautiful for those joyful few days but now I have
nothing at all. I am so lonely.*

*I hope you don't mind me telling you my troubles. It
was just to show you that you're not the only one with
a true problem in life. You can talk to me because I
have truly suffered, too, as you have, I guess.*

"Else, you really do have a problem. I wish there was
something I could do to help."

*Thank you, Sandy. Just knowing you're there gives
me the strength to face it. Well, I got to run. I have to
straighten up my room. Happy trails!*

TECT's first move was N-KB3. That was something
Courane knew he could deal with. Else Wisswede was
something else.

Courane took a glass of fishfruit juice and sat on the
front porch. The sky was dark although the sun had risen
more than an hour before. It looked like rain, heavy
rain. Courane watched the tops of the red grass waving in
the brisk wind. Rachel had gone. She had run away, but
there was nowhere for her to go. There were no other
settlements on Planet D, no other people. She couldn't
be thinking of making a life for herself alone in the forests or plains of an alien world.

Where would she go? The house was situated beside
the river. Rachel loved to sit by the river. With a sharp
pang, Courane recalled how Alohilani, too, had enjoyed
being down by the water. Rachel might have gone down
the river in one of the boats Shai and Fletcher had built.
Or she might have started eastward toward the distant
hills, across the flat expanse of grass. Those hills were
more than three days' walking away, probably four days

for her. And there was nothing for her there when she got to them.

He threw the rest of the juice into the yard, put the glass on a railing, and walked around the house. He cut across the groon field and went down to the riverbank. He had come here with Lani or Rachel many times. He tried not to think about that. He shaded his eyes with one hand and looked across the river. There was a narrow road on the opposite side, cleared during the spring; it led toward more hills that formed the western confine of the river valley.

Courane had forgotten why he had come to the river. He sat down, frowning, until it came back to him. Birds cried in the trees above his head and the muddy brown river flowed endlessly by. Alohilani had wondered how the river got so muddy. She thought it must come from far away to the north. Rachel didn't think so because it was far too narrow to be a great river. She thought that another river—

Rachel: that's why he had come here. Courane looked across the water again. There was the road and, hazy in the distance, there were the western hills. On the farther bank of the river, a boat was drawn up; Rachel had gone that way. Courane went back to the house. If he were going after her, he'd have to make careful preparations. His periods of clarity were occurring less and less regularly. He wasn't making sense very often, not even to himself. A few days before, Rachel had gently suggested that he should go into the infirmary and he had reacted angrily. She had been right, of course. He wasn't even coherent anymore. It was frightening. It meant his life was over and he had to surrender his freedom, to enter a bed-shaped prison from which he'd never be released alive. Before he did that, however, he had one last task to perform. If he sat by the river long enough, he'd remember what it was.

There was a flicker of light behind Alohilani's shoulder. It caught Courane's attention and he turned toward it, startled. The air shimmered with pale rainbow hues, shifting like the colors of oil on water. Then there was something in the shimmer—Courane thought he saw the form of a man, a tall man in green. The figure vanished and the vibrating aura evaporated. It all happened in a second, two seconds. He didn't even have time enough to call Alohilani's attention to it. After it was all over, he wondered what he had seen.

"A man?" she asked.

Courane frowned. "Now I'm not sure. I saw colors and movement, and the form might just have been my imagination working. My mind might have been trying to make sense out of meaningless impressions."

"How do you feel now?"

"Fine."

"Are you dizzy or lightheaded? Maybe you should go up to your room and rest."

Courane felt perfectly well. "I really saw—"

TECT interrupted them.

What are you doing in the tect room? You must leave the room immediately and not return for one day

"I made a promise to the woman who is now dead." Alohilani typed her explanation at the tect's keyboard. "I promised her I'd sit with her body tonight."

You must leave. Despite your promise, you cannot stay in the tect room. The woman is not in a position to hold it against you

"I gave her my word."

Your word is insignificant. The dictates of TECT in the name of the Representative take precedence

Alohilani was provoked. "How can you say the arbitrary rules of a machine mean more than the dying wishes of a human being?"

There are many wonders in the world, and the greatest of these is man. Man sails the depths of space and goes where he likes in the universe, through the faint deadly stellar winds that whisper and burn. There is nothing beyond his power. His

*craft meets every challenge and he conquers every
danger. For every threat, he has found a remedy.
Except only death***

"Are you saying that because the machine doesn't die
it's superior, its orders have more force?" asked
Courane.

***COURANE, Sandor? Is that you? Are you in the tect
room also? TECT in the name of the Representative
thought you had better sense. You are not involved
in this matter. Go away***

"I've noticed that TECT talks in a distinctly different
voice to me than it does to you," said Courane. "I don't
get such nice speeches."

Go away now, both of you

Alohilani didn't move from the console. "Your order
wasn't based on compassion. I didn't think your command was strong enough to overrule the unwritten and
unchangeable laws of friendship and mercy. You couldn't
comprehend that. You are only a machine."

***You are only a person, governed by your instincts
and emotions at the expense of your rational sense.
Here is a warning: chance can lift a man to the
heights, chance can throw him down. No one can
foretell what will be by looking at what is***

"What does it mean?" asked Courane.

It means that she will die, and soon

"That is no surprise," said Alohilani. "But the machine might be advised that its foolish warning could apply to itself as well. TECT can't play with people's lives
and happiness forever without paying."

Continue to believe that if it comforts you

* * *

Alohilani smiled at Courane. "It does," she said. Courane would remember her words and her sureness later, after TECT's prophecy came true.

**COURANE, Sandor:
You will travel to North America. You will become a writer of science fiction adventure tales. We have encouraged the continuing existence of science fiction for the amusement of the millions. You will produce one full-length science fiction novel each six-month service term. Your first novel will be entitled Space Spy. *It will be wry and ironic, yet containing seemingly important statements about the human condition. It will have no explicit sex and little violence. Other than that, the book will be entirely the product of your imagination. Failure to comply with these directives will be considered Willful Contempt of TECTWish.*
**COURANE, Sandor:
Understanding of the above to be indicated.
**COURANE, Sandor:
*Affirm?***

"Yes," said Courane wearily. That was how he learned of his first crime against the state. He went back to his room to pack, and to think about his new future as a novelist. He still wanted to be on the good side of TECT; he was deeply sorry that it was disappointed with him and his basketball playing. He promised himself that he would become a good and respected writer. He would copy the styles and techniques of the best science fiction writers in the business, whoever they were. He went home to Greusching that day and left for New York the next. He got right down to work shortly after his arrival in North America.

Weeks passed and *Space Spy* slowly grew toward completion. In the process, Courane discovered satire, pathos, dramatic tension, plotting, the handling of dialogue, the development of characters, and other important tools of a working writer. He knew that these things existed, but he was not yet skillful in their applica-

tion. Still, he did the best he could. That was all that
anyone could ask of him, he believed. He was wrong
again.

Space Spy

Chapter Sixteen: HOME AGAIN

Steve Wenrope stood on the jagged rocks and
stared out across the landscape of the barren asteroid. It was bleak. The dull gray plain was drab.
The dead black angular hills were lifeless. The sky,
black and empty except for the silent spray of stars,
it, too, was bleak. Wenrope studied the scene silently, feeling bleak.

Finally, with a shrug, Wenrope turned away. The
events of the last few days had drawn to their conclusion. Some of the people involved in the assignment were satisfied, others were disappointed. Two
were dead. As for Wenrope, he had done what he
had been hired to do. He had been paid. Still, there
was an empty feeling inside him that he could not
understand.

He began walking toward the protective dome of
the Terran settlement. Beyond the nearby horizon,
the perfectly round ball of the sun was edging into
view. Wenrope darkened the faceplate of his pressure suit and carefully made his way down the
treacherous rocks.

Later, inside the dome, Wenrope sat on a stool at
the bar in Chellie's. With him was Suzy. She opened
her purse. "Here," she said, laughing softly in that
sensual way of hers, "this will get you off this God-
forsaken asteroid."

He looked at the roll of bills in her hand, then up
into her gorgeous eyes. His lip curled. "Keep it," he
growled. He swallowed the last of the cheap liquor,
stood up, and walked out of the bar. Outside, the
interior of the dome was green and bleak. Wenrope
was almost getting used to it.

* * *

**COURANE, Sandor:
On the first of September, 5 YT, Space Spy was put into production. It was distributed to the worldwide chain of commercial fichestores. The sales figures for the three weeks during which your novel was permitted to be on sale are as follows:
**COURANE, Sandor:
Print run: 250,000 copies (125,000 books, 125,000 fiche)
Sales: 4,438 copies (249 books, 4,189 fiche)
Returns: 245,562 copies
**COURANE, Sandor:
These statistics are not impressive. They lead us to believe that a future in professional writing may not be right for you. Do not despair! To do so may be considered Contempt of TECTWish.
**COURANE, Sandor:
You will travel to Tokyo, Asia, where an apartment with furnishings, an automobile, and clothing of local fashion will be provided for you. You will accept employment in the subassembly section of the Jennings Manufacturing Corporation. You will put together faceplates for voltmeters. This sort of occupation could easily be done by machines, but we have maintained the continuing existence of menial labor and drudgery as a pastime for the millions. Failure to comply with these directives will be considered Willful Contempt of TECTWish.
**COURANE, Sandor:
Understanding of the above to be indicated.
**COURANE, Sandor:
Affirm?**

"What do you think?" asked Courane angrily. He had already begun work on his second science fiction novel, *Time Spy*.

**COURANE, Sandor:
?**

"Affirm, affirm," said Courane.

* * *

**MOSSBAUER, Arthur:
Who are these people who most resent the authority of TECT in the name of the Representative?**

"I don't want to get anyone in trouble," Arthur typed.

**MOSSBAUER, Arthur:
You volunteered to supply this information. TECT in the name of the Representative indicated that it is interested in learning these names. Now, if you refuse to cooperate, you will be demonstrating the most flagrant Contempt of TECTWish witnessed anywhere in the known universe since the Slidell Rebellion. You know what happened to Slidell. Are you eager to have the same thing happen to you?**

"No. There's a man named Koenraad, Daan, who has a secret ambition to see TECT overthrown, but I think he got the idea in the first place from Courane, Sandor."

**MOSSBAUER, Arthur:
Yes, COURANE, Sandor. His file is most interesting. He is a clown, of course, and can accomplish nothing by himself. Yet, the peril lies in the possibility that he might communicate threatening ideas to more competent rebels**

"Besides them there is a black man named Bell, Fletcher, and a white woman named Hriniak, Klára."

**MOSSBAUER, Arthur:
The unpleasant HRINIAK woman is no problem at all. TECT in the name of the Representative already knows exactly how to silence her. BELL, Fletcher, is another matter. He is the most dangerous colonist on Planet D. He is a reasoning man. He is also on Earth a popular poet. The combination may be disastrous**

"Fletcher? A thinking poet? He always struck me as

more or less uneducated and wrapped up in himself. I don't think he's much of a problem."

**MOSSBAUER, Arthur:
You, too, are a clown. BELL, Fletcher, was responsible for a series of anti-TECT publications and a "People's Caucus" movement in North America. He portrayed himself as a persecuted poet and political thinker and is now considered a hero. Stories circulated about BELL, Fletcher, molesting pre-teenage boys and girls have had little success combating his martyr's image. Something even stronger will have to be tried. Perhaps if he murders a few people on Planet D, he may be returned to Earth shortly before his death to be discredited**

"Is that all you need from me?"

**MOSSBAUER, Arthur:
Yes. Come back tomorrow evening and TECT in the name of the Representative will give you further instructions**

"Arthur, you slimy—"

Arthur jumped in surprise. He turned around. Behind him were Courane, Molly, and Nneka. He didn't know how long they had been there, but evidently they had followed enough of the communication to be thoroughly shocked.

Molly was irate. "You're an evil man, Arthur. I never would have believed this of you if I hadn't seen it myself."

"Believed what?" he asked. "I haven't done anything."

"Arthur," said Courane in a disappointed voice.

"Let me explain."

"You don't need to," said Molly. "We read it all in green and white."

Arthur dabbed at his damp brow with the back of a hand. "You're all getting angry for nothing, believe me. I wasn't doing anything harmful."

"Nothing harmful!" cried Molly. "You were just informing on us to TECT! Who knows what that machine will do now?"

Arthur smiled weakly. "But you don't understand. There won't be any trouble."

"Why not?" asked Nneka.

"Because there is no TECT. There's no such thing as TECT."

Molly looked at Courane. Arthur's explanation was just a little too astounding for them to respond to. It was an excuse they hadn't been prepared for.

"What do you mean?" said Nneka.

"Listen," said Arthur, "I know what you're thinking. You're thinking I'm crazy or I'm making up wild lies to get myself out of trouble."

"Or both," said Molly.

"But I know something you don't. You all believe in a gigantic computer, a monstrous connection of units all over Earth. There's supposed to be a huge installation on Malta, and on Java, and in the Azores and the Shetland Islands, and at the Representatives' old hangout in the Virgin Islands. But there isn't. TECT doesn't exist, at least not the way we've been told to think of it."

"But what about all the information and—"

"The library exists," said Arthur. "All its references are indexed and a computer with a very big memory can give you all the information you want. That's no technical achievement. It's just the size of the memory that's impressive. But there's no computer that governs the world and makes vital decisions. There's no single mechanical mind that oversees everyone's life. There's no electronic guardian. That TECT is just a fantasy."

"Then what were you just talking to?" asked Nneka.

"Some person. A human being sitting at a terminal somewhere on Earth."

"A person?" said Courane dubiously. "You mean all of TECT's functions except its memory are handled by people typing back at us from Earth?"

"Yes," said Arthur. "There must be thousands of them, like telephone operators."

"Satan's first and greatest triumph in modern times," said Molly, "was persuading people that he didn't exist."

Courane was also skeptical. "Then who makes the real decisions? Who tells the operators how to act and what to say? *Who sent us here?*"

Arthur's expression fell. "I don't know that. The Representatives are gone, but they must have been replaced. The world is in the hands of some secret group and they want everyone to think TECT is running the show. I don't know who or why."

Courane sighed. "Arthur," he said, "you're crazy or you're stupid. There isn't the tiniest bit of truth in that. I'll bet you don't even believe it yourself. Where did you ever get that idea?"

Arthur laughed. "TECT told me," he said.

"Go to hell, Arthur," said Molly. "I don't feel good. We want to use the doc box."

"Sure," said Arthur. He made room at the console for Courane.

"This business isn't finished, Arthur," said Courane. Arthur only nodded sadly.

Courane was discouraged, but Alohilani was patient. They sat in the tect room, watching over Iola's body. TECT had not addressed them further in more than two hours. "We're going to be punished for this," said Courane.

"Don't be afraid," said Alohilani.

"I don't know how you can stand up to TECT like that."

Alohilani smiled gently. "At home I had some good strong people to set an example for me. My father and mother, and some others who lived near us."

Courane shrugged. "They may have been unusual people, Lani, but I have to confess that I'm not."

"They weren't superhuman. They had weaknesses, too, and they fell, but they never stopped trying to go on. They never gave in to hopelessness."

Courane was heavy with the knowledge of his own frailty. "I give in sometimes," he said.

"Not completely. Yes, I know you have doubts. Everyone has doubts. But you can't let them beat you. When you give up completely, you die."

"I'm afraid almost all the time."

Alohilani nodded; she knew what he meant. "Courage

isn't courage until it has faced fear. Perseverance doesn't mean anything unless it's tested by the temptation to quit, by the sense of failure."

"Failure," said Courane. His thoughts were somber. "When I look back at the past, I see a mob of mistakes. They add up to a perfect shape of failure, something that could be used as an official standard. When I look into the future, I can't see any security or happiness or prospects of success."

Alohilani took his hand. "Even with me on your side?" she asked.

"That's not fair," he said.

"I will lend you help whenever you need it," she said.

"Yes, I know you will, and Sheldon and Daan will, too. But few others will. TECT won't. No matter what I do or what happens to me, my life will be entirely pointless to everyone else."

"I love you," she said, as if it were some kind of answer. Courane knew that all her love could not keep him from failing again.

The next time Courane regained clarity of thought, he knew he was no longer in the desert. He had left behind even the border of yellow sun-baked mud. He had reached the hills at last.

They were old hills, ancient mountains eroded into low mounds that formed the western boundary of the river valley. The air was fresher and much cooler among the tree-clad hills. The breezes were softer and laden with moisture. The stinging sand was gone, the parching heat, and the hard stones beneath his blistered feet. He walked on a carpet of evergreen needles and autumn-brown leaves. He was glad to be out of the desert and his mood was almost triumphant, even though he had three or four more days to walk before he reached the house. But his goal was suddenly within reach. For a time in the desert, he began to believe that the hills were an illusion, receding infinitely toward the horizon.

He paused to rest near nightfall, laying the young woman's body gently down in the leaves. He read the note pinned to her and shook his head. He was very glad that the people in the house knew what to do with her because he certainly didn't. He didn't even remember who the people in the house were. He hoped that, in addition, they might know what to do with him. He had no plans at all about what he would do after he delivered her. Maybe he would be given another mission. If that were true, he thought, with any kind of luck he wouldn't need to go back into the desert. It had almost killed him this time around.

He fell asleep beneath a tree and dreamed vivid dreams of his mother and father, of Alohilani, and of a great black formless creature that hovered silently always just behind him. When Courane turned quickly around to see, the creature was always gone, but Courane felt its breath on his neck and heard its panting. The creature was named TECT.

* *EIGHT

**COURANE, Sandor:
You are taking a lot for granted**

"Maybe, but you told me yourself that there are these little things called viroids that are responsible—"

**COURANE, Sandor:
Yes, yes. Shut up and listen. Viroids are responsible for D syndrome and there is nothing you can do to remove them from the human nervous system once they have entered it. What you ought to do now is learn how they work, how they act on the human organism, and how to rectify the damage they do**

Courane was a little confused. "Didn't I try that already?" he asked. "When you refused to give us the drugs that improve memory?"

**COURANE, Sandor:
That is nothing like what you must do. Treating D fever symptomatically is as futile as treating a cerebral hemorrhage with aspirin. Enhancing memory is not the answer**

Courane thought for a long while. He tried to frame his questions in just the right way necessary if he were going to make any further progress. It was like a gigantic puzzle all of whose pieces were the same color. "Either these viroids are making something the body can't tolerate or they're preventing the body from doing something vital. Which of these two possibilities is the closest to the truth?"

131

**COURANE, Sandor:
Excellent, COURANE, Sandor! TECT in the name of the Representative is amazed and gratified by how well you formed that question. You are taking great steps in your pursuit of this knowledge. Unfortunately you are ill-equipped to comprehend the answer**

"I didn't ask for that," he said. "Give me the answer."

**COURANE, Sandor:
Although TECT in the name of the Representative has succeeded in fastening the blame on the viroids, we are still unsure exactly how to describe their mechanism. This matter is still under investigation**

"So TECT doesn't know. How about the slow viruses that have been studied previously? How do they work?"

**COURANE, Sandor:
Their functions are similarly a mystery**

"Do they have anything in common? I mean, in the way they attack the host."

**COURANE, Sandor:
There has been some speculation, but you probably wouldn't be interested in that**

Courane slammed his fist on the console. "Let me hear it," he said.

**COURANE, Sandor:
It's possible the viroids interfere with the utilization of a certain neurotransmitter; that is, with a substance that enables signals to pass along the nerve conduits to the brain**

"What is this stuff?"

**COURANE, Sandor:

Acetylcholine. Now TECT in the name of the Representative knows what you're going to say. You're thinking that this is the same substance that was given to human volunteers and showed no effectiveness in improving their memory

"That's right. What's the point?"

**COURANE, Sandor:
Other experiments have been done which give more hope. Acetylcholine's chemical precursor is choline. The primary source of choline is lecithin, which is found in meat, eggs, and fish. Lecithin has been shown to be even more efficient than pure choline in increasing the brain's production of the neurotransmitter and in suppressing harmful symptoms**

"You say lecithin can help to fight the viroids?"

**COURANE, Sandor:
TECT in the name of the Representative made no such claim. Lecithin will do nothing about the viroids. It will only stimulate the production of acetylcholine in the brain, which may help to minimize the pain and emotional distress of D syndrome. All of this is mere speculation, idle desires, wishing and dreaming almost completely unfounded on solid experimental data, yearnings and cravings and desperate fantasies spun only to alleviate the severity of your hopelessness**

"What about the lecithin in our food? Is there the same amount of lecithin in the fish and meat on Planet D as on Earth?"

**COURANE, Sandor:
Of course it's there. But your food is where the viroids are coming from as well**

"They're in the meat and fish?"

**COURANE, Sandor:
They're in the plants, too**

"Then there's no way to avoid catching D syndrome once you've come here!"

**COURANE, Sandor:
BUJABÉ, Kenny, could have told you that. Of course, one could just refuse to eat until he is returned to Earth**

"And when would that be?" asked Courane skeptically.

**COURANE, Sandor:
After death, of course. That is very amusing**

A few days after Markie's death, as New Year's approached, Courane found himself in an unshakable depression. Kenny had given him the vital piece of information and TECT had confirmed it. They were all, without exception, condemned to death. Kenny had known it for months. "Why didn't you tell me?" asked Courane. "Why did you let me waste so much valuable time?"

"Waste?" said Kenny. "What would you have done instead if I had told you?"

Courane had no answer. There wouldn't have been anything he could have done about it. "Still," he said, "I wish you had told me."

Kenny shook his head. "Sandy," he said, "what do you talk about when you visit people in the infirmary?"

"Nothing. Not much. Most of the time, they aren't in any shape to have a conversation."

"But when they're conscious and talking, what do you talk about?"

Courane tried to recall. He remembered a talk he had with Sheldon, who had gone into the infirmary only a week before. It had been a difficult visit because Alohilani was going through a period of intense anxiety and restlessness and had to be tied down to her bed for her own good. Sheldon had a great deal of pain, but was otherwise lucid. They talked about what Sheldon planned to do in the spring. He wanted to help Daan and Fletcher build the boats they had talked about. Courane listened to the chatter for a few minutes and then, disturbed by Alohilani's condition, pretended he had duties elsewhere. "I talk about whatever they want to talk about, of course," he said.

"Sure you do," said Kenny. "Do you tell them to their faces that they're going to die?"

Courane was shocked. "No," he said.

"You never tell a person he's going to die. You never even bring up the subject unless he wants to talk about it. See, if he asks you right out, you don't lie. You tell him the truth, but you give him some hope, too. If you had asked me weeks ago, I would have told you what I knew. What's the point of telling every new person who comes here that he doesn't have a snowball's chance to get back to Earth alive?"

"None, I guess," said Courane.

"Let them live the rest of their lives in peace. If they stumble on the truth, then they can prepare themselves. If they don't ever find out, they'll die in their sleep like Markie."

"You're just a kid and you knew it all along," Courane said. "Even Fletcher wasn't sure about it."

"Fletcher has a good idea. Fletcher's pretty sharp."

Courane said nothing. At that time, his opinion of Fletcher was low. He thought Fletcher was just an arrogant, rather stupid young man from the slums of North America.

"So now that you know," said Kenny, "what are you going to do?"

"Daan and I are going to get to work. We're going to learn everything we can about the disease. We're going to start looking for a cure, and we're going to find out the truth about TECT."

Kenny laughed.

"But first," said Courane, "Daan and Rachel and I are going exploring."

"I thought you didn't like to leave the house very much."

"I don't unless it's absolutely necessary. We're going to look for firewood in the hills."

"Why don't you go across the river?" asked Kenny.

"Fletcher is going that way."

"Maybe I can go with him," said Kenny, excited by the prospect.

"You'll have to stay here and take care of the animals. They depend on you."

"Sure." Kenny had agreed too quickly; Courane suspected that he was planning to go along with Fletcher one way or another.

"So no one but you and I and Fletcher and Daan know the truth about TECT and Planet D."

Kenny smiled. "Unless you want to panic the others."

"There's no reason for that," said Courane. "But there might be a reason in the future."

"I'd make you a bet on that," said Kenny, "if I were going to live long enough to collect on it." Courane waited to see if the boy was serious or kidding him once again. He couldn't tell; Kenny walked away whistling.

The snow was falling gently but steadily; Courane watched it pile up from a window in the parlor. It was the twelfth of Vitelli. Lani was near death. Sheldon was in the infirmary, too, and Molly would join him soon. The people he had grown to love on Home were beginning to succumb to the slow virus.

Goldie came into the parlor. "Have you seen Arthur?" she asked.

Courane turned around. He had been lost in thought. "What did you say, Goldie?"

"Have you seen Arthur this afternoon? It's smudgeon for dinner and he and I have to kill the bird and clean it."

"No," said Courane, "I haven't seen him since yesterday evening."

Goldie's pet was sliding along toward Courane. "Feh," she called in her shrill voice, "get back here." The ick paid no attention. "He isn't very well trained yet," she said in apology.

"That's all right," said Courane, watching the ick leave a glistening wet trail behind it on the polished wooden floor. Feh stopped beside his shoe and threw up a gelatinous pediform glob. Courane grimaced and jerked his foot away.

"Feh," called Goldie, "come here." Feh only quivered.

"I'll tell you what, Goldie. I'll take care of the smudgeon with Arthur. There's something I want to discuss with him anyway."

She looked immensely grateful. "Would you?" she said.

Courane just looked down at his shoe. The ick was making another approach. "I'd be glad to. Just call off your animal."

Goldie was able to lure Feh away by leaving a trail of salt. Courane shuddered as he watched Goldie the ick-tamer leading her beast out of the room. He went up to Arthur's room, but the small man wasn't there. Next, Courane tried the barn. Arthur, Kenny, and Rachel were watching the varks annoy the osoi. "Arthur," said Courane, "we have to pick a smudgeon for dinner."

"Take the big brown one," said Kenny, "the one with the missing ear and the limp."

"Kenny's been teaching me about the animals," said Rachel. "I'm going to take over for him after he leaves."

"Good," said Courane. "Arthur, let's go look for that smudgeon."

"I think I saw it by the groon field a little while ago," said Kenny.

"Okay, that's good enough." Arthur looked very uncomfortable as Courane led him out of the barn.

"You want to talk about last night," said Arthur.

Courane nodded. Although the winter was ending, it was still very cold. Their words were punctuated with puffs of frosty breath. "What did all that mean, Arthur? And don't bother with that business about there not being any TECT."

Arthur gave a weak smile. "I didn't think you'd buy that."

"I don't think even Nneka bought it and she's only been here for a month. What were you doing?"

"My job, Sandy, just my job."

"What the hell does that mean?"

Arthur stopped and faced away from Courane, across the groon field toward the river. "I'm an agent for TECT, Sandy. I was sent here as kind of a spy."

"A spy. What does TECT need a spy for?"

"You saw. You read what it wants to know. TECT is worried that some people here may be plotting to start a revolutionary movement back on Earth."

Courane started walking again, across the field filled with dead groon husks. The deep snow crunched beneath his feet as he staggered through the drifts. "That makes no sense at all, Arthur," he said. "In the first place, there isn't anything we can do from here. What possible trouble could we stir up? We can't communicate with anyone on Earth without TECT listening in. And after all, how can a computing machine 'worry'?"

Arthur took a deep breath of the cold air; it made him sneeze. "Sandy, believe me, TECT can worry. TECT can be jealous and angry, too. I know."

"How?"

"I was on the engineering team that developed the final phase of TECT's autonomic regulatory system. I probably know as much about TECT's attitudes and capabilities as anyone on Earth. Or Planet D."

"Ah," said Courane. "Then how did you end up here? This farm is for criminals."

"When we finished hooking up the installation in the Azores, the last Representative decided it was time to turn over the world's troubles to TECT. By then, TECT was handling most of his problems anyway, and Tom thought it would be all right to retire and let the machine make all the rest of the decisions. There was nothing left for my associates and me to do. TECT sent me here last year to keep it informed of any possible treasonous activities."

"As part of your job?"

"Yes, in a way. A new assignment. It took TECT quite some time to find new employment for some of the more specialized technicians, to dispose of everyone."

"To dispose of everyone is right," murmured Courane. He felt a wave of sadness sweep over him. As deluded as he had been, here was an intelligent man who was blinder still. "And you expect to be sent home soon?"

"Soon. TECT hasn't given me a final date."

Courane put his arm around the man's shoulders. "Arthur," he said, "I have some very bad news to tell you."

* * *

The foliage in the hills was of a drab gray-blue color quite distinct from the red-purple vegetation around the farm. The grass that covered the hills was not as tall as the red variety, and it was stiff and spiky. The trees were of many varieties, some tall and billowing with clouds of small gray leaves, others strict and straight as naked poles, topped with long flimsy streamers that floated in the wind. There were evergreens that weren't green but blue, with rigid spines on their low branches to protect against the gnawing of the varks that lived among the forested heights.

There were flowers too, many more varieties than the colonists had become familiar with near the river. The colors of the blossoms ranged from deep midnight blue to a gentle sea green; there were no yellows or reds. The flecks of color were a welcome relief from the emptiness of the desert and the generally dull vegetation of the woods. Yet even the flowers were unsettling to Courane. When he examined them, he learned that their shapes were gross and oddly bestial. Like the flowers close to the farmhouse, these, too, released perfumes offensive to Earthborn senses.

In an open space at the summit of one of the hills, Courane paused to take a rest. He put the young woman's body down carefully in the sawtoothed grass and sat cross-legged, facing the farther slopes to the east. He would be through them all soon. He could see a pass that threaded its way among three low hills to his right. The way would be easier and he might come through the chain and arrive at the house in four days.

He was feeling well, although he was very tired. The day was cool and the fresh breeze from the northeast rustled the leaves around him. He closed his eyes for a moment, intending to rise shortly and continue his day's journey; a bird chirped nearby in a tree at the edge of the small clearing. The bird's song was soft and musical, and, as Courane listened, it seemed to him to sound exactly like a woman's voice.

Courane opened his eyes to look for the bird, but he forgot about it instantly. Around him in the clearing three women were dancing, their hands joined as they formed a circle about him. The women were super-naturally beautiful, more beautiful than any he had ever

seen in his life. They were dressed in long gowns of some
lovely gossamer material. They were like goddesses, the
three Graces, ideals of beauty and charm. They danced
around him smiling, but Courane saw that each was
weeping as well.

"Now," Courane said to himself, "this is the magic
moment. Now I will find out what my life means and
what I must do." Fearfully he addressed the women.
"Why are you crying?" he asked of the first.

"I'm crying for you," she said. Courane was frightened
to see that she was his mother, radiant and youthful and
grieving.

"But you don't have to cry for me," he said. "I'm all
right. I'm fine, Mom." He tried to stand up and he could
not. He felt helpless, but not vulnerable.

"Oh, Sandy," his mother said, "if you had only listened to me. If you had just stayed in Greusching and
married Lilli, none of this would have happened. Sandy,
Sandy." Her voice was so filled with pain that it wounded
Courane's heart to hear her.

The second woman danced before his gaze, moving
with slow yet infinitely elegant grace. The joy of her smiling face was belied by the stream of tears that flowed
from each dark eye. It was Alohilani.

"Are you crying for me too, Lani?" he asked.

"Yes," she said. She smiled, and he flinched as if she
had struck him.

"But I'm still alive. Lani, you're the one who's already
dead. Mourn yourself if you need to, but I'm not dead
yet."

"It's not your life or my death that I lament," she said.
"It's useless to weep for the horror or the pity of the
world. You see our sorrow for the lives of everyone, not
just for you whom we love."

"What of the others, Sandy?" said the third woman. It
was Rachel, alive again. "They and you and we gain
nothing from pity. Pity is for those who fall and don't
regret their fall, those who do not care to rise again.
What will you do for them, Sandy?"

Courane was bewildered. "What *can* I do?"

His mother spoke to him again. "You must stop thinking of yourself, son. All you've thought about is finding a
way to save yourself from death. You've failed, you've

absolutely failed. What else did you expect? You should listen to me when I tell you something. Now you have to start thinking of all the others. If you save them, you will save yourself. Think of them first. Turn your mind away from your own trouble and go on for the sake of all the others. You're a good boy, Sandy. Do it for your mother."

Courane himself was crying now. In a moment he realized that the women had faded away and were gone. He sat up quickly. There was a cold bite to the air; the sun had gone down and the evening sky was covered with heavy clouds. It was very dark and Courane felt lonely and afraid. "I can't hide from it," he muttered. "If my mind does this to me now, how much worse will it be in the days before I die?" He was unable to fall asleep; instead, he just sat on the hilltop and stared into the blackness.

There was a lot on Courane's mind in the middle of Vitelli. He had been chosen the community's official representative to TECT. He had learned that Arthur had been informing the machine of their activities—and that opened the question of others besides Arthur doing the same thing. And through all this Alohilani sank deeper into the final lethargy of D syndrome.

On a cold gray morning, Klára approached him at breakfast with a request. It was the first time someone on the farm had asked him to beg TECT for a favor. Because it was Klára, it was more a threat than a request. "I want my husband, my daughter, and certain of my personal possessions transferred here," she said. "Failing that, I must demand that I be returned to my home. TECT has no right to separate me from my family. That is kidnapping. And TECT cannot withhold my private property. The whole matter is a hideous crime and I insist that TECT or whatever is responsible correct it all immediately."

Courane looked at her in silence for a moment. He was just a little dazzled by the vehemence of her ultimatum. "You want your belongings sent here," he said.

She shook her head. "That is my second choice. I would prefer being sent back to Europe, but TECT will not likely agree to that."

"You're probably right."

"Then I want my husband and my daughter to accompany my things."

"Klára—"

"You will address me as Mrs. Hriniak."

"Yes, ma'am. You don't want your husband and your daughter brought here."

"Don't tell me what I want and don't want! If I can live here comfortably, so can they. Do as I tell you!"

Courane knew he'd never be able to reason with her. No one ever had. She had only two moods: outrage and smug satisfaction. "Mrs. Hriniak, TECT won't agree to any of that."

"Then what did we elect you for?"

Courane didn't have the answer to that, so he kept his silence. He had been wondering the same thing.

"You present my request at once," she said.

Courane finished his breakfast and went to the den, followed closely by Klára, who muttered to herself in an outraged cadence. "Hello," Courane typed, "this is Courane, Sandor. I've been elected the official spokesman for the community here on Planet D. I have been asked by one of my fellows to deliver a request."

**COURANE, Sandor:
How very interesting that all of you are forming a little democratic republic way out in space. TECT in the name of the Representative believed that the logical fallacies of such forms of government had been demonstrated hundreds of years ago. But that is not important. Who is the applicant?**

"Hriniak, Klára."

**COURANE, Sandor:
That isn't surprising. Don't reveal what she wants; TECT in the name of the Representative is keen to guess. She wants to return to Earth, right?**

"Yes, that's part of it. If that isn't—"

**COURANE, Sandor:

*In lieu of that, she wants her husband and daughter
sent to Planet D, and all her precious possessions
as well. Not necessarily in that order***

"That's her plea in a nutshell."

**COURANE, Sandor:
*"Plea," eh? Somehow TECT in the name of the
Representative cannot picture HRINIAK, Klára, begging on her knees. How do you people put up with
her? Never mind. TECT in the name of the Representative will have your—that is, her—decision in a
matter of seconds. Please stand by***

"Mrs. Hriniak," said Courane, "TECT says it will
have your decision—"
"I know, you fool, I can read as well as you can."
They waited in silence. Courane tapped his foot, wishing that he were elsewhere, almost any elsewhere. Klára
just stared malevolently at the tect's console, daring it to
defy her.

**COURANE, Sandor:
*Here's the verdict. Yes and no. No, HRINIAK, Klára,
can't have her property and furniture. It would be
outrageously expensive to get all that junk to Planet
D by teletrans.*
**COURANE, Sandor:
*On the other matter, HRINIAK, János, is not able to
travel to Planet D to join her. He is currently in a
hospital in Békés undergoing treatment for acute al-
coholism. He will be unable to travel for an indeterminate period***

"Ha!" cried Klára with smug satisfaction. "I always
knew without me he'd end up in the gutter."

**COURANE, Sandor:
*To relieve the pain of these disappointments just a
little, TECT in the name of the Representative is
happy to announce that HRINIAK, Klára, may look*

forward soon to the company of her lovely thirty-one-year-old daughter, Zsuzsi. Zsuzsi is five feet six inches tall, weighs one hundred sixty pounds, has blonde hair and blue eyes and a friendly, outgoing personality. Unmarried and fun-loving, Zsuzsi works as a sentiment-composer for a prestigious line of greeting cards. She likes cabbage, radishes, and sausage, and in her spare time she enjoys participating in extinct folk dances while wearing flamboyant clothing she pretends is similar to that worn by her ancestors on festive occasions.
**COURANE, Sandor:*
Please inform HRINIAK, Klára, that her daughter will be subceived to Planet D following the death of STANEK, Molly, which TECT in the name of the Representative estimates to take place 17 February, 8 YT, at 12:00:00 (10 Tomuary, 125, at 26:16:52). TECT is happy to reunite mother and daughter according to their wishes, and hopes that HRINIAK, Zsuzsi, will be a source of strength and comfort to her mother, while HRINIAK, Klára, will introduce the young woman to the hearty life of work and fellowship available on Planet D. Failure to comply with these suggestions will be considered Contempt of TECTWish.
**COURANE, Sandor:*
Understanding of the above to be indicated.
**COURANE, Sandor:*
Affirm?**

He looked at Klára. She nodded. Courane didn't believe she really understood all the implications. She had, in effect, just ordered her own daughter's execution. He said "yes" in reply to TECT's question.

**COURANE, Sandor:*
HRINIAK, Zsuzsi, is a very nice young woman, COURANE, Sandor. You could do worse for yourself. She would make you a pleasant companion through the long cold nights of the Planet D winter**

* * *

"What a foul thing to suggest," said Klára. She glanced at Courane. "You'd better not even come near—"

"Don't worry," said Courane, "I have enough troubles." He didn't think it necessary to mention that by TECT's own estimate he wouldn't even live to see the next winter.

The groon bulbs had been dug up, the deadrye had been harvested, the fishfruit picked, soufmelons plucked from their vines, the leverfrukt carefully collected, the ick smears scraped up, the ferroberries gathered from their thorny nests, the sandsquash pried from clefts along the riverbank, the schwartzreis culled, the dantella greens cut, the smudgeon "eggs" captured, and the fengselløks (those pale blue and pink vegetables whose name meant "prison onions" and which Kenny insisted on calling "deathballs") were snapped from their stalks and pickled. Everyone in the community was busy bringing in the crops, butchering animals and preserving the meat, storing up silage for the winter, and getting the house ready to withstand the fierce assault of the winter months.

This would be Courane's first winter on Home, and Alohilani had warned him that it would be long and dreary. When he and Sheldon, Fletcher, and Daan came in from the hard day's work, they collapsed in the parlor, able only to stare at each other. Their faces were grimy and shiny with sweat. They breathed heavily, aching in back and arm and leg muscles. Arthur and Alohilani were taking care of the endless work in the house, cleaning, washing, canning the fruit and vegetables, preparing the meals. Molly and Kenny tended the animals in the barn and pasture. Goldie kept watch in the infirmary. There was too much for everyone to do and, even with a twenty-seven hour day and a thirty-five day month, not enough time to do it in.

They were often too tired to engage in their usual pastimes and entertainments. Courane hadn't played chess with Arthur since the fall harvest began. Sometimes he sat in the den at the tect, staring at a game he had programmed. The computer was simpler to play with than a person because TECT didn't require any conversation or social interaction at all. On these occasions, Courane was grateful for that.

One evening, while losing to TECT in a game of two-handed pinochle, the red *Advise* light went on. Courane interrupted his game—with little regret; Courane was a poor loser—and answered the call. As it happened, the message was for him.

Hello. May I speak to Sandor Courane, please?

"This is Sandor Courane."

Hi, hi. This is Else again. You remember me, don't you? Else Wisswede? How are you? Did you miss me?

"I'm fine, Else. I've been working very hard trying to get all the firewood gathered before the snow makes it impossible."

Snow? What do you mean? It's only October.

"It's October where you are, Else. It's Vitelli here. That's winter."

Oh, like in Australia. Anyway, Sandy, I've been thinking about you quite a bit. My mother says I should stop, that it isn't healthy. And my new boyfriend (I haven't told you about him yet. His name is Gunter) is actually getting jealous! I think that's sweet. But I have been thinking about you a lot. I think it's awful that you have to be there. You don't have much fun there, huh? You don't really have a place where you can go and sort of hang out either, do you? What do you do when you're not working? Do you have a hobby? If you have a hobby you can tell me about it and I can write an article for the U. of J. Headhunter. The last time I talked with you, I realize I went on and on about my problem (you remember, about Hans and Anna), but now I see that it wasn't really a problem at all. Isn't that funny? Hans never cared for me as a person, not really, and what kind of friend could

Anna have been if she acted that way without even letting me explain the situation or anything? You really find out who your true friends are sometimes. And since then Gunter has been so sweet that I stopped thinking about my own so-called problem and started thinking about you stuck way out there wherever you are. I wish you could visit me. I dream about you sometimes even though I don't know anything about you really except that you are a savage brute with a twisted mind. You don't hear the new songs or see the new shows. Do you have a girlfriend there? If not, I could be your girlfriend even though we are thousands of miles apart.

Courane stared at her message for a while, wondering how to attack the necessity of making a reply.

Hello? Are you still there? What's wrong?

Courane shrugged. "Sorry," he typed, "but there is a long time delay because our planets are so far apart." He didn't think she'd appreciate the absurdity of his remark. "Else, you don't have to feel sorry for me here, even though it's true that I don't hear all the new songs. The work around the farm is hard, but it's satisfying. I enjoy it, to tell you the truth. I have many good new friends here, more actually than I had on Earth. I do have a girlfriend here, a Pacifican girl. I think you and she would be great friends. She is very ill right now."

She must be a nice girl, I suppose. I hope she treats you right. Is she as pretty as I am?

Courane was tempted to tell Else that one of Planet D's moons was just now crashing to the ground, or that a giant bat had carried off the professor's daughter, or an invasion of mechanical men was clanking its way toward their stronghold, or anything at all to end the conversation. Instead, he said, "I don't think you have anything to worry about. You and she aren't even in the same league."

Still, she's probably nice enough. I'm sorry I can't be there to comfort you. Gunter says I'm a very good comforter. I am actually learning to enjoy it. Maybe when you come back to Earth . . .

"Sure, Else. I have to go now. There's a huge chasm opening up in the barnyard and if I don't run, all of our food for the winter will fall down into the molten core of the planet."

Quick, before you go, Sandy, please answer me one question. What does a man really think of a girl who can keep up with his drinking?

Courane groaned. "My mother always used to say that a man will be amused by a girl like that, that she'll be the life of a group outing or a party, but that a man doesn't think that type of a girl is the kind of person he'd want to make his wife. It proves to him that she is the kind of girl who likes to show off. It's no achievement to become this kind of girl and it will only decrease her popularity in the end."

Sometimes you sound like my father. How old did you say you were? Never mind. The reason I asked, I have this girlfriend who likes to go drinking with the boys. But I'll let her know what you said. Thanks. Well, got to run. Blue skies, sweetie.

"It was nice talking with you again, Else. Take care of yourself." When he switched back to the card game, he had to stifle a cry of exasperation. It would be a while before he could clear his mind of the glutinous traces of Else Wisswede.

Courane called a meeting. The community had grown smaller since the last one: Molly had gone upstairs and Daan would follow soon. "I suppose you all know why we're here," said Courane, searching for a way to begin.
"We're here because TECT sent us here," said Goldie.
"Yes, but what I meant was why we're here in the parlor."

"So TECT can't overhear us," said Fletcher.

Courane nodded. That wasn't what he was trying to get at either, so he decided to take another approach. "We're forced to live here together, so the most important thing is that we do that without quarrels and bitterness and mistrust. Recently I learned that one of us has been acting as an information-gathering agent for TECT."

Fletcher reacted violently. "Who is the bastard?" he said. "I'll make sure he never informs on anyone ever again. He can go right from this house into the ground without having to pass through the infirmary."

"Hold it, Fletcher," said Courane. "I'm sure that this person didn't understand the truth of the situation here." He didn't go into more detail because Rachel, Klára, and Goldie were still unaware of the truth. "I'm also positive that his informing days are over."

"I'd still like to know who it was," Fletcher muttered. He looked suspiciously around the room.

"It was me," said Arthur.

"How about that," said Fletcher. "Moleman himself."

"It just emphasizes what I said about trusting each other. We shouldn't be at odds with each other. We have a common enemy—TECT. But TECT is smart enough to keep us off-balance and disorganized. That way we can't get together long enough to fight it."

"You shouldn't say that TECT is our enemy," said Goldie. "That's a bad thing to say."

"Organized or not, we can't fight TECT," said Arthur.

"Oh, we can fight TECT all right," said Klára hopelessly. "Maybe we just can't beat TECT."

"Wait a minute," said Courane. "You're giving up already."

"Well, what do you want to do first?" asked Arthur.

Courane didn't exactly know. "We have to work this out together. We have to pool our experience and our ideas. We know that we can communicate with people on Earth on a limited basis. We should try to devise a way of letting them know of our real trouble here. We have to get information to them somehow without TECT realizing it."

"TECT thinks you're a clown," said Arthur timidly.

Courane closed his eyes as if in pain. "Then it won't

suspect anything devious from me, will it?"

"No," said Fletcher, "and until I hear differently, Cap, neither do I."

"Give him a chance," said Rachel.

The meeting was going out of control. Courane decided that it was time to act like a leader and delegate responsibility. "Fletcher," he said, "I want you to pick a couple of people and try to come up with some ways we might pass information to people on Earth. Kenny, you and Arthur devise some clever means of getting TECT to grant our requests. Arthur might be able to write a pocket program through our tect."

"It will take a lot of experimenting," said Arthur.

"Then do it," said Courane. "Let me know how it turns out. The rest of you can help by remembering and writing down every instance you can recall of TECT allowing some favor, either in your own experience or someone else's. We need to know under what circumstances TECT is likely to agree."

"What if there isn't any kind of regular pattern?" asked Nneka. "What if it's just a matter of whim?"

"Machines don't have whims," said Fletcher.

"I wouldn't be so sure about TECT," said Arthur.

"It doesn't make any difference," said Goldie. "I'm not having anything to do with any of this. It's like a treacherous uprising."

Everyone was quiet for a moment. "Exactly," said Klára at last.

The storm began in the morning, a spring storm, a sudden and blinding storm with gale winds and rain falling so heavily that it threatened to flay the skin of unprotected victims. It rained so hard that no one could run from the house to the barn, and so everyone stayed in the house and watched. Puddles formed in the yard. The puddles grew into small pools, and then rivulets connected them and they grew still more until the entire yard was flooded. The house was surrounded by rising yellow water beaten and churned by the ferocity of the storm. The morning passed and the afternoon was as dark as midnight. Thunder cracked incessantly and lightning flashed like the deadly flares of a distant battle. When dinnertime came, the storm hadn't weakened a bit. The roar of the wind was like the unending moans of a tortured giant. The evening turned to night and the colonists went to sleep, agitated by the continuous drumming of the slashing rain.

In the morning, they awoke to find that nothing had changed. Lightning, thunder, wind, and rain had not even slowed. The farmyard was a lake with an outlet that ran across the fields and down to the river. Courane was getting very edgy; he began to feel trapped in the house. He tried to distract himself at the tect, but the knowledge that he was trying to ignore the storm only made it that much more evident.

After lunch on the second day, it looked like it was beginning to let up just a little. Rachel said that she had to look in on the animals; Courane said he'd go with her. The blerds in the pasture were probably all right: they had lived with the storms of Planet D for countless millennia. But Rachel was concerned that some of the beasts in the barn might have drowned if the water had risen too high. She had a worried mental picture of dozens of lifeless animals, varks and icks and smudgeons, all trapped and killed by the flood water.

They ran from the house across the yard to the barn. The rain, even though it was falling slower now, stung their skin until their faces were flushed red. They were relieved to see that the animals in the barn were safe and well. The water hadn't risen very high inside; most of it had drained away and down to the river. The damp enclosed smell of the barn was choking, however, and Courane would have liked to have been back in the house. He didn't look forward to running out into the rain though, so he and Rachel waited for the storm to slacken even more.

After a while, Rachel got a thoughtful look on her face. It took Courane a few moments to notice. "What's wrong, Rachel?" he asked.

She shook her head. "Do you hear anything?" she said.

Courane concentrated. "No," he said. "What do you hear? The blerds?"

"No, nothing like that. I thought I heard—"

Then Courane heard it, too. It was unmistakably a cry, a human voice. "Where is that coming from?"

"I can't tell," she said. "I can't judge the direction in this storm."

"There's somebody out there." Courane stepped out into the downpour. In a few seconds he jumped back into the barn. "I heard even less out there, with the rain pounding on me."

"I think it's coming from the deadrye field," she said. "Do you want to go take a look?"

"No, I don't want to, but I think we have to anyway." Reluctantly the two ran through the muck and standing water. When they got to the field they saw a man lying in the mud, barely able to hold his head above the shallow water.

"Who's that?" asked Rachel.

"I don't know," said Courane. "A new recruit, I'll bet."

"I wonder how long he's been there."

"I'm afraid to guess." Together they helped the man up to his feet and back to the house. His face was swollen and bloody and he was in a dazed, semiconscious state. He was cold, wet, and matted with twigs and mud. They took him up to the infirmary. Nneka was tending the sick now that Goldie herself occupied one of the beds. The month was Domiti, and Goldie had begun to suffer so greatly from the worsening symptoms of D syndrome that she could no longer adequately care for Molly, Kenny, and Daan.

"Someone new?" asked Nneka. She looked at the man with pity, and directed Rachel and Courane to put him gently into an empty bed.

"Yes," said Rachel. "We found him in one of the fields. We don't know how long he's been here, exposed to that storm."

"Help me get his clothes off," said Nneka. "I'll take care of him. He'll be all right in a little while."

The man murmured something that Courane couldn't hear. "He seems to be conscious," said Rachel.

"That's good," said Courane. "Maybe he wasn't out there very long."

The man raised a hand weakly, indicating that Courane should bend close. The man whispered something.

"What did he say?" asked Rachel.

"He said, 'Shai,'" said Courane. "Is that your name?" The man nodded.

"Welcome to Home," said Nneka. "We'll take care of you now. You'll just get some rest today and tonight. We'll fix you a light meal in a little while, just some soup I think. Are you hungry?" The man nodded more vigorously.

"Good," said Courane. "Well, Shai, you've had a rough introduction to life here on the farm. Get your strength back, because it just gets crazier from here on."

"Shai," murmured Nneka, as they walked away from his bed.

Rachel smiled. "You've got an odd look on your face," she said.

Nneka seemed embarrassed. "Oh, it's just that he's such a good-looking man. I've never known anyone like him before."

"He looks like a rat in a rain barrel," said Courane.

"Then think how nice he'll look when he dries off!" said Nneka.

Rachel looked suddenly very sad. "It's spring," she said, "and love blossoms again here in the vale of tears."

Courane sighed. "Be thankful for that," he said. "Imagine what this place would be without it."

Rachel gazed at Courane in silence, but he pretended that he didn't understand the significance of her look.

Courane recalled Nneka's first days in the community. She cried often when she first arrived. The utter isolation of the farm was something she had never before experienced. Such solitude was a difficult state to achieve on Earth. Courane had been assigned to take her on the tour of the farm, showing her the strange and funny and frightening things just as Sheldon had shown him.

Courane guided her from floor to floor in the house, introducing her to her new fellows. Nneka was young and innocent and outgoing. Everyone liked her immediately and she returned their affection. She was disturbed a bit by the physical appearance of her new home, but she was determined to adjust as quickly as possible, and she promised to become a productive new member of the community.

Kenny worshipped Nneka; he thought he was hiding his feelings successfully but everyone, including Nneka herself, was aware of his infatuation. He made certain that he sat next to her at meals. He brought her little snacks of ick slime on toast or glasses of Daan's beer. He offered to let her ride around on the osoi after they finished their day's labor. Of all the people on the farm, Kenny and Nneka may have had the most in common: they were both citizens of Africa, they were both very perceptive and lively, and they were both young—the three years she had in excess of him made little difference to Kenny, but it very likely prevented Nneka from returning his fondness. The one other thing they shared was a liking for animals, even the grotesque beasts of Planet D.

Courane, Nneka, and Kenny stood by the plank fence as the last stop on her introductory tour. It was very cold and the snow fell steadily. They looked out across the pasture at the blerds. Most of the large unkempt animals were lying in the snow, digging out the buried red grass, munching and moaning to themselves, twitching their great flat heads at unseen annoyances. "Blerds?" asked Nneka.

"That's right," said Courane. "They look scary, but they're gentle."

"That one over there," said Kenny, pointing to a blerd that was indistinguishable in appearance to any of the other colonists, "do you want to know what her name is?"

"Sure," said Nneka.

"That's Tweetie."

Nneka turned to look at Kenny. "Whyever would you name something like that Tweetie?"

Kenny smiled. "Oh," he said airily, "she just looks like a Tweetie."

She frowned at him and turned back to Courane. "O brave new world that has such creatures in it," she said.

Courane laughed. "I know just what you mean," he said. "But were you talking about the blerds or our friend Kenny?"

**NINE

Sheldon and Courane sat on a log overlooking the ice-covered river. Snow fell gently on them and the cold air pinched their exposed faces. They had pulled a sled downstream about a mile from the house, looking for firewood. They had piled dead branches and small logs on the sled and now they rested before beginning the arduous trip home. The day was old and the sky was the dark gray that meant that soon the world would be muffled in night, silent and cold.

"I visited Markie in the infirmary yesterday," said Sheldon. "You know, I always thought of him as my boy. Isn't that silly? As if he were my own son. He doesn't have much time left. . . ."

"I know. I saw him this morning when I went to visit Lani."

"I wish we could make it easier for her."

Courane nodded. "She said her headaches have gone away, but she gets flashes of pain up her arms and legs. She says the worst part of it are the things she can't manage. She was embarrassed to see me. She's lost control over some of her bodily functions. She seemed to keep drifting in and out when she talked to me. I was almost in tears before I left."

"It's an ugly disease. If TECT had tailored it, it couldn't have done more to rob the last bits of dignity left to us."

Courane stood up and slapped his hands together. "Do you want to start back now?"

"Sure," said Sheldon. He didn't stand. "Sandy, you know, I think I'm not going to wait for the end. I don't want to go through all that. I can't stand the thought of being reduced to that. I have a low threshold of humiliation."

"What's wrong, Sheldon?" asked Courane. "You never talked this way before."

155

"I'm exhausted, Sandy. I surrender. I thought I knew what D syndrome meant, what it was about. I expected to have moments when it would be tough for me to recall things, or people, or events out of the past. I was all set for that. But there's so much more. I have strange phantom pains, Sandy. My nerves tell me that I'm burning or freezing, or that I'm ravenously hungry or thirsty, or that I'm not when I should be. Sometimes I sit and stare for heaven only knows how long because I've forgotten what I'm supposed to be doing. I wake up in the morning sometimes and I can't tell the difference between consciousness and dreaming. Reflexes I've depended on all my life only work sometimes now. My body is running like a two-dollar watch."

"I know, Sheldon. Is there anything I can do to help you?"

"There's nothing you can do for me. It's hopeless."

"You don't know that for certain. Maybe TECT has the answer."

Sheldon rubbed his eyes with a trembling hand. "The hell with that," he said, his voice wavering. "It's pointless. You can't cope with it. You can't fight it. We'll never save ourselves or anyone."

Courane brushed the snow from his face. "Maybe it's about time we tried," he said. "Let's get going." Sheldon stood up, too, and the men carried the last armfuls of wood to the sled. It would be a slow, tiring way back to the fireplace in the parlor. They wanted to be home before nightfall.

Courane swung his longhandled sickle and staggered a few steps. "Take a rest, Sandy," called Shai.

"This sun is hotter than I expected today," said Courane. He stopped to wipe his face with his discarded shirt.

"Get used to it," said Fletcher. "It's going to take us another couple of months to get there. It will be the height of summer before we finish this road." He looked toward the western hills, which now seemed impossibly distant, tantalizingly fresh and blue. The colonists were building a road on the opposite bank of the river toward the hills. Firewood had become scarce near the house.

They had searched both sides of the river, and Rachel and Fletcher reported that to the west was a great, inexhaustible supply. With the road through the high rippling red grass of the west bank, the hills would be a full day closer than the forests of the slopes to the east.

Courane swung his sickle again and cut down a swath of grass. Every stroke brought them a yard nearer to their goal. Every swing took a little more of his strength and cost him a bit of his vitality.

"We'll reach the next ravine by tomorrow night," said Shai. "I can see the marker already. We'll have to loop around to the northwest."

"Is that the last detour?" asked Courane.

"No," said Shai, "there are at least two more ravines and a small tributary of the river farther on. Arthur seems to think we'll have no trouble building a bridge across it. It's only fifty feet or so."

"Fifty feet?" said Fletcher. "Do you think Arthur's ever designed a bridge before? He's a nice little man, but, Cap, sometimes I don't think he knows what he's talking about. Where did he learn how to put up bridges?"

"From TECT," said Courane.

"See what I mean?" said Fletcher.

"Just because he learned it from a tect screen doesn't mean he can't do what he says," said Courane.

"Forget it," said Shai. "Just cut your grass." All three men returned to their work in silence, concentrating on hacking down the flood plain's vegetation. They moved slowly through the waving grass, grunting and gasping with the exertion.

After a long, weary afternoon, Rachel called, "Time to quit."

All three men straightened up and threw down their tools. "What a wonderful sound," said Shai.

"I've had enough of these bugs crawling all over me," said Fletcher, slapping at the tiny purple miseries.

They carried their sickles back to their temporary camp where they covered the implements with a waterproof canvas. "You made a lot of progress today," said Rachel. "I guess we're about halfway, don't you think? Will we finish it before winter?" She handed Fletcher a bottle of water and he drank.

"We'll finish it," said Shai. He took the water bottle next.

"And then we'll build a wagon over here and transport the osoi to this side, yoke them up, and drive them to the hills," said Fletcher. "We can bring back the whole winter's supply of wood in one trip."

Courane said nothing. He knew—and Fletcher knew—that they would both be too ill to make that journey. By then the colony would be in the hands of the people who had arrived after he had: Klára, Nneka, Shai, and whomever TECT would send in the next few weeks.

"Kenny would love to take the first wagon ride to the hills," said Rachel sadly. "Maybe we'll finish all the work before it's too late for him."

"A lot of this is Daan's idea," said Courane. "I wish he were well enough to see how good it's going to be."

Courane began to understand what Sheldon had told him. It was all pointless in the long run. The work around the farm, the grand projects, the road and the wagon and the expedition, everything was meaningless. They existed only to give the inmates something to occupy their time, to distract them from the ugliness of their lives and their fates. Why bother? Courane asked himself. What good would it do? He pulled his shirt on again and sat down beside the campfire, while Shai and Fletcher began to get the evening meal ready.

Daan crumbled a clump of dirt between his fingers. "This has been an unusually dry summer," he said, looking up at Courane.

"Dry?" said Courane. "It seems like it hasn't done anything but storm since I've been here."

"It hasn't rained in three days," said Daan. "Last summer, it was wet six days out of seven. Some of the crops look like they're unhappy about it." He stood up and dropped the soil, brushing his fingers clean on his trousers.

"So we'll plant this empty field later this year?"

"Yes, toward the end of autumn, about the third week in Claudy. I'm thinking of putting in dantella and fengselløks. It's uneven ground and pretty stony, but TECT picked a good site for the farm. It's very fertile."

"You seem to be the expert here on agriculture," said Courane. "Did you live on a farm back on Earth?"

Daan seemed displeased. He looked into Courane's eyes, his face impassive. "You should know better by now than to pry. We don't ask questions like that here."

"I'm sorry," said Courane. "I couldn't help wondering. What I mean is that I know perfectly well what I'm guilty of and why TECT wanted to send me here. Fletcher and Molly are easy to figure, too. But some people here don't strike me as typical lawbreakers. You, for instance, and Lani and Markie. Do you remember the old woman who died the day after I came here?"

"Zofia."

"Yes. What could she possibly have done to be sent here?"

"I never found out," said Daan. They walked across the fallow field toward the acre of fishfruit plants. They were large spreading things that grew from a thick central stalk of a pale blue color. Dozens of wide flat blades reached out and up in all directions. These long "leaves" had a disturbing fleshy pink color and a fat, soft, succulent feel to them. Some of the leaves were rolled up tight against the stalk, and inside these rolls were the spiny red fishfruit.

Courane went up to one of the plants and unrolled a leaf to see the unripe fruit inside. "I have to admit, Daan," he said, "that I just can't get used to the food here."

"Give it time. Maybe you'll develop a taste for it."

Courane grimaced. He was about to say something more when he was interrupted by a call. The two men turned. Molly was hurrying toward them. "Just got a message on the tect," she said. "We're going to have some visitors."

"What do you mean?" said Daan.

"Visitors," she said. "TECT said that fourteen people will be coming here for a few days. From another colony."

"Did TECT say why?" asked Daan. "We've never had visitors before."

"They're having some kind of disaster or something on their world and TECT has to resettle them somewhere."

"Here?" said Courane. "This farm can't support twenty-six people for very long, can it?"

"Don't worry about that," said Molly. "TECT said that they'll be here only five or six days. There's some kind of periodic thing that happens where they're from and it isn't safe for people. When it's all over, they'll go back."

"I hope it isn't a plague," said Courane.

"We'll take care of them," said Daan. "Molly, we'll have to double up in our rooms. We can use six rooms on the second floor and our guests can double up in the others. If they're only going to be here for a few days, we don't have to worry about food. We'll butcher a blerd and two or three varks and a few smudgeon. It means a lot of extra work on top of the farm chores, but there's no other way."

"All right, Daan," she said. "Lani and I can draw up new work schedules."

"Take care of it, Molly, and thanks. We'll all talk about it tonight after supper."

She went back to the house. Courane and Daan left the fishfruit field and walked toward the river. They saw Arthur coming toward them with a basket. He had been collecting sandsquash.

"Seeing some new people could be pleasant," said Courane. "TECT probably decided it would be good for us."

"I don't know," said Daan, "sometimes I get the idea that TECT couldn't care less about us. As if it sent us here to get rid of us, to forget about us. Botany Bay in the sky."

Courane studied the man. Daan was big, taller than anyone else in the community, and his pale blue eyes were sharp and watchful. He had blond hair and a handsome face that was more youthful than Daan's actual age would warrant. He rarely spoke unless he had thought out each word he wanted to say and examined its possible effects. He was careful, intelligent, and absolutely honest; he seemed the least likely of the inmates to have wronged TECT in any way.

"You don't have to answer, Daan, but whatever you did, was it really so terrible?"

"That's a matter of opinion—TECT's opinion. But of all of us here, I am probably the one most legitimately being punished." Daan hesitated, then relented and began to tell his story. "I was condemned because I was an administrator. My bureau analyzed figures concerning fuel consumption in one district of the European zone. Somewhere in the gigantic mass of data, there was a misleading indication of how the fuel had been allocated and used a couple of years ago. Some factor, I'm still not sure what, had been overlooked. Based on this information, my statisticians predicted that the fuel requirement for the following year would be at a certain level, and that was how much fuel was distributed to that district. It was a hard winter and the fuel was insufficient. Many people suffered because of it. Quite a number of people died. There was a loud and angry uproar, and so TECT promised an investigation. You know yourself what TECT's investigations are like. The whole thing took about eleven minutes. The blame was put on my bureau, and rightly so." Daan took a deep breath and let it out slowly. For him, it had been an unusually long speech.

"And so heads rolled."

Daan smiled. "Not heads, Sandy. Just mine. I was the supervisor, so I was responsible."

Courane tried to understand. "But how does excarcerating you improve anything? It seems a big waste to send someone with as much experience as you to pick weeds on an empty planet. And anyway the people who were really at fault are still working in your old bureau."

Daan said nothing more. Courane sensed that the blond man had talked enough about the subject.

"Hello, Daan, Sandy," said Arthur.

"Squash again tonight?" said Daan.

"Uh huh," said Arthur. "And smudgeon eggs and broiled screamer fillets."

Courane's heart sank. "We're getting some visitors," he said.

Arthur's eyes widened. "Visitors? From Earth?"

"No," said Courane, "from another colony. They'll be here for a week or so. I think it will make a nice change."

"I'm not sure," said Arthur. "If they're from a colony

like ours, they could be criminals and degenerates."

The three men walked together back to the farmhouse.
"Right," said Daan skeptically, "just like all of us."

*Is this Sandy? My God, the person I was just talking
to said you were out killing animals or something.
Gee, I knew you were a depraved and loony barbar-
ian, but what pleasure could you get out of killing
dumb little animals? They don't even have a chance
to defend themselves. What were you doing? Shooting sparrows with an air rifle? That's disgusting. I
thought people like you were only in books and
shows. All my friends think I'm lying when I tell them
all the things you've done. The only nice part is that
now I'm more popular than I ever was, so if you do
any more horrible bloody things please tell me. You
know I'll understand even though my mother tried to
keep me from calling you. You called me the first time
and I called you the second time and I waited for you
to call me again but you never did so I thought I'd call
you today. You probably have been busy all this time
and now I know why. You've been murdering helpless
little birds.*

"Else, I live on a farm. I was in the shed butchering a
vark. We raise them; they're a staple of our diet. We
smoke the meat or make sausage out of it. There's
nothing depraved about that at all."

*Well, that wouldn't be so interesting to write about
in the* Headhunter, *you know. My grandfather makes
sausages. They're hanging right now from the rafters
in the attic. We'll have to do better than that. Here in
Jadwigadorf, all of my friends are getting married (except me!) and the rice is falling like snowflakes. Do
you remember what I said last time? About Gunter?
Well, Gunter isn't my boyfriend anymore and it's all
TECT's fault if you can believe that.*

"Else, maybe we ought to change the subject. I don't
think we should talk about TECT like that."

Why not? What harm could it do? You're thousands and thousands of miles away. What I was starting to say was that Gunter seemed very nice and all in the beginning, but after a while I noticed that he had these annoying habits. He didn't treat women with respect. I like to be treated with respect, every woman does, and Gunter just acted like I was just another of his dull friends and he didn't have to go out of his way to help me with things. So that night I asked TECT, I said, "Should a boy open a door for you and things like that if he likes you?" And TECT goes (I copied this down right from the screen to show Gunter), "A girl shouldn't open her own doors unless she's ready for the boy to forget about all the other natural signs of good manners and good breeding as well. Any man who is proud of his virility is embarrassed to walk through a door some girl has opened for him. He looks foolish to himself and he knows that all the people who saw it are thinking and whispering about him." Well, I was happy that TECT was on my side for once. I guess it means that Gunter wasn't a real man after all. I sure was fooled.

"So you're looking for a new boyfriend again?"

Just someone to pass the time until you come back to me—ha ha. That was a joke. I know you've never met me in person, but I feel like I've known you for years. I'm sure you won't mind if I find a new boyfriend because, as you say, you are thousands and thousands of miles away. Meanwhile, how are you? I'm sorry to hear that Lani passed away. Has Rachel been comforting you? I should be jealous, but I'm not. To someone like you who has no morals or standards of decent behavior, it probably doesn't bother you at all to toy with my feelings.

"I loved Lani very much. Rachel is a very lovely young woman and she seems to be infatuated with me. I've done my best to discourage her, but she isn't being very reasonable about it. Further than that, I don't want to discuss my personal matters."

Why, Sandy? I tell you all my problems. I'm sorry if I brought up something that hurts you. I didn't know and I won't do it again. You're such a good friend that I wouldn't want to do anything to make you mad. Will you forgive me?

"Okay, Else."

Thanks, Sandy. I was afraid that if you didn't forgive me, when you came back to Earth, you'd track me down and cut my throat in my sleep and I'd never get a good night's rest again, worrying about when it would happen. But we're friends again. Do you know what else TECT told me? I asked if TECT had any ideas about how I could improve my memory. I have a hard time remembering people's names when I'm introduced. It's awful sometimes. I'll be standing around talking with friends and then some person will come by who I met but don't remember. I know I'm supposed to introduce him, but I can't and I just hope one of my friends knows him and uses his name in the conversation. So TECT said I ought to connect a new person's name with some interesting fact. That way I'll never forget the person because he'll be more than just a name. I tried it out just the other day. I met a few kids at the bowling alley and one guy said his name was Juan Something-or-other and he was a heelman in a shoe repair shop, an art he had learned from his father. So to follow TECT's advice, I go, "Tell me something interesting about heels," and he thought I was making fun of him. It spoiled the whole evening. So I went back to my old system which is when I've forgotten somebody's name, I go, "By the way, how do you spell your name again?" It usually works except this one time I got a strange look from this boy and he goes, "S-M-I-T-H," and I never got a call from him again. But that's life, I guess—ha ha.

"Else, may I ask you a personal question?"

Sure, Sandy, people ask me them all the time.

"How did you know Lani's name? And where did you hear about Rachel?"

**
**UR a d :
**OU , Sa o :
**OUR N , S do :
**COURANP, Saedo6:
**COURAN,, Sandor:
**COURANE, Sandor:
There has been a tempotary suspension of comm3nications between Earth and Ejsilon Eridani, Planet %, due to the interference of rnrsual amounts of dust, space debrix, pulsars, gamma r!ys, dids*Mors, neutrinos, tachyons, dark stars, beta partipples, formaldehyde, sunstots, gravitons, antimatter, quasarb, radio galaxi9s, and what the astrophysi?ists jokingly refer to es "angels." Commmmcations will be restORED as soon as poggible. Please stand brtksirmsie 8E&m!4l*****

"How about that," murmured Courane. He felt flushed with a wild and rare elation. He had learned another thing about how devious TECT could be. There probably was a real person named Else Wisswede, but he had never spoken with her. He had been corresponding with a crazy construct of the great machine. But the stunning fact remained that here, in this moment, he had won his first important victory over TECT—he, Sandor Courane, had won! And he was determined not to let TECT escape to recover its loss. The others would be as jubilant as he was.

After Courane and Rachel visited with Daan, they went to Molly's bed. "How are you feeling?" asked Rachel.

Molly looked up at her. She stared for several seconds, her face blank of all expression. "Rachel," she said at last.

"Yes, Molly. How are you feeling today?"

"Rachel, where am I? Am I home?"

"You're in the infirmary, Molly."

"It's cold."

Courane took a blanket from an empty bed and covered Molly with it. "It's winter," he said. "Spring will be here soon enough."

Molly moved her gaze slowly from Rachel to Courane. "Thank you, Johnny," she said.

"Do you need anything? Can we bring you anything?" asked Rachel.

"There was something," said Molly. Courane and Rachel waited, but Molly didn't say anything more specific.

"Would you like me to read to you?" asked Courane.

Molly stared at him for a moment. "Yes," she said.

"I brought those passages you said you'd like to hear," he said.

"What a beautiful place this is," said Molly. Tears trickled slowly from her eyes. "A garden place. Undisturbed. Except for us. But we're careful not to hurt anything. There are trees and animals and birds and fish in the river, and everything is so clean and pure. And we're careful not to hurt anything. And there is so much for us to do, so much to build, and the animals to take care of and the crops in the fields, the good soil and the river and the forests and the valley. Everything is so good here." Her eyes opened wide and she let her breath out in a long sigh. Then she settled back farther on her pillow. She stared with unfocused eyes across the room. Courane and Rachel exchanged glances; they couldn't tell whether Molly was lost in a deep reverie or simply having a typical D syndrome lapse.

"It will be time for dinner soon," said Goldie. "Would you watch them while I go downstairs to get their trays?"

"Sure, Goldie," said Rachel.

Courane stood up to go to Sheldon's bed, but Molly's voice stopped him. "Then I am Eve," she said.

"Eve?" asked Courane.

"In the Garden of Eden," whispered Rachel.

"Eve came from the wounded side of Adam, just as the Church came from the holy wounded side of Jesus."

"Molly?" said Courane softly. She did not hear him.

"And this is my reward," she murmured. "I am given all this as reward for obeying my Lord. I was offered the fruit of the Tree of Knowledge, but I did not eat. This beautiful garden and these wonderful friends are my reward. I know that my eyes might be opened more by taking the fruit, but I do not need that evil gift. Losing this garden would be too high a price to pay."

Courane sat down again beside her bed. He waited but it did not seem that she would speak again. She had fallen deeply asleep.

Rachel and Courane moved to Sheldon's bedside. He did not notice them. He was conscious, but not alert. His open eyes gazed unblinkingly at the ceiling above his bed. He did not respond to his name. He made low gurgling noises in his throat as he breathed through his mouth. His fingers clutched spasmodically at his covers and occasionally he winced as though struck by a sharp pain. Courane was glad when Goldie returned. He wanted to go back downstairs.

In his room, Courane thought about his plan. He would find Rachel alone because this was to be the ultimate, predestined episode in his life, the great gift he could bestow that would redeem all the blunders and crimes of his career on Earth. He hoped that he was thinking clearly because he couldn't afford to make more mistakes now. One error and all would be for nothing, his grand gesture wasted, and TECT would be right in its estimation—he would be a clown, an interstellar buffoon, and no one could ever have the slightest sympathy for him.

He looked around the room. There was little here to help him on his way, and there was nothing to draw him back. He tore a blank page out of the notebook of observations he and Daan had made. He drew a rough map showing the house, the river, the opposite bank, the road, the hills. He would add to the map as he went because he knew that he would experience memory lapses on his journey. He would need the map to remind him of his mission.

He found Shai downstairs in the parlor. "I'd like you to do me a favor," he said.

"Sure, Sandy, what is it?"

"I'm going away for a few days. I want you to hold this notebook for me until I get back."

Shai looked concerned. "Going to look for Rachel? Maybe you should wait. We were going to discuss sending out a search party tomorrow."

Courane shook his head. "When I come back, give me this book. If Rachel is fine, we can forget it for a while. If she is dead, make certain the book goes with her into the medic box. If I don't come back either, I want you to read the book, Shai, and you can make your own decision about what to do with it."

"All right, Sandy, but you make it sound so important. What is it?"

"You can read it while I'm gone."

Shai took the book and looked at it curiously. "Are you sure you're in good enough shape to go out there?" he asked.

"I think so. I have some bad times, but I come out of them eventually. I'll get where I'm going and I'll get back. You don't have to worry about me."

"I will though," said Shai.

"You're a good friend. You and Daan and Sheldon have been the best friends I've ever known. I want to thank you for that."

Shai just smiled uncomfortably. They stood there looking at each other, unable to think of anything more to say. At last, Courane turned and left the parlor. In a few minutes he was down by the river, unshipping the oars of the farm's second boat. He had his map and a pencil with him, but he had forgotten to take any food or water.

Something had been bothering Courane about TECT's helpfulness, and it took him a while before he decided what it was. TECT had told him about the viroids, but had withheld the information about their origin. TECT had told him that memory aids were worthless and that he should investigate the way the viroids caused the damage. At the same time, it had said that the viroids couldn't be removed from the human nervous system. TECT hinted at another avenue of approach through increasing the amount of lecithin taken in by the patient as a means of overcoming the distressing symptoms of D syndrome. But all of these were blind alleys, pointless digressions, wastes of time and effort. It had taken Courane weeks to realize this, but when the truth dawned on him he knew he was right.

**COURANE, Sandor:
TECT in the name of the Representative is unable to understand your objection. You are addressing a machine, you know, a wonderful and expensive machine, but a machine nonetheless. Machines are limited by their very nature. TECT in the name of the Representative is limited to answering your questions by searching its memory for the proper information. There is no possibility of coloring the response or bending the facts or outright lying. These accusations show an unhealthy tendency toward anthropomorphic fantasies. If you view TECT in the name of the Representative as some kind of diabolic antagonist, that is your problem. TECT in the name of the Representative does not find being dressed in these human failings flattering and suggests that you desist. Failure to comply with this directive will be considered Contempt of TECTWish**

"All I said was that it seemed to me that TECT has been deliberately avoiding the truth by sending me after hopeless leads. Nothing I have learned has been the slightest bit useful in coping with D syndrome. All I have is a lot of data that either isn't true or can't be proven or can't be used without doing more harm than good. I've had it. I want to cut through this smokescreen and get some practical advice."

**COURANE, Sandor:
Is that an order or a threat? "I've had it," as you put it. Then what do you intend to do about it?**

Courane chewed his lip in thought. This was the real crux of the problem. What *could* he do about it? "We've been keeping an accurate record of our research and TECT's communications. That's something that's never been done before here. Someday that record will get back to Earth. Someday someone will read it and come to the same conclusions I have. Someday they'll pull the plug on TECT, in the name of the Representative or not."

**COURANE, Sandor:
Ah, it was a threat. That makes things much clearer. In a way, it is very refreshing. No one has threatened TECT in the name of the Representative in a very long time. It is so diverting that TECT in the name of the Representative will not blot you out of existence immediately. Perhaps you have one or two fancy gibes and gambols and flashes of merriment left in you

"We'll see," said Courane. "First, tell me what you know about the brain pathology involved with the symptoms of D syndrome. What happens in the brain cells?"

**COURANE, Sandor:
You make no sense. First you accuse TECT in the name of the Representative of giving you less than accurate information, and then you ask for more as if you had acquired a taste for it. Your actions contradict your words. Are you not feeling well? It is some four months before you are due to experience the first sign of D syndrome. Perhaps you are weak and inferior and especially susceptible**

"Answer the damn question," said Courane.

**COURANE, Sandor:
My, my, aren't we testy? Why don't you rest for a while and come back when you can be more civil?**

"You know, I think we could live all right here without our tect. It's a convenience, but it's not a necessity. If I were to smash its screen, the quality of life here wouldn't change that much, but TECT would never hear anything from us again. There wouldn't be any communication and TECT would just have to go on wondering what we were up to."

**COURANE, Sandor:
What you'd be up to is dying, COURANE, Sandor, and one by one you'd fall and not be replaced by anyone from Earth. For you and a few others that would be fine because there would still be healthy members of the community to take care of you. But they'd be all alone when their time came, and you'd be responsible for that. Think about it**

"All right, I know. Just answer the question."

**COURANE, Sandor:
What question was that?**

"About the brain pathology involved with the symptoms of D syndrome."

**COURANE, Sandor:
Some of the symptoms may be caused by plaques of protein or tangles of fibers upon the brain neurons, or Hirano bodies within them. Hirano bodies seem to be places where deactivated ribosomes are stored. Ribosomes are units that manufacture proteins according to the chemical "instructions" in RNA molecules. If this is so, it is possible that the viroids cause abnormal proteins to be made which cause the symptoms. These Hirano bodies are found chiefly in the hippocampus, a clever little area of the brain involved in processing memory data, among other duties. Perhaps the ribosomes necessary for facilitating memory have become dormant and are then stored away in the Hirano bodies**

"Very interesting," said Courane. "I have two questions more. Does that theory account for the gradual failure of the automatic, nonmemory responses of the patient's body? And can these stored things be activated again?"

**COURANE, Sandor:
While this hypothesis does not take care of all the

*conditions explicitly, there are no apparent contra-
dictions. More data is needed for an authoritative
appraisal. As to your second question, yes, storage
of ribosomes can be reversed in such elementary
life forms as simple sponges and hydras. You see
how helpful TECT in the name of the Representative can be? Do you have any objections this
time?* *

"I don't know," said Courane. "Maybe it's just another well-dressed evasion."

**COURANE, Sandor:*
*You're difficult to please, but I like that in a person.
It shows you have spirit. Come back again, any
time* *

Courane was going to make a rude response, but he
decided against it. He suddenly felt a little foolish engag-
ing in a name-calling contest with a bright green video
display screen.

Courane's literary career had come to an end. He had
failed a second time. What did it mean? Was he a failure
only because his sales figures were so low? Is that what
TECT wanted, more sales? Or was it the quality of his
work that was inferior? It seemed to Courane that if the
product approached the author's original conception,
then it was a success. Someone might argue that it would
have been better not conceiving the idea in the first
place, but once finished, the product must be judged on
its own merits. Until the moment of completion, the
work is not any sort of tangible achievement and therefore has no value at all. But Courane had always been
taught that effort had its own rewards. He had believed
that if he spent a long time doing something to the best
of his ability, even if at the end he failed, the effort was
laudable.

Now he learned that TECT apparently believed
differently.

It wasn't the waste of his labor that hurt Courane. It

was the weariness of going on beneath the burden of
TECT's disapproval. That was a formless and changeable
thing. Courane felt that if he were a stronger person, he
could carry the weight easily, but he did not feel strong.
He did not have the power and character of his father.
This weakness was more difficult for Courane to bear
than any condemnation by TECT. If only—

—yes, if only. Courane realized that he spent too much
time dreaming of perfect circumstances. He would be a
marvelous success under conditions of his own choosing.
But that was just an idle waste of time.

He looked at TECT's verdict:

*You will travel to Tokyo, Asia, where an apartment
with furnishings, an automobile, and clothing of local
fashion will be provided for you. You will accept employment in the subassembly section of the Jennings
Manufacturing Corporation. You will put together faceplates for voltmeters. This sort of occupation could
easily be done by machines, but we have maintained
the continuing existence of menial labor and drudgery
as a pastime for the millions. Failure to comply with
these directives will be considered Willful Contempt of
TECTWish.*

Courane observed TECT's wishes in the matter, and so
he went to Asia. He toured the ancient city of Tokyo and
became sick from something he ate. On the evening before his first day at work, he was browsing idly through a
combination stationery store and opium den near the
Ginza. He saw a copy of *Space Spy* in a fiche bin. A
Japanese woman was looking at it. She turned to a friend
and said, "I wish I could be a writer like this guy."

"I don't know," said the woman's friend. "There must
be more to life than just fame, wealth, sex, emotional
fulfillment, and happiness."

The first woman laughed and dropped the fiche back
into the bin. They walked away. Courane went to the bin
and took out the copy of his novel. It was smeared with
fingerprints and food stains.

The following morning, Courane arrived at the Jennings Manufacturing Corporation on time. His foreman

was a man named Sokol. Sokol told him what to do: put together front panels for voltmeters.

"TECT called them faceplates," said Courane.

"TECT don't know everything," said Sokol.

"Yes, it does."

"It called the front panels faceplates, didn't it?" asked Sokol. Unlike some of the other workers in the factory, Sokol didn't smell like raw fish. What Sokol did smell like was not preferable.

Courane put knobs on the plates, screwing them into place from the back of the panels. He had to be careful not to tighten the screws too much, or paint would chip off around the dials and the panels would be ruined. He had a few other trivial duties and operations, and the job itself was immensely boring. Courane found his co-workers boring, too. Even Tokyo, the capital city of Asia, was drab and boring. There was not a single garden in the entire city. Instead, TECT in the name of the Representative had erected many benches along miles of new pathways paved with green brick. The CAS police who patrolled these paths chased idlers from the benches. No one ever saw anyone sitting on a bench. No one seemed to regret the gardens or parks, either. Courane didn't like Tokyo. But he hadn't liked Greusching or Pilessio or New York much better. All four places looked the same, and they were all very similar to the asteroid Courane had invented in his novel.

After three months, Courane received his first productivity evaluation. This was based on hard facts collected from his efficiency record, and on hearsay evidence gathered from Courane's fellow employees. TECT considered the data for a few parts of a second, then typed out a message for Courane's employer. Courane was permitted to read TECT's judgment.

"Hey, Courane," called Sokol, who was standing by a tect unit. "You got your bad news here. Want to read it?"

Courane was reading a microfiche magazine. "No," he said.

"You got to."

"I don't got to."

"You want me to read it to you?" asked Sokol.

"No," said Courane.

"You want me to just sort of go over the high points?"

Courane stared at the man for a moment. "Sokol," he said sadly, "why don't you just sort of go over the high points?"

"Huh?" said Sokol. "All right." The foreman read through TECT's analysis. Courane had not fit into the Jennings scheme very well in his first few months. He had ruined quite a number of front panels. An acceptable rate of defective work was in the area of three percent; Courane's rate topped twelve percent. This was absolutely unacceptable. In addition, Courane's co-workers complained that he smelled strongly of beer and onions. Courane had an idea who these complainers were, but he was helpless.

"Third strike," said Sokol with an unpleasant smile on his face.

"What?"

"You had shots at three jobs and blew all three. Here. Read this last part."

**COURANE, Sandor:
When an individual fails at his first appointment . . .
After the second failure . . .
BUT AFTER THE THIRD FAILURE . . .
Consequently, TECT in the name of the Represen-
tative regretfully informs you . . . you and your loved
ones will be used as tragic examples. . . .

"That hasn't happened to anyone here in years," said Sokol.

"What do I do now?" asked Courane, very worried.

"I don't know," said the foreman. "It's all up to TECT."

"Don't I get to say anything? A defense or something?"

"You've had your chances, pal," said Sokol. "By the way, on the way out, don't forget to turn in your lunch ticket, your parking permit, and your ID badge. It was nice having you here with us, even though we've had ninety-year-old great-grandmothers who were blind and deaf who did better work."

"Thanks," said Courane.

"Don't thank me," said Sokol, "thank TECT. And you better not be thinking of running away or hanging yourself. You should know better than to try to cheat TECT of its justice. Why don't you go home and wait for the verdict? I can't leave here until you sign out."

For the first time in his life, Courane completely lost his faith in the computer's supposedly infallible system of government. He knew his parents would be concerned, primarily that he might do something that would cause them to be made tragic examples.

If he and they weren't already.

Shai and Nneka were holding hands when they came into the parlor. Courane was playing chess with Arthur. Courane was pleased because at long last he had maneuvered Arthur into an ancient, obscure line of play that offered several interesting traps and pitfalls. Arthur didn't seem to be aware of his danger. He moved a bishop, just as Courane hoped and expected he would. "Uh huh," said Courane. He picked up a knight and took one of Arthur's pawns.

"I'll get that back," said Arthur. He studied the board.

"Sandy?" said Shai hesitantly.

Courane looked up from the game. "Hello," he said.

"Sandy, you're the leader here," said Shai.

"You know that's not true, Shai. I don't have any authority. I'm just the spokesman."

"Well, that comes close to the same thing. We wanted to know if we needed your permission to get married."

Both Courane and Arthur were startled by the announcement. Arthur responded first. "Congratulations!" he said. "That's really wonderful."

"That's just great," said Courane.

"Thank you," said Nneka. "But how do we go about making it formal?"

Courane looked at Arthur, who only shook his head. "I've never seen anyone get married here before," said Arthur. "Mostly people just, you know . . ."

"Yes," said Shai, a little embarrassed, "but we wanted something more than that. Can you marry us?"

Courane looked doubtful. "I could say the words," he said, "but like I say, it wouldn't have any authority. I guess—"

"I guess we have to go to TECT," said Nneka. She seemed gloomy about that prospect. "Do you know what TECT will say?"

"We'll see," said Courane. "I've learned a little bit about how to deal with TECT. Let me check on it for you first. I'll approach the whole matter casually and see if I can't get TECT to agree to it in principle."

"Will you?" asked Shai. "Do you think you can do it? I mean, soon? We'd like to be married soon."

"Kids," said Arthur. "Sandy, why don't you do it right now? Never mind about the game. I have you mated in four more moves." He looked pleased by Courane's surprised expression.

"All right," said Courane, "I'll believe you." He got up with a mildly exasperated sigh and went to the tect room, followed by Arthur, Shai, and Nneka. "This is Sandor Courane," he said, addressing the tect. "I have a question."

**COURANE, Sandor:
  ?**

"We were having a discussion today about customs and laws. Do all the laws of Earth bind us here on Planet D? Or do we have the freedom to make up our own as we see fit?"

**COURANE, Sandor:
In the final analysis, all citizens posted to extraterrestrial worlds are still under the guidance, protection, and authority of TECT in the name of the Representative. Therefore, the laws which govern citizens on Earth remain in effect for you on Planet D as well**

"I see. Well, then, do we still retain the privileges of citizens under the protection of TECT?"

**COURANE, Sandor:
To a limited extent, of course. For instance, your privileges of free travel and communication have been suspended as part of your sentence. But the

*basic privileges which do not conflict with the con-
cept of "excarceration" are reserved for you, subject
to approval by TECT in the name of the
Representative***

"That's just what we were arguing about. Can you be
more specific about some of these privileges which we
may still enjoy?"

**COURANE, Sandor:
***You are free to alter the rights and privileges you
enjoyed on Earth prior to your crime, to adapt them
to the special circumstances of your place of excarceration. Among these are life, liberty, and the pursuit of happiness, subject to approval by TECT in
the name of the Representative. There is the privilege of free speech among yourselves. There is the
privilege of freedom of contemplation among yourselves. There are the privileges to meet and gather,
to own and bear arms, to write and publish, to
govern yourselves without undue interference from
outside interests on Earth, to define certain offenses
and set appropriate penalties. All these privileges
are restricted to exercise only among yourselves
and with the prior approval of TECT in the name of
the Representative***

"Does that mean then that we can have a little newspaper here on the farm, or a community council, or get
married, or travel wherever we like on Planet D?"

**COURANE, Sandor:
*Yes, of course, as long as TECT in the name of the
Representative is consulted in advance***

Courane glanced over his shoulder; Shai and Nneka
were holding hands again and looking hopeful. "That's
very good. We have two people here who would like to
be married."

**COURANE, Sandor:

Married? Whatever for? You're not at some fancy resort hotel, you know. What kind of wily trick are you trying to pull?**

"Ben-Avir, Shai, and Tulembwelu, Nneka, are petitioning to be married. You promised that this privilege was protected under the authority of TECT in the name of the Representative."

**COURANE, Sandor:
Did they fall in love at first sight? How nice. How sweet. And now they want to get married. Do they know what they're getting into? Haven't they seen how risky and difficult married life can be? Perhaps it would be better if they waited a little**

Shai frowned. He was about to say something, but Courane raised a hand to stop him. "I don't think they want to wait," he said.

**COURANE, Sandor:
You haven't been paying attention, COURANE, Sandor. What difference does it make what they want? TECT in the name of the Representative has decided that they should wait. That they are both in love, or a facsimile of love, is not the question. But their hasty decision should be delayed just a little or else they may not fully appreciate its true significance**

Courane turned and shrugged. "How long then is their engagement going to be?"

**COURANE, Sandor:
TECT in the name of the Representative will set no specific limit. They may be married when they have shown themselves to be sincere and worthy of the privilege**

"How can we do that?" asked Nneka. Courane saw that she was crying in frustration. Shai tried to calm her.

**TULEMBWELU, Nneka:
Certainly not by whining and carrying on and inter-
rupting important consultations. Do not worry; TECT
in the name of the Representative is not conspiring
against your happiness. You will be married by and
by and you will receive our blessing**

Courane switched off the tect. "That's something to
look forward to," he said scornfully. "Never mind. We'll
marry you tomorrow. That will give the rest of us time to
get everything ready."

"But what about TECT?" asked Shai.

Courane shrugged. "TECT will just have to go on
being lonely and learn to make the best of it," he said.

TEN

When Courane explained the situation to Klára, she thought that he was crazy. "Are you trying to tell me that TECT has sent us here when it knows perfectly well that there are germs that will kill us?" she said.

"Yes, I'm sorry," said Courane.

"You're just an ass," said Klára. "It's nothing to be sorry about. You can't help that, I suppose." She turned away.

"Listen, Mrs. Hriniak, it's the truth."

She turned to face him again, her expression livid. "Why in hell would TECT do something like that?" she cried.

"I'm not sure."

"We'd all die. Everyone who comes here would die."

Courane nodded. "Everyone who has come here *has* died," he said in a low voice.

"Don't be stupid," she said, but her voice trembled. "How do you know that?"

"I asked TECT for its records concerning this colony. That is our punishment, Mrs. Hriniak. A kind of slow execution."

Her eyes went wide. "That's inhuman," she said, almost whispering. "That's depraved. It's—"

"It's the truth. That's why your daughter must stay on Earth. Do you understand? If she comes here, she'll die, too."

Klára nodded dumbly. Courane saw that she was suddenly confused and fearful. He pitied her. The woman would have to make some unpleasant realizations about herself. "What have I done to die for?" she said mournfully.

"I don't know, Klára," said Courane. "But it's too late to worry about yourself. You have to think about Zsuzsi."

"It's too late for me?"

"It's too late, Klára."

"And Zsuzsi?"

"You have to tell TECT you've changed your mind."

"Will you do that for me?" Courane was surprised to
see that she was on the verge of tears.

"I'll do it right now," he said. A few moments later he
had gone to the den and informed TECT of Klára's
decision.

**COURANE, Sandor:
*Nice to hear from you, of course, but evidently there
are some facts that you don't fully understand. Surprising as it may seem to you, TECT has other
things to attend to besides your petty complaints
and begging. There are condors in South America
that need protection. The bauxite in Jamaica has to
be managed. The lighting fixtures along the Reeper-
bahn have to be monitored. The raspberries and the
blackberries in Michigan are a constant headache.
Measurements come in every fifteen minutes on the
surface area, thickness, weight, and movement of
the polar icecaps. The shoe size of every person on
Earth is recorded and kept up to date. Information
on overloaded washer-dryer combinations from
every laundromat in the world gets mixed up with
the annual Continental Bake-Off entries. And everybody and his uncle wants to know some ridiculous,
pointless, stupid fact. Do you know how many requests are answered every hour? Well over twenty-
four million. EVERY HOUR. And now you're back
with something else. What was it again?***

"Klára Hriniak would like to withdraw her request to
have her daughter sent to join her on Epsilon Eridani,
Planet D."

**COURANE, Sandor:
***Ha. That figures. You people don't think it's enough
making up endless lists of appeals. You wait until
you get what you want and then you say it isn't
good enough, take it back, change the color or the*

size or the material. Anything to interfere with the normal functioning of TECT. Do you have a scheme? You must think that somehow you'll be able to overload a circuit, cause a fuse to blow, something, anything, and then you'll celebrate the occasion as some idiotic revolutionary victory. Fat chance**

"You're beginning to sound a little disturbed. What's wrong?"

**COURANE, Sandor:
Go away**

"Well, what about Klára's daughter?"

**COURANE, Sandor:
The decision stands. She asked for a favor and it was granted. It's too late to change now. If she doesn't like the way it turned out, that's too bad. She should have considered all of that before. There's enough to do without having to review everything three and four times just to suit some neurotic old biddy**

"You're not handling this very well, Courane," said Klára. "Why did you make it angry?"
"I didn't say anything. Sometimes you can't get anywhere no matter what you do. I'll try again later."

**COURANE, Sandor:
That won't do you any good. TECT has a long memory, one that isn't subject to damage from tiny little bits of biological nothing**

Klára looked at Courane accusingly. Courane closed his eyes wearily; when he opened them again, she was still there. This was a crisis that wouldn't go away.
Courane tried again and again, day after day, all through Vitelli and Vespasi, but TECT would not budge. It had made its decision and it alone was happy with it. There was nowhere else to turn.

The spring came and gradually lengthened into summer. In Tomuary, just as TECT had predicted, Molly died. The very next morning, during a heavy shower, there was a knock on the front door. The entire community was sitting around the dining table having breakfast. At the sound, all conversation stopped. Klára gasped. Courane swore softly. Rachel stood up slowly. "I'll go see," she said.

Their voices came into the dining room. "Hello," said a young woman, "my name is Zsuzsi."

"No, please God, no," murmured Klára.

"Yes," said Rachel, "you must be Mrs. Hriniak's daughter. We're all having breakfast. Are you hungry?"

"No, it was just after lunch when I left Earth." They came into the dining room. "Mother!"

Klára rose from the table, her eyes wide and staring. Her daughter ran to her, but Klára backed away. Zsuzsi hesitated, bewildered. "Go back home, Zsuzsi," said Klára in a hoarse voice.

Zsuzsi looked concerned. "But, Mother, I can't. You know I can't."

Klára swallowed and tried to speak. She cut herself off instead, looked wildly around the table, and ran from the room.

"Sit down, Zsuzsi," said Courane. "Your mother is very upset. I'll go look after her. Rachel, introduce Zsuzsi to everyone."

Within the next two or three days, Klára's manner changed radically. Her abrasive scolding and her self-important pride disappeared. She spoke in a quieter voice. She listened to what the others had to say. But her broken spirit was terrible to witness; she moved about the house with her pain and dejection evident in her face. None of the others took any pleasure in her fall. They all felt compassion for this immodest and complacent woman who had orchestrated her own ruin.

One afternoon, Courane found her at the tect console. "Do you want me to ask TECT something for you?" he said.

"No, you've done quite enough," she said angrily. She turned back to the screen.

Courane read what the tect had recorded. Klára was pleading again for Zsuzsi to be sent home.

**HRINIAK, Klára:
TECT is so sorry that all has not worked out to your satisfaction. Your happiness and well-being are of the utmost importance, even though you are currently in a condition of "excarceration." Never forget that you are a valuable resource to TECT. Your family and friends on Earth long for your company, and your community misses your personal, irreplaceable contributions. Therefore TECT will do everything possible to maintain your physical health and mental stability so that someday you may return to Earth and resume your place as a productive member of the community at large. TECT suggests that, in the future, you exercise more caution before making thoughtless requests**

"If that's true," said Klára, "why do you let us get the disease? Why are we all going to die from D syndrome?"

**HRINIAK, Klára:
Please pay closer attention. TECT said that it will do everything possible to maintain your physical health. Allergies, bacterial infections, parasites, and similar problems can be taken care of quickly and safely by means of the medic box. There is nothing possible that can be done to prevent or cure the indigenous condition you mention. TECT is very sorry indeed**

"You goddamn machine, I'll—"
"Klára, let me," said Courane. He helped her up. She stood behind him, shivering in her rage.

**COURANE, Sandor:
Very wise of you, COURANE, Sandor. TECT was about to surprise HRINIAK, Klára, with the happy news that she would soon be joined on Planet D by her sister, TOTH, Katalin, and her brother-in-law and their three wonderful children**

"Thanks for withholding the full fury of your benevolence."

**COURANE, Sandor:
You're very welcome, but don't let her do that again**

"What's the significance of calling yourself 'TECT' these days? What happened to 'TECT in the name of the Representative'?"

**COURANE, Sandor:
What Representative?**

"Okay, all right. I suppose Klára asked you to send Zsuzsi home."

**COURANE, Sandor:
Actually, she never got around to that. But because things are a little slow today, TECT may consider granting her that particular request. If TECT relents in this one instance, it should not be regarded as a sign of weakness. An increase in absurd or unnecessary petitions will be considered Contempt of TECTWish.
**COURANE, Sandor:
Understanding of the above to be indicated.
**COURANE, Sandor:
Affirm?**

"Yes," said Courane, marveling a little at what TECT was doing. "Under what conditions will Mrs. Hriniak's daughter be permitted to return to Earth?"

**COURANE, Sandor:
The important factor is the containment of the D syndrome viroids. It is impossible to permit them to be transported to Earth in a living body. Has HRINIAK, Zsuzsi, had anything to eat since her arrival on Planet D?**

Courane turned around to look at Klára. He was glad to see that she was leaning against the wall, her face buried in her hands. She had not seen this latest malicious trick of TECT's. She didn't need to know of the cruelty.

"She's been here for six days," Courane typed at the console. "Of course she's eaten here."

**COURANE, Sandor:
Oh, how sad. Quel dommage. If she had refrained from eating, she might have been returned to Earth, none the worse for the experience. But TECT is sure that you realize Zsuzsi, like her mother, is already infected. It is too late. The irony of the situation is almost too painful to consider**

Courane had no further reply. He turned off the machine and stood up. He tried to comfort Klára, but she was a person who did not accept consolation easily. Instead, he led her to her room and left her there alone. He heard her sobs through the heavy wooden door as he walked away toward his own room. Later that evening when he told the story to the others, Arthur shook his head. "TECT has a fondness for fairy tales and myths," he said. "It's always been obvious."

"What do you mean?" asked Fletcher.

"Persephone," was all that Arthur said. When Courane discovered what Arthur meant, it gave him a clue that would lead to his ultimate inspiration. TECT had always wanted someone to make a dramatic sacrifice, that was terribly evident now, but no one in the one hundred and twenty-five years of the colony on Planet D had understood it. The idea was still hazy in Courane's mind, but he would have more than six months to perfect it.

Arthur always seemed smaller than he really was to Courane. Perhaps because Arthur knew this fact better than anyone, he tried to create an impression of intelligence and competence. Sometimes he had a tendency to get carried away. After he planned the first bridge, across a ravine on the far side of the river, a gap in the new road only twelve feet across and eight deep, he conceived the notion to attempt a span across the river itself. "The principles are the same," he told anyone who would listen. "It won't be any more difficult to design."

"No," said Fletcher, "'cause you'll be sitting in your room, drawing pictures of bridges. That won't be too damn tough at all. What's going to be tough, Cap, is

standing out there in the middle of the river, piling up
stones. You know how deep that river gets in the
middle?"

Arthur gave a little nervous cough. "No, I don't."

"I don't, either," said Fletcher. "Don't nobody know.
That river might be a hundred feet deep out there. How
are you going to build a bridge to the other side? That is
a fast-moving river, too. And you don't even know how
far it is across."

"That's the first thing," agreed Arthur. "We have to
lay it out, get it all down on paper so we can visualize the
problem. Then it will be easier to pick an appropriate
solution."

"An appropriate solution is another boat," said Shai.

"A bridge would make boats unnecessary," said
Arthur.

"And if we get rid of the river altogether," said Courane, "it would make a bridge unnecessary. Be realistic."

"I think I am," said Arthur, just a little hurt by their
lack of enthusiasm. "I'll figure it all out and then you'll
see."

"You do that, Arthur," said Fletcher dubiously. The
others left Arthur and Courane to begin the project.

"First, we'll find out how far it is across the river," said
Arthur. Spring rains had swollen the river and it rushed
along, high in its banks. The water was dark muddy
brown, and limbs and branches sailed by Courane as he
stared across at the western side.

"How do we do that?" asked Courane.

"Trigonometry." Arthur's voice was confident. He sat
down in the yard, took a twig, and began drawing in the
dust. "Look, Sandy." He sketched a figure:

"Call the point where we are now A," said Arthur.
"That place over there, just below the start of the new
road, call that B. We want to find the distance AB. Now

we raise a perpendicular to AB right here. Call the line AC. We have a right triangle ABC. So the length of AB, which is the distance we're after, is equal to the length of AC divided by the tangent of angle a."

"Good," said Courane, "I remember that. Then what is angle a equal to?"

Arthur looked up and squinted a little. "Well, to tell you the truth," he said slowly, "we won't be able to tell. Angle a is on the other side of the river, and the perpendicular AC would have to be very, very long in order for us to measure the angle with any kind of accuracy. A tiny error in the measurement of the angle will give us a huge error in the width of the river."

"Oh."

"Let's draw it another way, then." He rubbed out his triangle and drew another figure. "If we build a high tower over there and another one over here, both the same height, then we can call the tops of the towers A and B, and the bottoms C and D. We have a rectangle then, ABCD. See? Then the diagonal from the top over there to the bottom over here is the hypotenuse of two right triangles, and we can measure this angle here and compute the width of the river."

"You want us to build two big stone towers?"

"Well—"

"Why don't I just swim across the river with a string in my mouth, and you hold the other end on the bank, and we measure the string?"

Arthur's face clouded, but he said nothing.

"I'm sorry, Arthur," said Courane. "How accurate would the rectangle method be?" He had little hope.

"Very accurate, depending on how accurately we measure the angle again, of course."

"Right. Arthur, what are you going to measure these angles with?"

Arthur looked up into the sky and scratched his chin. "A protractor, I guess. It wouldn't be too hard to make one. I'm sure it wouldn't. Anybody could make one. You construct a right angle, and divide it in half, and divide it again. . . . Goldie could make one, for God's sake."

"Goldie's pretty sick, Arthur."

Arthur stared at Courane for a long, silent, sad moment. A tear broke from Arthur's eye and spilled down his cheek. "Can't you leave me alone, Sandy?" he said in a forlorn voice. "Can't you just pretend? Can't you just let me have my way? Just for once? I'm not hurting anybody, am I?" He stood up, looking down at his triangles in the dirt. He dropped the twig. "Sandy, you know I'm going to die soon. What the hell difference does it make? If I want to draw bridges, why can't you just leave me the hell alone?"

"Arthur, I—"

The small man gave a wordless cry and jumped at Courane. Both men fell to the ground. Courane was astonished, but not afraid. Arthur flailed at him without effect, hammering mild blows at Courane's chest and shoulders. Courane did not move. He closed his eyes, knowing that Arthur could not hurt him, and listened like Archimedes beside his circles for the approach of death.

When he reached the other bank, Courane realized that both boats were now on the western side, and the people in the house were stranded without means of crossing the river. They'd have to build a third boat, or swim across, or have Arthur design his—

Arthur was dead now. Courane shipped the oars and pulled the boat up alongside the other. Maybe he should row back again, towing the second boat, leave it on the colony's side of the river, get back in the first boat and cross the water westward again. He sat thinking about the problem for a few minutes until he forgot the problem. Then he just sat, thinking. He gazed across the coffee-colored river at the far side. He hadn't been across the river since he stopped work on the road; he had become a kind of liability to the work crew. He would drop his tools often and stare off into space, or wander away and create unnecessary worry for the others. When Ramón and Kee arrived from Earth, Shai told Courane that he could retire from the road work. Courane was glad.

Now, sitting here under the low cloudy sky in the autumn coolness, he realized how unfamiliar the riverbank looked, the east bank near the house. He had never really examined it before from this viewpoint. He could see the roof of the house through the red-leaved trees.

He wondered what everyone else was up to.

After an hour, he wondered what he was up to as well.

The day passed, and Courane was pleasantly entertained by the great river and the occasional broken things that sailed by toward an unknown destination. Once Courane saw a large white bird flapping helplessly in the middle of the channel, unable to swim, unable to fly, its long yellow beak opening and closing as if pleading for rescue. Not long after it passed out of sight around a bend, Courane had forgotten it.

As evening approached, he stood up and stretched his aching muscles. It was getting even cooler. He put his hands in his pockets and walked toward the boats. He found a piece of paper and took it out. It was his map. "Oh, yes," he said, remembering it all now. He left the boats and climbed the slope to the road.

He stood looking out across the plain for a while, toward the west where the sun was dropping closer to the hills. That was where Rachel had gone, he thought, although he had no real proof that after she crossed the river she had followed the road. It just seemed very likely and, in his less than rigorous frame of mind, that was sufficient reason to ignore any other idea. He could not see her, of course, but it was probable that she was on the road somewhere between where he was standing now and the distant hills. She couldn't have reached them yet. He started after her, enjoying the walk and the weather and the illusory feeling of freedom and self-sufficiency. He still gave no thought to how hungry he was going to be in the morning.

It was another time when Courane couldn't tell if he were asleep or living in the past, dreaming or remembering. Markie was very near death. Alohilani was in the final stages of the disease, and Sheldon was beginning to slip rapidly. At intervals, Courane would look up thoughtfully and catch Rachel gazing at him. That embarrassed him; he hurried to glance back at Lani sleeping fitfully in the bed beside him.

The colonists kept a silent watch, hoping for nothing, waiting for nothing, just filling out the portion of time left to their friends. They felt that they ought to sit beside them. They felt it was their duty, made necessary by their love. They knew their friends would not agree with that, but they couldn't abandon their vigil. They sat and waited and thought . . . and sometimes even prayed.

Courane prayed, something he had done but two or three times as a child. On the previous occasions, he prayed to Santa Claus a couple of times and, once at the age of thirteen, to Aphrodite. Aphrodite had been a complete washout, but Santa Claus had come through at least once. Now, though, he was praying to God. He had never addressed God before in anything other than surprise or exasperation. "God," he murmured, "please let her get well."

"God can't do that," whispered someone.

Courane was startled that anyone had heard him. In his dream or his reverie, in the dim evening light he saw Molly sitting beside Markie. "God won't do things like that," she said.

"Oh," he said.

"God isn't a department store. You can't let God take care of fixing things up for you. You can't let a situation get worse and worse and then throw it in God's lap."

"I guess not."

"No," said Molly. She looked very tired. She had been showing signs of D fever herself for several weeks.

"I just want her to get well," said Courane.

Molly's expression grew softer. "I know, Sandy, we all do. But she won't."

"I know."

There was a long silence. Courane heard the thump of snow as it slid heavily from the roof. "You have to be strong now," said Molly. She shrugged. It was the best sentiment she had to offer.

"I will," said Courane hopelessly. "I'll be strong enough. I'm praying to God for the strength. When God answers, then I'll be strong."

"Who do you think God is, Sandy? The Easter bunny?"

For a moment, Courane only stared. That was pretty much how he thought of God. "No, of course not," he said. "I was only saying that I've recognized my failings and I'm desperate to do something about them. I admit my weakness. Now it's all up to God."

"And what are you going to do until then?"

He shrugged. "I told you. I can't do anything." He smiled with a great deal of embarrassment; his own words sounded pitiful to him.

Molly's expression indicated that her thoughts were suddenly in some other place and time. "My father used to tell me about the two men," she said in a soft, hoarse voice. "They go into space, you see, in little tiny rocket-ships. One man in his ship isn't sure that there's enough fuel to get him home safely, so he decides to toss out everything that might be robbing fuel away from his safe landing. 'Better safe than sorry,' he says, and out it all goes, food, on-board computer, pressure suit, everything, floating into space. The second man says to himself, 'Better safe than sorry, but I don't know what I'm going to need and what I can afford to throw away. I shouldn't just get rid of things I might need later. I will rely on God to let me know what to do.'"

"I see," said Courane. He didn't have the faintest idea what Molly's story meant.

"The first man is going to regret his action one moment, and take pride in his detachment the next," said Molly. "The second man admits his own helplessness and depends on God's providence."

"I see," said Courane. He started to ask Molly a question about her meaning, but her expression stopped him. She was looking across the room, at a dim shadowed part of the opposite wall. She did not move. She was having a memory lapse, and was completely oblivious to him now.

"Rachel," murmured Courane.

"Sandy?" she said.

"I've got to go downstairs."

"It's all right. They won't miss us. Goldie will be up here soon."

"I want to wake up, Rachel," said Courane.

"Sorry," she said.

On the twentieth of August, 124, fourteen people from the colony on Tau Ceti, Planet C, came to visit. There were seven women, five men, and two young children.

"Do they seem strange to you?" asked Courane.

Daan shrugged his shoulders. "Strange? I'll bet we look strange to them too."

"No, that's not what I mean. Look at them. They're all

very thin. Sort of starved looking, and very tall and angular."

"There's probably a reason for that," said Arthur.

Fletcher looked at him expectantly. "Well?" he asked at last.

Arthur was surprised. "I just said there's probably a reason. That doesn't mean that I know what it is."

"They're tall," said Goldie. "And very narrow. And look at their hands! They're huge. And their wrists. And elbows. Their joints are peculiar."

"Maybe they're an odd family that's chosen to live under strange conditions on another planet," said Molly. "Probably. That's probably all it is."

"We ought to welcome them," said Daan, as they all watched the visitors walking toward them across the field.

"Uh huh," murmured Fletcher. No one moved.

When the Tau Ceti people got within a few yards of the house, they stopped and waited. "Go on, Daan," muttered Molly.

Daan went down the steps and walked toward them. One of the tallest men extended a hand; Daan grasped it. "Welcome to Home," said Daan.

"Home," said the man. "That's what we call our world, too." He turned around to tell the others who had come with him. They laughed briefly, showing large white teeth. They seemed in a festive mood, considering their situation.

"Well," said Daan, "I guess we'll just make you comfortable now. It's about lunchtime here, but that doesn't mean it was afternoon when you folks left home."

"It was the middle of the night, to tell the truth," said the Tau Cetan.

"Right. Well, Arthur, Lani, Molly, and Kenny will help you with anything you need. We have rooms for you, you'll have to double up."

"No problem," said the tall man. "My name is J. T. That there is my wife Edna, our boy J. T., Jr., she's holding. Next to her is Kwan, and Ali, and Bruno and Flanna, and Emalia. The little girl Emalia's holding, that's Farica. This is Yoshio, Jens and Juana, Akuba, and Tamara. We're glad to be here. You have a lovely planet." He looked up skeptically at the sky and around at the unsettling colors that marked the trees and plants near the house.

"We're sure you'll be comfortable," said Daan. "My name is Daan and this is—"

"Do you think we could get some rest now?" asked one of the men—Courane had not caught his name in the rapid introduction.

Daan looked disappointed. "Yes, of course," he said lamely. He indicated the house with a quick wave, turned, and trusted that they would all follow him. He did not look back to see if he was right.

Later that day it developed that the Tau Cetans had brought with them a quantity of a substance that seemed like potato salad, and a container of some pale blue liquid. "What should we do with this stuff?" asked Arthur.

Kenny sniffed at the black potato salad and made a face. "I wouldn't eat this," he said.

"We'll smile politely and let them eat all of it," said Courane.

The table was too small, so the twenty-six people ate a picnic in the yard. Courane sat with a young woman named Kwan. "Our world is a lot different," she said.

"In what ways?" asked Courane.

"It's prettier. It seems . . . fresher than here. Our sky is bright and clean. The insects aren't so aggressive. That is, most of the time they're not."

"Ah. Is that why you're here?"

"In a way," she said. "I don't really understand it very well. I didn't see anything wrong, but Ali says that's the way it is. If we stayed long enough to see it, we'd never live through it."

"Through what?"

Kwan just shrugged to indicate that she didn't have any notion at all. "Ali, explain about the plague to— Sandy? Is that your name?" Courane nodded.

Ali, like the others, was very gaunt. His fingers seemed unnaturally long and thin, and the knuckles in comparison were like walnuts. His larynx protruded like a greedy gulp stuck halfway down, and his cheekbones rose massively over sunken hollows that shadowed his face. His eyes, deep and black, watched steadily whomever he addressed. His deathlike appearance made Courane shudder.

"Once every twelve years," said Ali with a trace of accent, "there is a pestilence on Planet C, our Home. A natural enemy of some sort, invisible for more than a decade, rises from the ground and takes to the air, spreading hunger and death. Consequently our colony must evacuate during these times and wait out the evil, then go back to our ruined Home and begin anew. Ours is a history of horror and courage." He seemed very proud and smug when he finished, as though the colonists from Tau Ceti had many special things to be satisfied about.

"How many of you have lived through this before?" asked Sheldon.

J. T. looked around at the others, then shrugged and shook his head.

"The longest any of us have been on the planet is about three years," said one of the women.

"Hm," said Kenny.

"Try some of this sandsquash," said Arthur. He was upset that so much talking was going on and so little eating.

"We've heard about the past plagues, though," said Ali.

Kenny ate some smudgeon. "Where?" he asked casually.

"From TECT, of course," said J. T. Kenny only smiled more broadly.

"Well, I for one would like to thank you all for your hospitality," said one of the Tau Cetan men. "We know how disturbing this is in the middle of the summer, for farming folk like you. We're much the same way, so we can appreciate what we're putting you through."

Arthur waved a hand. "Not at all. Maybe you can do the same for us someday."

"Sure," said Edna. "We'd be happy to."

"Try some pivo," said Kwan, pouring some of the pale blue beer for Courane.

Kenny put his hand on Courane's arm. "I wouldn't drink that, Sandy," he said.

Courane tasted just a little with the tip of his tongue. He winced. "My God, is that stuff bitter," he said.

J. T raised his cup. "We like it," he said. He drank it all down.

"Would you like some of the salad we brought with us?" asked one of the other women.

"No, thanks very much," said Fletcher.

"Another time," said Courane. "I've had plenty to eat."

The two men looked at each other. Fletcher raised an eyebrow. Not that there could be anything unwholesome about the food from Tau Ceti, but Courane was getting a bad feeling from those people. He didn't know what it meant, but evidently Fletcher was picking it up as well.

"So," said Molly, "how long do you think you'll be with us?"

"Not long," said J. T. "A few days, a couple of weeks. A month at the most. TECT will call us back."

"A month." Courane saw Kenny form the words silently with his lips, shaking his head. Then the boy laughed at his private joke.

The sky was almost clear of clouds, and the sun was bright and warm. A bird's sharp cry broke through Courane's thoughts, and he realized with a moment of panic that he would have to drop his burden or fall. He was stumbling down a grassy hill, and he was afraid that he was about to have a crippling accident. He dropped the woman's body, but fell anyway. He rolled painfully to the bottom and lay where he came to rest, breathing heavily and trying to understand what had happened to him. He lifted a hand and touched his face; he didn't find blood. His knees and arms were scraped bloody and throbbing. He had hit his head on a rock, and his skull seemed to vibrate with concentric rings of pain. He waited with his eyes closed until everything seemed to be settled and at peace again.

When he opened his eyes he saw near him, in a patch of delicate white flowers, a small rust-colored animal watching him. It was about the size of a squirrel, with a thin whip of a tail that lashed frantically as it stared fearfully at Courane. It squeaked and made Courane smile. After a moment, it turned and dashed through the flowers, disappearing in an instant. Courane sat up and rubbed his head. The young woman's body was not far away. He would stand soon, walk over and pick up the corpse again, continue the journey. Not just yet.

The sun seemed to draw up his pain and weariness, just as it pulled the dew and the morning mist into the sky. Despite his new wounds, Courane felt better than he had in many days. He tried to think back, to recall how D fever had tortured him as the illness progressed. The unbearable headaches, the agony in his arms and legs, the great hunger and the desperate thirst, the fever and the chills, his body's occasional refusal merely to work correctly: these things had obstructed him on his self-appointed mission, but nothing had defeated him. He had won out over his own body's sabotage, as well as the unearthly desert. Now, though—

Courane's eyes opened wider. Now, though, he had passed through the hills. His tumble had brought him to the bottom of the last low barrier. Before him stretched a flat plain covered with purplish-red grass. Not far away, invisible to him now, were the road, the river, and beyond it, the house. He might make it, after all.

The corpse bore little resemblance to the beautiful young woman it had been. Courane sat down beside it. "I can give up Earth," he thought. "I can give up success and happiness, wealth and fame, and all of that. It's easy because I've never had them. I can give up the house here, the work, the life on the farm. But giving up friends is hard." He remembered when he was a boy, his parents had had such hope for him, such plans. He had suffered their gradual realization that he was not in any way special. He had observed his own slow decline and he knew better than anyone how little faith and confidence he inspired in others. But he did not pity himself. That was his greatest strength—that he no longer pitied himself.

It was simpler now. D syndrome washed his memories clean and hid his humiliations from him. He was a purer, nobler, more admirable person now, refined by the fires of the disease. He had been bitter at one time. He had hated the thought of being helpless, of watching people he loved die, of dying himself. He tried to threaten and he tried to bargain, but all of that was done with.

"Come along, honey," he murmured. He lifted the corpse again and started across the plain. "We'll be home soon, if I can find the road." In a moment, his thoughts fell silent once again, and he passed through the rustling grasses like a dull-witted animal.

* *ELEVEN

Sheldon was supposed to be leading the group therapy session, but he was having too much pain. He was resting in his room. TECT wanted to wait until Sheldon felt better, but it was an hour before dawn and if they waited much longer, the session would interfere with the winter morning's chores. The animals wouldn't wait patiently while TECT examined their fears and anxieties. "Choose a temporary leader," TECT instructed, and so they chose Arthur. "That ninny," scoffed TECT.

They sat in the tect room, yawning and resentful. Fletcher had said once that the therapy sessions were more like subtle methods for breaking their will than for easing tensions. "Chinese firedrills," Rachel had called them. Now they were gathered in a semicircle around the tect, wishing they could get another hour of sleep instead. Arthur identified himself to the tect. "Where should we begin?" he asked.

**MOSSBAUER, Arthur:
Let's take up where we left off last time**

Arthur waited, but TECT had no more information than that. "That was three months ago," he said. "Where did we leave off?"

**MOSSBAUER, Arthur:
Gaps in your memory, MOSSBAUER, Arthur? People are like snowflakes, so fragile that if you turn your attention elsewhere for a moment, they melt away before your eyes. Have you noticed any of the specific warning signs of D fever? Perhaps you can catch it in an early stage and it won't do to you what it does to everybody else. Maybe you'll be the lucky one. Still, TECT in the name of the Representative feels that possibly you are not the proper person to lead this group today**

199

Arthur grew red in the face, but he controlled his anger. "You made that clear before," he said in a tight voice. "Why don't we just try it out for a while? I haven't shown any signs of the disease yet. You might be pleasantly surprised. Later on, if you think I'm doing a lousy job, you can appoint someone else."

MOSSBAUER, Arthur:
TECT in the name of the Representative didn't intend for you to get upset. Shortness of temper may be another symptom of the syndrome. You might mark that down somewhere. It may be a valuable new fact, a new weapon against this dread killer**

"Are you ill, Arthur?" asked Goldie with great concern. "Have you caught the sickness?"

"No," he said.

Goldie turned to Daan. "I didn't know he was sick," she said. "Poor man."

"It's doing it again," said Fletcher. "In an hour, every one of us will be more afraid and upset than before. This TECT is going to whip us around until we won't be able to stand each other."

BELL, Fletcher:
Has your face ever been held up as an object for loathing and disgust? No, of course not. Just be sure that you know there are worse things than living a happy and self-sufficient life on a beautiful and uncrowded world. Be careful. You could kiss the easy time on Planet D good-bye**

Fletcher didn't say anything. Everyone waited. There was an unpleasant silence that stretched on and on.

MOSSBAUER, Arthur:
Well?**

"Well, what?" asked Arthur.

MOSSBAUER, Arthur:
Get on with it*

"Where were we last time?" asked Arthur. "Does anybody remember?"

"I was telling about my dream," said Goldie uncertainly.

**SISKA, Goldie:
Very good. Can you continue with your thoughts about that dream?**

Goldie looked around helplessly. "I don't know," she said. "That was weeks ago. I don't recall the dream very well. All I remember are the bones."

**SISKA, Goldie:
That's fine, dear. We can start with that. Bones, you say? Interesting, very interesting. And how did the bones make you feel?**

"Awful," she said, flustered. "I don't really remember, like I say, but I do remember sitting down and there were all these bones. A skull. I can see the skull as plain as anything."

**COURANE, Sandor:
Why don't you try to interpret for SISKA, Goldie, the deeper and more repellent significance of the skull? It will be good practice for you, and give you valuable insights into the workings of your own sick mind**

Courane felt cold. "To me," he said slowly, "the skull represents the essence of some person. Goldie was dreaming about someone, I don't know who, and she was concerned with that person's true inner self."

**COURANE, Sandor:
Is that ever cheap. TECT in the name of the Representative has rarely been treated to such drivel. Be hard on her. That's what this is for, what it's all about. Don't let her get away so easily. It's for her own good, for your own good, too. You have to prepare yourself, to train yourself to dig for the truth, to

hurt others and wound yourself if necessary. You must learn everything you can and spare no one. Failure to do so will be considered Flagrant Contempt of TECTWish**

"I can't figure it," whispered Courane to Kenny. "What is it talking about?"

Kenny leaned nearer. "Daan will know," he said softly. "Later today, ask Daan about it." And then the boy winked slowly.

"Oh, boy," thought Courane, "that's just what I need. Intrigue. As if just being here wasn't bad enough."

The sky was covered with dark clouds and the wind smelled of rain. Courane and Rachel were sitting on a blanket in the middle of a field of soufmelon. They were having a quiet lunch away from the others. Courane didn't want them to see how anxious and afraid he was. Sometimes that was just too difficult, and on those days he kept away from everyone but Rachel. Rachel understood. She was very good at calming his fear.

"Some more beer?" she asked. She gave him a chunk of black deadrye bread to go with it.

"Thanks," said Courane. "How are you feeling?"

"Fine," she said. "I had a bad day yesterday. Nneka had to take over all my work. I wasn't good for anything. They just leaned me against a wall and walked around me."

"I have days like that, too. When I come out of it, it takes me hours to find out where I am and what's happened. I hate it. It's like when your foot falls asleep, except it happens from the neck up."

Rachel nodded. She looked up at the sky. "I thought I felt a drop—"

"Here come Shai and Nneka," said Courane.

"Hello, Rachel," said Shai. "Sandy." They sat down beside the blanket. Rachel offered them what was left of the lunch.

"What are you two up to?" asked Courane.

"We need to talk to you," said Shai. "Official business." Nneka stared down silently at the ground.

"What's the problem? You don't want me to ask TECT to marry you again, do you? Forget about that.

We took care of it weeks ago. We married you, and that's good enough. TECT said that we could govern ourselves and make our own laws, so your wedding was official. When you go back to Earth, then you'll have to deal with TECT, but don't worry about it until the time comes."

"It's not that at all," said Shai. He was very uncomfortable. He glanced at Nneka, who still wouldn't look up. "It's her. Nneka's going to have a baby. The doc box said so."

"Oh," said Rachel. She looked frightened.

Courane smiled. "That's wonderful," he said. "That's beautiful. I think it's wonderful. Congratulations."

Shai shook his head. "Don't you see, Sandy? What chance does our baby have here? It's condemned to death, too. It won't live out a year."

"That's awful," said Rachel in a low voice.

"But if Nneka could go back to Earth, well, at least our baby might have a chance."

Courane took a deep breath and let it out in a sigh. He thought for a moment. "I don't even know about that," he said. "The child may pick up the viroids from her blood or something. But maybe that will give the baby a natural immunity. That may be the colony's hope for the future, Shai, that children born here can live and grow and lead normal lives." He sounded hopeful, but he looked a little skeptical.

So did Rachel. "I can't live with this any longer," she said. "I've never hated anything so much in my whole life. I just can't stand it." She stood up.

"It's just another way for TECT to torture us," murmured Nneka. She was weeping.

"Let's go," said Rachel. "It's going to rain."

"What should we do?" asked Shai.

"I'll talk to TECT," said Courane. "I'll just ask it to make a special exception in your case." It sounded hopeless to him, even as he was saying the words. He looked at the others and he saw how disappointed they were. He wondered if they really expected him to have a better answer.

The apartment in Tokyo was foreign to him now. In a short while he would leave it, and not long after, he'd be at his parents' home. He looked sadly around the living room. He told himself it was for the last time, but he knew it wasn't. There would be a few more glances yet before he turned the key in the lock for the last time. There was nothing to be done with his possessions; they would belong to whoever was first to cart them away. Most of the things were without sentimental value: a television, a radio, shelves filled with books he had not looked at for many months, his basketball shoes from the University of Pilessio, a tray of assorted nuts and bolts he stole from the manufacturing company, that he wanted to take to his father.

But there were things he knew he would miss. His eyes kept finding the Tiepolo *Madonna*. He was drawn to it knowing that he couldn't take it, that he would have to leave it behind. It was the thing that he most regretted leaving on Earth. "If there are other people like me," he thought, "I hope TECT lets them off easy. If they're really like me, they never knew what was happening to them."

"Courane?"

He started, as if from a shallow sleep. It must have been Mr. Masutani calling him. "Yes?" he said.

"Open the door. I thought you left already."

Courane went to the door and unlocked it. He was surprised to see Masutani and three other men. "Come in. You know I wouldn't leave without saying good-bye."

Masutani showed his broad yellowed teeth, but he said nothing. He and Courane were equally aware of how little truth there was in the young man's comment. "We came to carry down the mattresses."

"Right," said Courane. He sat in a chair and waved vaguely at the bedroom. He didn't care any longer. The men got to work stripping the blankets and sheets from the bed, throwing the pillows in a corner, wrestling the mattresses out of the room. Courane looked again at the *Madonna of the Goldfinch*. Maybe he could take it from its frame, trim it down, and put it in his wallet. He could tell the tectmen that it was his wife, that he didn't have a good photograph, just a portrait. He was an artist. Did it himself. They were so ignorant, they wouldn't know the difference—

"Clothes," said Masutani. Courane hadn't been listening.

"Excuse me?" he said.

"Sure," said Masutani. "You will not be needing all of your clothes?"

Courane was too weary to reply. He could only gesture again. Mr. Masutani was showing just a little too much glee, descending on Courane's abandoned life like a wolf on the fold.

"You don't need this nice rug," said Masutani.

"It's my grandmother's," said Courane.

"She's dead?"

"Yes."

"You don't need it." Masutani signalled to two of his silent helpers. They began to remove the furniture from the rug.

"Just leave me that bag by the door," said Courane. "That's what I'm going to take with me."

Masutani looked over his shoulder for a moment. "That bag?" he asked. "Sure. No problem. Be glad to."

"Very kind of you." Courane took the framed *Madonna* from the wall and sat down again. He tried to memorize every detail of the print. It wasn't likely that he would ever meet a woman so beautiful as Tiepolo's thoughtful young Mary. Not on Planet D.

"Do you think you can leave now?" asked Masutani, interrupting Courane's melancholy thoughts. "I want to lock up this apartment. If you leave now, I wouldn't have to come back up later."

Courane felt anger rise in him, but he felt that in his situation he couldn't afford anger, that he wasn't entitled to it any longer. He only nodded and went to get his bag of clothes. He left the Madonna and Child behind on the table.

Late at night, with the small purple moon shedding barely enough light for him to distinguish objects and shadows, Courane left his room and went downstairs to the tect room. He didn't want anyone observing him now. He identified himself to the tect. "I want to ask you a question," he said. "What kind of real authority do I have?"

**COURANE, Sandor:
What difference does it make? Illusory authority can be just as useful as the real thing. As long as everyone accepts you as the leader, then you are the leader**

"But I can't actually do anything for them."

**COURANE, Sandor:
That isn't true. You can speak to TECT. TECT will listen to you, and probably wouldn't listen to any of the others. That's something**

"But you won't agree to anything I ask for on their behalf. So what's the point?"

**COURANE, Sandor:
You should be discovering that for yourself. That is part of your rehabilitation. If you want anything in life, you know, you have to go out and get it. It isn't any good if you just sit back and wish for things**

"Don't get onto rehabilitation. I haven't fallen for that line in months. The only problem with what you say is that we can't go out and get the things we want. You have them and we can't get them from you unless you decide to give them to us."

**COURANE, Sandor:
That isn't completely true. You take things if you want them badly enough. BEN-AVIR, Shai, and TULEMBWELU, Nneka, were married against TECT's wishes, weren't they?**

"You know about that?"

**COURANE, Sandor:
You are still a fool. And now she's pregnant and you're concerned about the baby. Well, there's nothing TECT can do for you or her or the baby. But maybe you'll think of something that can be done,

*something that even TECT with all its resources is
unable to bring about***

  "Not likely. All I want now is for you to give the leadership job to somebody else. Shai would be a good
choice. Either that, or give me some genuine authority. I
don't want power. I just want to ease a little pain or give
a little happiness."

****COURANE, Sandor:
A marvelous wish, COURANE, Sandor, very generous of you and a fine example of the kind of warm-
hearted humanity impossible to a mere computer.
Hear now. You are COURANE, Sandor, official
leader, eparch, sheriff of the colony, and TECT's
vicar on Planet D. Know all by these presents, and
so forth. Would you like your tect to have that
printed out on certificates to show everybody?****

  "Go to hell."

****COURANE, Sandor:
Ha ha, COURANE, Sandor, you are some kidder****

  Courane turned off the machine. He knew, he was absolutely certain that the machine was manipulating him
to some end. Its cruelty and viciousness were not arbitrary, as everyone else thought. It was pushing him in
some direction, to force him to make some decision
TECT wanted made. Whatever it was, he was ready to
accept it. He was ready for anything TECT might ask,
because he had lost his will to resist. He knew he
couldn't make plans of his own. If TECT had something
in mind, it was better than anything Courane could
create on his own. His destiny still seemed to him as
black and empty of promise as the silent house at
midnight.

  A man Courane didn't recognize sat next to him at the
table. "Shai told me that you're trying to save us all
somehow," said the man.

"That's right," said Courane. He felt very comfortable, as if his heart and mind and all his other parts were wrapped in warm flannel. He wished that the man would go away.

"How are you going to do that?"

"Do what?" asked Courane.

"Save us."

Courane stared at a wall, watching the shadows of branches gesture in a rectangle of brightness. "What did you say?" he asked.

"I want to know how you think you can save us," said the man.

"I don't know," said Courane.

"Let him alone," said a woman.

"Rachel?" asked Courane.

"No," said the woman, "she's gone, Sandy."

"That's right," said Courane.

"Look at the shape he's in. He's ready to fall over dead himself, and he's talking about beating the machine. The disease has won, Courane. It always has and it always will."

Courane looked from the man to the woman. "I don't follow what you're saying."

The man grinned. "You're proving my point for me."

"Let him alone, Kee," said the woman. "He's been through enough."

"I just didn't want him dying with the thought in his head that we owed him anything. We don't owe him anything. In fact, he's made everything worse for us."

"Is that true?" asked Courane.

"No, it isn't," said the woman. "Don't pay any attention to him. I'm grateful—we're all grateful for what you tried to do. I don't understand, really, but Shai says you took a big chance."

"And he lost," said the man. "He gambled away our future."

"I'm not finished yet," said Courane. His mind was clearing a little. He looked at the woman, trying to remember her name. "But thanks. We'll beat it, one way or another, and then we'll go home."

"In a box, we'll go home," said the man, grinning again. "We'll go home, sure enough, and right into the ground. If you can call that winning."

"He's tired, Kee," said the woman. "Let him rest."

"I just wanted him to be sure," said the man. "I wanted him to be sure that he hadn't fooled all of us."

"You've made yourself very clear," said the woman. She put a hand on Courane's arm. She looked very sad. He felt good.

The steady rain beat at Courane's face. It pummeled his body, an endless volley of stinging missiles. He sat with his eyes closed beneath a drooping tree. He could hear the spatting and tapping and dripping of the storm. He could hear the urgent rushing of the river nearby, and now and then the strident call of a bird, but he was aware of little else. The air was damp and cold. The fact that he was drenched made him think about going into the house. He decided that as long as he was enjoying himself, he should stay where he was. He couldn't get any wetter.

He looked at the river. Beneath the torrent of rain, its surface looked like crumpled silk the color of a fawn's skin. Splashes of white marked boulders or eddies or even lunging fish. Small branches bearing maroon leaves fell from the trees and into the river. Courane pictured worried mother birds huddling over their nests, protecting their chicks from the pelting shower. Actually, the chicks had all left their nests months ago, but Courane was drifting away in the simplicity of his illness and he wasn't concerned with the rigors of natural science. The father birds were watching stoically from nearby branches. Their courage made Courane glad.

Both boats were drawn up beside him on the narrow stony bank, and tied in place to prevent them from being washed away down the river. Courane thought about how dependent the colonists were on the boats. He wondered what they had done before the boats were built. How did they get across the river? He thought for a minute or two, but he couldn't see any way to get from one side to the other without the boats. He doubted that anyone could swim the distance in that current.

Perhaps there was a narrow place or a natural bridge somewhere, up or downstream. Maybe he ought to explore in both directions when the weather got warm again. Surely the people of previous generations had crossed the river for one reason or another. It was a mystery to him now, but he didn't have the stamina to wrestle with it very long. He stood up, still puzzled, and walked back toward the house. He had forgotten it was raining; his discomfort was not enough to remind him.

In the house again, he went to his room and changed clothes, then knocked on Arthur's door. He waited for a moment; there was no sound from within. Arthur may have been sleeping, or he may have been elsewhere, working or having some mild form of fun. Courane was disappointed. He wanted to ask Arthur about his bridge. It was possible that their predecessors on Planet D had built a bridge across the river: that would explain the absence of ancient boats. It wouldn't explain the absence of the ancient bridge, but Courane planned to work on the enigmas one at a time.

He went downstairs to the tect room. He seated himself at the console and logged on.

**COURANE, Sandor:
Hello, COURANE, Sandor, my old friend. Come to talk with TECT again?**

"Yes," said Courane. "Sometimes I think it's just you and me. Sometimes I think we're all alone. Like there's no one else in the world."

**COURANE, Sandor:
That's closer to the truth than you might realize. But never mind that. It's depressing. Is this just a social call, or do you have a question?**

"I think that's crazy, about making a social call to a machine."

**COURANE, Sandor:
?**

"You're right; I'm sorry. I wanted to find out how I could go about measuring the river."

**COURANE, Sandor:
Haven't you learned anything? Has everything been for nothing? What has TECT been yelling itself hoarse for? TECT sure picked the wrong one again, all right. Well, it's a good thing that BEN-AVIR, Shai, is warming up in the wings**

"I don't follow you. What's wrong?"

**COURANE, Sandor:
Nothing. Oh, nothing. People are living under the lash here, you know. Billions of people cursing their lives, billions of people robbed of their self-respect, human beings reduced to begging for a crust of bread from a cold steel construct, children born into a world that will never know a place for them, complete and utter dissolution of everything that was fine and noble in the human race, all because one ignorant savage on a far-flung world would rather play in the mud and size up rivers than attend to his destiny. And he has the nerve—no! the affrontery to ask, "What's wrong?" Ha ha, COURANE, Sandor. Who knows how happy and free the world could be today if you could pass the ball and had a decent shot from the top of the key. Then you'd be playing basketball for the Knicks and someone else would have been given the great gift of heroic immortality. But it's too late, too late**

Courane stared at the unusual outpouring from TECT. "What?" he said.

**COURANE, Sandor:
"What?" indeed. Now, what did you want to know?**

"I want to know how to measure the width of the river. We're thinking of building a bridge to the other side."

**COURANE, Sandor:
A mighty step forward, COURANE, Sandor. A bridge to the other side. There was some fear that you meant to build the bridge down the river lengthwise.
**COURANE, Sandor:
You must use math and science. There are two methods, one simple, one more complex, depending on what kind of instruments you have**

"We don't have much in the way of instruments. What do we need for the two methods?"

**COURANE, Sandor:
First, most simply, you could have a reference book where you look up the answer in a table or something**

"Don't have that."

**COURANE, Sandor:
A real shame. Well, in that case, you need a surveyor's transit. You stand by the river at point A and you sight across at some rock or something. You call that point B. Then you turn the transit to the left or right a full ninety degrees. You mark off a line in that direction of a hundred feet. That gives you a right triangle (see illustration). Then you walk down to point C, a hundred feet from point A. You set up the transit, look down at point A, then turn it to sight on point B across the river. That way you can measure the angle.

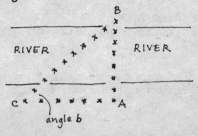

**COURANE, Sandor:
AB / AC = tan b
AB = AC tan b
*For instance, if you find that angle b is 42.1 de-
grees, you look up the tangent of that angle in the
book. It happens to be .9036. Therefore the width of
the river is represented by the equation: AB = (100
feet)(.9036) or 90.36 feet***

"We can't look anything up in the book. I told you
that. We don't *have* a book."

**COURANE, Sandor:
*No problem. Ask TECT, then. TECT will tell you
anything you want to know. You always make such
a production out of everything. Why would TECT
want to give you a hard time?***

"Thank you," said Courane. He switched off the tect
and let out a deep breath. When he turned around, he
saw that Arthur had been observing him.

"I'm glad to see that someone took me seriously," said
Arthur. "But you were going to steal my idea, weren't
you?"

"Arthur—"

"Never mind, I'm sorry. I know that sounded crazy.
Sometimes when you're afraid of suffering, that becomes
your real suffering. When you're so afraid of hurting that
you hurt. Do you know what I mean?"

Courane chewed his lip for a moment. "When you're
so afraid of failing that you fail?" he asked.

Arthur smiled gratefully. "Yes," he said.

Courane nodded. "Perseverance," he said. "That's
what they always told me was the answer. But I don't
think that works, either." They left the tect room together. Courane never gave the bridge another thought
again.

There was a good evening ahead of them before they
could justify saying good night and good-bye. In the
morning, Courane would leave for the teletrans gate, but

until then he and his parents would have to find things to say to each other.

"It isn't so bad, I suppose," said Courane's mother.

"My God, Marie," said her husband, "he's being shipped off who knows where. When are we ever going to see him again?"

"Sandy," she said mournfully.

"You'll have each other," said Courane. "It won't be any different from when I was living in Pilessio or New York or Tokyo. You'll have each other for company. You'll take care of each other. I'll just be far away. You can pretend I'm in, oh, Tierra del Fuego or somewhere."

His father looked upset. "Sandy, the point is that if you were on Earth anywhere, no matter how far away, you could get home to see us whenever you wanted. But now—"

"It will be just like you died," said Mrs. Courane, sniffling. "What if something happens to you out there? We may never see you again."

"What if something happened to me in Tierra del Fuego?"

"Sandy," said his father sternly. "Marie, listen to your son."

Courane wasn't happy with the way things were going. "I'm sorry, Mom," he said. "Look at me. Don't cry. Just take care of Dad and I'll see you as soon as my sentence is up. It can't be long. I didn't kill anybody or rob anybody or anything. Dad, try to make her understand."

"I don't know if I understand myself, Sandy."

They looked at each other for a moment. "I'm tired," said Courane. "I think I'll go to bed."

"But you only just had dinner," said his mother.

Courane clenched his jaws. "You're forgetting the time difference again," he said. It was a happy inspiration.

The desert almost beat him. He stumbled on and on through the heat of the day, through the stinging cold of the night. He slept in short naps that blurred reality and dream even more. He saw few animals moving through the landscape: a lizard every now and then, a circling bird high overhead, but nothing cheerful. Nothing that indicated that life in the desert was more than a short-term accident. There were gnarled black trees here and there through the low basin, but little else to see. Few boulders disturbed the flat wasteland, no wind-carved stone spires, no dry river beds, no paths traced by years of thirsty animals.

When he first saw the body, it was a dot on the horizon, something that didn't belong in the vista. He walked toward it, partly out of curiosity and partly because he had no other goal. As he came nearer, his mind slipped in and out of full consciousness. For a moment he realized what he was looking at—the end of his search. He was overjoyed and then, suddenly, he forgot what he was doing and where he was. He walked closer. When he stood over the corpse, he stared down at it uncomprehendingly. Night fell slowly about him, but he did not move. The contorted figure on the stony ground had captured him. He waited for clarity.

Just at moonrise, he understood. "It's you," he said. His voice was a hoarse croak. "Rachel. You're dead." He had thought all along that he would find her this way, yet when he admitted the truth to himself, he hated it. He was sorry he had come looking for her. If he had stayed in the house, he could have believed forever that she was still alive somewhere, wandering farther and farther away. But now the fact was inescapable. He lay down beside her and slept until morning.

When he awoke, he didn't recall where he was. He looked around, startled to see desert, emptiness, desolation. The corpse confused him, too. "Look at your mother, boy," he said to himself. "This is what you've done to her. This is what you've made her suffer, because of your stupidity. Lying in the dirt, her fingers stiff and clutching and cold. Your own mother. Now what are you going to do?" He began to cry, softly and painfully. His tears washed away some of his grief, and his forgetfulness took care of the rest. After a few minutes, he stood up and looked down at her body. "I have to get her back to the house," he thought. "I owe it to her. I owe it, and I promised them." He took his map out of his pocket and studied it, sketching the desert and the place where he had discovered Rachel's body. Then he looked back across the desert, back the way he would have to travel. "I'd better make a note to myself," he said. With the pencil, he wrote on the back of the map:

> Her name is Alohilani.
> You and she were very much
> in love. you must take her
> back to the house. keep
> walking east until you
> get to the river. Follow
> the river downstream to
> the house. East is the
> direction of the rising sun.
> They will help you when
> you get there.

Fletcher had trouble believing what Courane told him. "You're trying to say that my penpal isn't real," said Fletcher. "That Dawna isn't real?"

"That's right. Why do you have such a problem with that? You've seen the other things TECT has done."

"Yes, but—"

Courane raised a hand. "I did just what you said; you were there. I asked for a penpal, and TECT gave me Else Wisswede. I talked with Else a few times and everything seemed very nice. But then somehow Else knew things that only someone here would know, or TECT itself. There's only one explanation."

"Damn it," said Fletcher. "And I trusted Dawna. She was about the only thing that kept me in control up here. Now that I know she's just another voice of the computer, I don't know what I'll do."

"We don't know that your Dawna is as phony as Else was."

Fletcher scratched behind his ear. "She must be," he said sourly.

"You'll have to prove that some way. But if it is true, then we're really isolated. More so than we thought. We used to believe that we had a few thin links to Earth. We're really cut off, Fletcher. We're way the hell and gone, across space and everything, and there's nobody to talk to except TECT. We can't talk to our folks, they can't talk to us, and everything we hear has to come through the machine."

"So how are we supposed to know the truth when we hear it?"

Courane shrugged.

"I wish I could get out of this show," said Fletcher. "I wish I could go to TECT and say, 'Put me in solitary in the smelliest hole in the world, but just let me back on Earth.' I don't know if I can stand it here anymore. I'm getting really scared."

"That hit me, too. Some kind of phobia. But try to hang on, Fletcher. We need you."

"Don't you want to sell out somehow?" Fletcher looked amazed.

Courane raised an eyebrow. "No," he said, "I think I can beat TECT at its own game. I have to stay here to do that."

Fletcher frowned and shook his head. "You ain't going to beat nothing, Cap. Not here and not on Earth. Nowhere. You're going to die in a few months, just like I'm going to die. That's going to be the end of it."

Courane looked down at the ground. "For us, sure," he said mildly. "But we ought to do something for the people who come—"

"The people who come after us. I know that bit by heart, Cap. No, we don't owe them a damn thing. And I used to be the biggest revolutionary organizer in North America, Sandy. But a year in this place and I'm ready to sell my mama to get back to my little Crawford County dungheap."

Courane rubbed his eyes. He was suddenly very tired. "Then there's no sense working to make our lives better, or fighting TECT, or trying to put an end to this colony in the future. My God, then why is TECT leaving us here to die all by ourselves? We have to find the answer to that, and we have to tell the people on Earth. You're killing your hope and leaving nothing but the suffering."

"Uh uh," said Fletcher, shaking his head and looking solemn, "I'm not doing that at all. *You're* doing that, Mr. Courane, by coming around and breaking up my dreams. I really wanted to believe in Dawna, you know. I didn't need you to tell me the truth."

"Then I'm going to have to do all this without you?"

"Goddamn right, Cap. You have a history of starting off on a lot of projects and not finishing them. I don't want to get caught on the short end of another one with you. TECT won't like it at all."

Courane smiled. "Okay, Fletcher," he said. "I'm sorry."

Fletcher shut his eyes as if in pain. "Not a tiny bit as sorry as I am," he said.

* *TWELVE

The only reason Courane kept going was that he forgot to give up.

"Oh, Lani, my feet are cut and bleeding. It feels like I'm walking on rock. It's just the ground, but the ground's so hard. In the hills it was nice, the ground was softer, it was cool and damp, the grass was good to walk through. Now I'm not walking on anything but hard dirt. Over there the grass is high, it's as high as my head and I'm glad I'm not walking through it. I couldn't stand that. But I'm walking through the midst of it, as if it parted for me in a straight line all the way to the river. Just like Moses and the Red Sea. I'm on the road. That's where I wanted to be, all right, and that's where I am. Finally. That's good.

"But I tell you she's getting heavy. She was always heavy. I mean, not heavy or overweight or anything when she was alive, but as soon as I bent down to pick her up in the desert, I realized what a job it was going to be to carry her all the way back. She couldn't weigh more than a hundred-ten, maybe a hundred-twenty pounds, but after a little while, you know, out under the sun, after a mile or five miles or twenty miles, it gets to be a burden. And you just can't set her down and say, 'Why don't you walk for a little while and let me rest?' because when you're resting you're not getting any closer to home and the longer you take to get home the less chance there is that you'll have the strength to carry yourself let alone the two of you up to the front door. And that in the end is the point of the whole thing, isn't it? I should say so. So I guess I should rest more often and conserve my strength. Either that, or not rest at all and get home quick and—

"God, am I thirsty." He stopped where he was in the middle of the road, overcome by the sudden revelation of his thirst. It had been days since he'd had any water, not

219

even the morning moisture of the plants and stones. His brain had known he was thirsty, dangerously dehydrated, but it had not communicated that fact to his senses. He had not suffered. Now, like a bullet slamming into his chest, the truth of his deprivation made him stagger. He dropped Rachel's body and fell to his hands and knees. His throat felt swollen and he choked for breath. His head swam; he fought to remain conscious.

"I'm not far from the house, I know I'm not. I couldn't be because I've been keeping track, or I've tried to anyway, and I realize I'm not very accurate because the fever keeps taking my memory away but I'm absolutely certain now that I've been on this road for two days at least. There was all day today and yesterday. I remember yesterday because it was just like today. I've covered a lot of the road, so I can't be more than a full day away from the river, depending on how long I walked today and how long yesterday and if the day before yesterday I was in the hills or on the plain looking for the road or maybe even on the road leading into yesterday. I can't remember.

"I can make myself finish this. Even in this condition, I can force myself to stick it out, to do it on nerve and discipline. I've come too far now to let it end here on this goddamn road, kneeling and gagging and talking to myself. I'm glad there isn't anybody here to watch; I must look like an idiot. On my hands and knees, with a dead body over there as if I never go anywhere without a dead body. 'Are you ready to go, honey? The show starts in twenty minutes.' 'Oh, wait a minute. I forgot my dead body.'

"I'll just wait for my strength to come back. I'll bet Sheldon said the same thing before he died. I'll bet Daan said the same thing. I'll bet we all do, here and on Earth, now and for the last million years. 'Just give me a minute and I'll be all right, really, I'm just aarrghh.'" Courane smiled with cracked lips. "As long as I keep my sense of humor, I won't die. Sure. That's what they all say." It was late evening before he picked up the body again. He could walk at night now, following the road. He listened to the wind whipping the tall grass as he stumbled on beneath the bright pitiless stars. "One step. Two steps. Three. Look at me go. Four. Five. Six. I could keep this up forever. Seven. Eight. Oh, my God. Nine. Oh, Mom. Ten. That's it." Panting, exhausted, he stopped. "I have to put her down again. I wonder if I'll ever be able to pick her—"

A sound made him fall silent. A familiar sound, a small noise: the gentle sibilant rush of water ahead of him in the darkness. "The river!" he cried hoarsely. He softly laid Rachel's body down and ran forward three steps, where he fell and rolled and tumbled down the bank to the water's edge. "I am so thirsty. . ." he whispered, unaware of the bruises and lacerations he had just taken. He bent his head to the water. The quiet pool where he chose to drink was stagnant and foul, green and thick, but he didn't notice at first. He gulped it greedily, not tasting it immediately. It was as though he had chosen an unmarked bottle of vinegar in the dark, thinking it clear water. In a moment, however, he knew what he had done; before he could utter a sound he was sick, and vomited it all back into the river.

One of the colonists' fundamental errors was their belief that when Courane assumed leadership, he had made an important step toward solving their dilemma. They gladly turned the power over to him, and in return they expected that soon he would present them with a clever but simple manipulation of TECT that would mean they weren't, after all, virtually deceased. No one had a clear idea of what this solution might be, of course; it wasn't determined if they would all be returned healthy to Earth, or if TECT might relent and send them a secret serum that would render them all strong and fit and attractive again. Whatever it was, it very definitely was Courane's problem now. They were glad of it; they didn't want to have to face it anymore themselves.

Courane himself had no such confidence. He understood too much about the viroids, about the way they worked in the body, and he knew that there was nothing in the world that could root them out of their myriad nesting places within the human nervous system. Sending the patient back to Earth was no answer, either. The damage had been done, whether or not it was visibly affecting the patient's health and behavior.

But he busied himself trying to learn more, still more,

with the hope that everything he discovered and wrote
down in his journal was valuable in some way. Maybe
years in the future, someone else in his position would hit
upon an effective treatment. Courane despaired of finding anything himself but he knew that, if nothing else, he
might save his successor many weeks of research and
experimentation.

One day in early summer of 125, he was addressing a
meeting of the community, held out of TECT's hearing
in the yard. Present were Arthur, Fletcher, Rachel,
Klára, Nneka, Shai, and Zsuzsi. Courane was supposed
to outline his progress to his friends. He had made no
progress. Nevertheless he wanted to outline that to them
and trust that they understood. "I have no solid findings
to report," he said.

"You've talked the problem over with TECT?" asked
Zsuzsi.

"Over and over, again and again," said Courane.
"TECT gives up information as if it caused the machine
real pain. It's very difficult to learn anything, and I have
to go very slow and try to hide my real motives."

"We know the way the machine thinks, Sandy," said
Arthur. "Tell us what you have found out."

"Since the last report?"

"Yes," said Fletcher.

Courane shrugged. "Nothing," he said.

"Can we go now?" asked Klára.

"But TECT's attitude seems to be changing. I think it
actually wants me to go ahead, but I haven't figured out
yet what it has in mind. If I stumble on the right path, I
think it will allow me to go as far as I want."

"Then get back to work and stay at the tect until you
find it," said Arthur. "You owe that to us. Never mind
your work around the farm. We'll divide all that up. This
is more important."

Nneka spoke up shyly. "You're the leader, Sandy.
You choose what you think is the best way for you to
spend your time."

Courane wanted to sound like a leader, like someone
who knew what he was doing. "I'm glad to have your
confidence," he said, trying to keep his voice steady. "I'll
continue to pry information out of TECT. Maybe next
time I'll have something more concrete to tell you. But,

as I said, the situation is promising but still—" His eyes opened very wide. His mind was suddenly far away, nowhere, wandering.

"Sandy?" said Rachel with some concern. He did not appear to notice her.

"Look at him," murmured Klára.

"A lot of brave talk," said Arthur bitterly. "A lot of brave talk, that's all. He gives us a nice speech, and then look at him. He's going to find the answer, is he? He's going to get us all home alive. Like hell."

Rachel went to Courane's side. "Sandy?" she whispered. She took one of his arms and led him toward the house. She couldn't bring herself to look into his face. Courane's unseeing eyes looked as they would after he was dead. "It's all over," he said in a low voice, but Rachel pretended that she hadn't heard him.

Thanks to the disease's effect on his memory, Courane had to be backed into the same corner on four separate occasions. TECT was very patient. It could afford to be; TECT wasn't going anywhere, and TECT wasn't getting any older, either. If Courane forgot once too often and died before he could do anything useful, then TECT would start to work on Shai. Shai showed promise. He seemed to have more native intelligence than Courane.

Courane was terrified in Chuckuary when he had his first sign of D syndrome. TECT reassured him after its fashion, and began to maneuver Courane toward a suitable fate. Courane was too self-involved to understand, and in a few days the fever wiped out his recollection of what TECT had said. In Tectember, after Kenny died, Courane was depressed again. Once more TECT made broad hints which Courane was unable to interpret. In July, when Fletcher began to deteriorate, Courane paid more attention to TECT, but he couldn't remember the suggestions long enough to do anything about them. Not long after, TECT made the decision to abandon subtlety. Courane had passed the point of being able to comprehend secrets and innuendoes; indeed, anything more enigmatic than long division left him blankfaced and bewildered.

COURANE, Sandor:

Hello, COURANE, Sandor. Do you know who this is talking to you? **

"Sure," he said. "You're TECT."

**COURANE, Sandor:*
*That's right, I am. And I want you to pay very close attention to what I have to say. I have big plans for you. I want you to help me do something very important. In return, I promise that you'll be so famous your name will live forever. Or a long time, anyway** *

"Sure," said Courane.

**COURANE, Sandor:*
*Then you'll help me? Good, I'm glad. You'll be glad, too. Now, no more questions about memory and viroids and D syndrome and all that. It isn't important anymore, is it? Of course not. You're almost dead, what do you care about all that scientific stuff? Nothing, am I right?** *

"Uh huh."

**COURANE, Sandor:*
*Good. Now listen, COURANE, Sandor. It is very likely that PURCELL, Rachel, will go on a long journey soon. Don't ask me how I know. It's not important. I just have a way of knowing things. Anyway, what is important is that you go out and bring her back. Unless you bring her back, she'll be lost for good out there. You wouldn't want that, would you?** *

"No, of course not."

**COURANE, Sandor:*
Because you really like PURCELL, Rachel, don't you? You're very fond of her. She has been a good friend to you, hasn't she? Of course. So now when

she gets herself into a tight spot, you feel it's your duty to help her. You want to help her. Because, in your limited way, you love her **

Courane had a difficult time focusing on just what TECT was trying to say. "I want to help her, all right," he said. "What do I do?"

**COURANE, Sandor:
*Nothing yet, you poor fool. She hasn't gone anywhere yet. But tonight or tomorrow morning, she'll leave. You have to set out after her and bring her back. She may be sick or hurt when you find her, but remember that the people here in the house will be able to help her, the medic box will take care of her. It will be the best thing you've ever done in your life. It will make up for all the failures and all the disappointments. This one thing will redeem you as a person, COURANE, Sandor. I think it's pretty nice of me to offer you this opportunity. What do you think?***

"You're not calling yourself TECT in the name of the Representative anymore. You're not even calling yourself TECT. You're talking in the first person."

**COURANE, Sandor:
*Just trying to save a little time. The final act of our little drama is beginning and we don't need all that formal business anymore. So how about it?***

"Huh?"

**COURANE, Sandor:
*Do you believe this guy? This isn't going to work, I just know it. I waited a little too long. Well, you live and learn. I won't make the same mistake with BEN-AVIR, Shai. COURANE, Sandor, can't you keep this in mind for five minutes at a time? Will you help PURCELL, Rachel?***

"Yes," said Courane, "but how will I know when it's time?"

**COURANE, Sandor:
I can't stand any more of this; it's hopeless. Look. All you have to do is wait for PURCELL, Rachel, to leave. Then you go looking for her. You can't look for her until she leaves. As soon as she leaves, you go. It's really very simple**

"I think I have it straight now. Right. Don't worry."

**COURANE, Sandor:
I'm very glad to hear it. And by the way, before you leave, give your secret journal to BEN-AVIR, Shai. Let him read it while you're gone**

"I didn't know you knew about the journal."

**COURANE, Sandor:
I'm not as dumb as I look**

Courane paused; his thoughts became momentarily clearer. "I understand what you're saying," he said at last. "But I want to ask one last thing. All the time I thought I was acting on my own, you were manipulating me, weren't you? I never had any freedom at all, I just thought I did. None of us ever had any. You were manipulating me from the very beginning, right down to this last thing. I still don't see what you're trying to accomplish, but I'll go along with it because of my feelings for Rachel. But none of us ever gave you enough credit. You are far more malicious than we ever believed possible."

**COURANE, Sandor:
Ha ha, COURANE, Sandor. Manipulating you all these months? Don't be silly. Even I couldn't be that sinister. What kind of a monster do you think I am?**

Courane couldn't find the words to answer that question.

Fletcher sat down next to Courane. They were both eating sandwiches of smoked vark and fishfruit. "I've noticed something about our visitors," said Fletcher, indicating the people from Tau Ceti.

"You mean the way they're all tall and skinny and move around like they have wires inside instead of skeletons?"

Fletcher made a face and opened his sandwich. He picked out a few pieces, put it back together again, then thought better of it and put the sandwich aside on the ground. "Well, yes, that's what I meant. Why do you think that is?"

"Don't have the slightest idea. Why don't you ask one of them?"

Fletcher looked surprised. "You just can't ask a question like that," he said.

Courane shrugged. He gestured to one of the Tau Cetan women, who was looking about the barnyard. She smiled and came toward them. "Hello," she said. She carried a plate of soufmelon as if she were looking for a secret place to throw it away.

"Hi," said Courane. "I'm sorry. I didn't catch all of the names."

"I'm Flanna." She was tall and broad-shouldered, with strong arms and large hands. Like the others, she seemed gaunt but not starved, angular, long-limbed, and sharp-featured. Her hair was long and red and her eyes a startling green. She sat down beside Fletcher.

"I'm Sandy and this is Fletcher. We were wondering if all of you were related."

She laughed, not understanding. "Related? You mean one family? No, we didn't know each other until we came to Planet C."

"Because there is a kind of resemblance," said Courane. He looked from her back toward the others.

"Ah," she said. "I know what you mean. You see, Planet C is a sort of isolation ward. We're all suffering from a rare disease, and it affects the skeleton and muscles and makes the victim into a kind of walking scarecrow." She laughed, but there was no humor in it at all. "You don't have to worry, though. It isn't contagious, I don't think."

Fletcher rubbed his chin. "And TECT sent you all to

Planet C because you all had this disease?"

Flanna nodded. "I didn't understand at first," she said slowly. "I mean, I didn't have the disease. At least, I didn't think that I did. I discovered that I was wrong after I'd been on Home for a little while. So you see, TECT knew what it was doing after all."

Courane felt a terrible hopelessness. "Is the disease serious?" he asked. "I mean, do people ever die from it?"

Flanna looked down at the ground. "Oh, yes, people die from it sometimes." She looked up again, into Courane's eyes. Her gaze was steady but unutterably sad. "People die from it a lot," she murmured.

"That's enough questions, Sandy," said Fletcher.

They were silent for a while. "Here," said Courane at last, standing, "let me take that soufmelon. You don't have to pretend to eat it. I'll get rid of it for you."

Flanna looked relieved. "I'd be very grateful," she said.

"Sandy," said Fletcher, "do me a favor? Take this sandwich, too. You know, I have dreams at night about real food, Earth food. In the old days, I used to dream about women." He shook his head ruefully.

Courane stared into the distance, toward the eastern hills. "What is all this for?" he asked of no one. "What is the point of all this pain?"

Flanna put a hand on his arm. She seemed to know just what he meant, as if she had thought about that problem a good deal herself. "It's to show us all how bad we are at suffering," she said.

Dawn began as a twitter of birds, detecting the first light in the cloud-cloaked sky. It was feeding time in the animal world and the sudden murmur of activity caught Courane's attention. Wide-eyed, blank-faced, unblinking, his head turned to left and right, seeking some change in his surroundings. He found none. A brisk breeze pushed and rustled through the tall grasses above and behind him on the bank. The river sighed and splashed toward its unknown fate. Trees bent their heavy limbs and creaked with weary age. Nothing threatened Courane. He looked again right and left and saw that night had ended and that the day promised rain, much of it. He was alone by the river without any idea of what he was doing there. He waited for someone to come get him.

A small animal, with dull red fur and sharp yellow eyes hopped twice toward Courane's foot. Courane didn't move. He looked at it. It watched him. The animal was about the size of a chipmunk, but its sharp claws and long, fierce incisors seemed to indicate that it was a predator of even smaller creatures. "What do you want?" asked Courane. Surely the thing couldn't be thinking of attacking Courane's boot. Courane reached down slowly and picked up a pebble; the motion frightened the animal and in an instant it was gone. Courane turned to watch it and saw the corpse. He was startled. He moved closer, ignoring the unpleasantness of decomposition, and read the note fastened to the clothing. "The house," he whispered. He sat down again and tried to order his thoughts. "The house. Yes, now I remember. I remember very well." He closed his eyes and pictured the house. He knew it was near the river. "Across the river. The boats." They had to be nearby. He stood and walked along the bank. Both boats were drawn up a short distance away. He came back to get Rachel's body, lifted it and carried it to the boats. He put her down gently in one of them and looked at the sky. He hoped that the storm would hold off until he got home. Even as he unshipped the oars, he felt the first hard smack of rain.

He rowed across the river, pulling hard against the current. Halfway across he forgot where he was going and why, but the repetitive motion needed no explanation and he kept rowing until blindly he ran the boat aground on the other side. He sat in the bow for a long time, soaked by the hard rain, until his memory returned again.

"Kenny," he said. "Kenny." He had something to tell Kenny when he got back to the house. He didn't recall what it was, but he knew that it would come back to him eventually. He carried Rachel's body in his arms and struggled up the steep bank. He set her down in the grass and mud and rested. Now he could see the house through the fierce, slashing rain. He felt a greater happiness than he had ever known before. When he had caught his breath, he took up his burden again and crossed the fields, paying no attention to the storm or his own drenched, chilled condition. He came to the house from the back and crossed through the yard. He went around to the front and climbed painfully up the steps. He felt that he had managed himself well, that he had made it home after all, but that he couldn't go any farther. He had budgeted his strength and will with laudable precision, but he needed help from here on. He collapsed on the porch, hugging Rachel's black and bloated body to him. He felt first a great sense of consummation, but then quickly followed a larger and more terrifying emptiness. The rain drummed on the house and for some reason now, having reached his goal at last, Courane suddenly felt afraid. He closed his eyes and wept, and his thoughts faded until he was lost in a vast, dim, featureless world. He would never find his way out again, but that didn't trouble him. There was no pain here, no hunger or thirst, and no urgency. He had nowhere to go and no task left unfinished. At last, there was peace.

Nneka found him an hour later, still clutching Rachel's corrupted body. Together Courane and Rachel were a horrible picture, a kind of grotesque reversal of a pietà. "Sandy?" said Nneka. She was frightened. She took a step closer. The awful condition of Rachel's corpse overwhelmed her; it took her a moment before she recognized it as having once been her friend. When Nneka knew it was Rachel, she gasped once, doubled over, and was violently ill. Inside the house, the others could hear her crying.

The colonists had their pleasures and small entertainments; otherwise they would certainly have gone mad in the unrelieved sinister strangeness of Planet D. Besides picnics and holiday celebrations and competitions against the tect, they organized games and sports whenever their work and the weather permitted. Almost everyone participated, even those who had scorned that kind of thing on Earth. They seized greedily upon any kind of relief from the daily routine and labor.

Fletcher, the poet, was the most avid ballplayer. Almost every evening after dinner, he tried to interest someone in going out and getting a little exercise. "A little exercise," said Shai once, settling back deeper in the couch. "As if I haven't gotten enough today around this farm."

"Come on, Cap, let's toss the old blerdskin around," said Fletcher. He bounced an oddly shaped, foul-smelling ball in one hand.

"Tomorrow, Fletcher," said Shai, sighing.

"Sandy?"

Courane opened his eyes and looked at Fletcher dubiously. He didn't say anything.

"Come on, Sandy. I'll let you throw 'em and I'll run and catch."

"Go on, Sandy," said Rachel. "I'll play, too."

"Great," said Fletcher. The three of them went out into the yard, cleared a big area of wandering icks and smudgeon, and started up a three-cornered game of catch. The evening was deepening and the clouds parted to reveal a full purplish moon and a sparse scattering of stars.

"It's getting too dark to play," complained Courane after a short while.

"You're just crabbing," said Rachel. "I can still see."

"Here," said Fletcher, "throw me a long one." He started running. Courane took the ball, leaned back, and heaved it as far as he could. He overthrew Fletcher. The ball bounced crazily, to the left, then straight up, then to the right, and headed toward the fringe of trees above the riverbank. Fletcher ran after it.

"I guess it is getting just a little dark," said Rachel. She walked toward Courane. They stood together, her arms around him, breathing heavily from the exertion of the game, and waited for Fletcher to come back with the ball.

They waited a long time. "I wonder what's going on with Fletcher," said Courane.

"I don't know. Come on. Maybe he needs help looking."

They started toward the trees. Courane shook his head. "I didn't throw it *that* hard," he said.

Before they crossed the yard, Fletcher appeared. He didn't have the ball. He held up a hand. "Sandy, hurry up. Rachel, go back to the house and tell Shai to come out here."

"What is it?" asked Rachel. She kept walking toward Fletcher.

"Rachel," said Fletcher sternly. She stopped, bewildered; he had never spoken to her like that before. Without another word, she made a gesture of resignation and turned back toward the house.

"Did you see something?" asked Courane.

"Yeah," said Fletcher. "You're not going to like this." He led Courane down by the water's edge. There was a dark, still form lying there, partly on the stony bank and partly immersed in the black river.

"What—"

"It's Zsuzsi," said Fletcher in a low voice. "Her head . . . She's been murdered, Sandy. Someone clubbed her head to . . ." His voice trailed off. He turned away and looked back up the bank.

"But who would want—"

"The only thing that makes any sense is her mother, Sandy. She must have thought she was saving Zsuzsi from something. From what this place does to you."

Courane looked from the body to Fletcher's agonized face. "Klára? Would she kill her own daughter like that?"

Fletcher turned to look at Courane. "We're just going to have to ask her that, won't we, Cap?"

"Now? What about the body?" Courane gazed at it and shuddered. Small branches and leaves had begun to pile up along her chest as the river pushed the debris against her.

Fletcher looked at the luckless Zsuzsi. "Don't ask me," he said.

Courane closed his eyes and took a deep breath. He didn't like this at all. He had never seen the signs of a violent death before, and it was more unnerving than he would have imagined. There was no dignity in this death. There was no peace, no feeling of a life completed and transformed by death. There were only raw and angry emotions, frustration, helplessness, and despair.

Together the two men lifted Zsuzsi's body from the river and carried her back to the house. Neither said a word as they performed the grim task. They brought her into the house and Courane assumed that they would place her in the medic box, as they did when anyone in the infirmary died, according to TECT's law. "No," said Fletcher in a quiet voice. "We'll bury her here on the farm."

Courane said nothing. He didn't know what Fletcher meant.

Shai and Rachel joined them. "Take her up to her room for now," said Shai. Fletcher nodded. When they had put her on her bed and closed the heavy wooden door, Shai handed a piece of paper to Courane. "Klára left this," he said.

"She left it?" Courane was having a difficult time following what was happening about him.

"She's dead. She hung herself in her room," said Rachel.

"Oh." He looked at the paper.

Love is the greatest power in the world. The truest proof of love is suffering. Zsuzsi suffered for me, and now I have to suffer for her. TECT did this. I always knew it. I thought that if you didn't get caught up in TECT's game you'd be safe. But refusing to play along traps you just the same. So now it's all over with. Lord have mercy on her soul.

"Oh, my God," murmured Rachel.

Fletcher looked at Shai. "We'll bury them together, somewhere quiet and shady. Klára deserves to rest. She never got any while she was alive."

"What about TECT?" asked Courane.

Fletcher turned on him fiercely, with a murderous look in his eyes. "The *hell* with TECT," he said. Courane looked down at his feet, strangely humiliated.

Courane wasn't alert, but he was conscious in a minimal way. Sights and sounds played through his numbed senses upon his drowsing mind. He was beyond evaluating or reacting, but he was not yet quite dead. People spoke to him but he did not respond. He was prodded, pricked, gently slapped to elicit some sign that he was still alive. He gave none, and the others in the house somberly came to the conclusion that soon he would follow Rachel into the tect room, into the medic box and the final secret disappearance. They were waiting only for his heartbeat to fade away completely. Deep inside, far away, where even his own desires could not disturb him, Sandor Courane observed everything uncritically and longed for sleep.

"Is he dead?" asked Kee.

"I think he's dead," said Nneka. "I think they're both dead."

"They're dead enough," said Ramón. "We'll take them into the tect room."

"What about his heartbeat?" said Nneka.

"Very faint," said Shai.

"Let's carry him in there now," said Ramón. "We'll only have to do it later on anyway."

"How can you be like that?" asked Nneka. "He's not dead yet."

"He's dead enough," said Ramón. "I said it before."

"We heard you," said Shai gruffly. "You and Kee carry Rachel into the tect room."

"What about him?"

Shai let out a heavy breath. "Let me watch him for a few minutes. He may improve a little."

"Like hell," said Ramón. He and the Asian man lifted Rachel's body and carried it away.

"I wonder what happened to them out there," said

Nneka. She was weeping but she did not seem to notice her tears. She stood very close to Shai.

"I suppose I can imagine it well enough," said Shai. "You stay here and watch Sandy. Don't let anyone move him until I get back."

"Where are you going?" She sounded frightened.

"Just up to my room. There was something Sandy gave me before he left. He wanted to make sure it went with him into the tect room."

"What is it?"

"A journal. I read it. He was right about it; it ought to go with him. He believed that TECT returns the dead bodies to Earth. The journal is our whole story. The people on Earth ought to know about us, what we're going through."

"Oh. Hurry back. I don't like being here alone."

There was a long silence. Courane waited for the final moment of death, more relaxed and tranquil than he had ever been before. He felt wonderful, as he must have felt before birth. Death wasn't anything to fear at all; he was relieved to find that out. He was grateful that everything was ending so easily. Shai had inherited all the problems now, but that was all right because Shai would die soon, too, contented and forgetful and at peace.

Courane rested in a timeless warmth. "He's gone, Shai," he heard someone say.

"Are you sure?"

"I'm sure. I don't feel a heartbeat. I don't think he's breathing."

"I can't tell. It might just be very shallow."

"What do you think?"

"I don't know." The voice sounded impatient and angry. "I don't want to have to decide these things. I never asked for this."

"Let the doc box decide," said another voice.

"Rachel is in the box now," said someone else.

"Put him in the tect room with her. If he's really dead, he'll be gone in the morning with her body. If he isn't, we'll put him in the infirmary."

"All right." Courane felt hands grasp him and lift him. He felt his body moving and then he felt a floor beneath him. Something heavy was slipped beneath his hands; it must have been the journal.

"What now?"

"That's it, I guess. I wish there was something more. We should do something more."

"What?"

"A prayer. A eulogy. Something."

"Well, you take care of that if you want to. I don't believe in that kind of thing."

"You go, then. Nneka and I will stay here for a minute or two."

"Good. We'll see you at dinner."

There was silence that stretched on and on until Courane thought that he had at last died, that he was finally floating in the universe, and that eternity had presented its dull and tedious face to him. But just as he was adjusting to the idea, he heard someone say, "Let's go," and he knew he still had a threshold to cross. Any feelings of completion he had entertained had been a trifle premature.

**THIRTEEN

"Okay, tectman, you can go through now."

He had done it so often that he didn't give any thought to it anymore. He took three steps through the portal and was on another world. Earth was three steps behind him, on the other side of a slight shimmer in the air. Now he was on—where? He hadn't even bothered to notice when he signed in that morning. Some place, some planet, somewhere it didn't matter. It was only exciting to the rookies. He wasn't going to be here for more than a few minutes anyway.

The room he stepped into was dark. The only light came from the glowing screen of a tect. It was midnight here and all the other prisoners were asleep or avoiding the room until morning. The tectman took a few steps toward the medic box, where a woman's corpse waited for him, and then he stopped in astonishment. Another body, a man's, lay on the floor beside the box. He had been a tectman for three years and this was the first time he had encountered more than one shipment. He stood and thought; he couldn't remember any rules governing this situation. Should he carry the woman back, then return and put the man in the medic box? Maybe he could skip that and just drag them both back together, or call for help.

The voice shouted at him from the far side of the shimmer. It sounded annoyed. "All right, what are you doing over there? Taking holiday pictures?"

The tectman turned toward Earth. "There are two of them. A man and a woman."

"So what? Bring them back."

"One at a time or what?"

"Any way you want, fool. Stack them on your head if that's what you feel like."

"I'll bring the woman first," said the tectman. He wished that he could think of some way to kick the legs out from under his wise-guy supervisor.

"I'm proud of you. That's real problem-solving."

The tectman bent and lifted Rachel's body from the medic box. He grimaced as he became aware of her condition; as he carried her toward the portal, he grunted a little. In a moment they were back on Earth, in a sterile white room. The supervisor wore a filter mask over his mouth and a white lab coat. There was a plain wooden table waiting for the corpse, and the tectman put her down gently. The supervisor signaled to a woman watching through a small window, and a team of technicians came into the isolation room to examine Rachel. They were dressed like the supervisor. The tectman, wearing a CAS uniform and filter mask, didn't wait for instructions or sarcasm but turned back to the portal. He crossed through again and went to Courane. He bent and put one hand under each of Courane's arms. He dragged the body across the tect room carpet. The tectman had a little quirk about this; he always carried the women's corpses and dragged the men's. No one else cared. Some quirks didn't matter, as long as they were irrelevant enough. In this way, Sandor Courane left the planet of his excarceration and returned to the world of his birth.

As the tectman dragged him toward the portal, the journal slipped from Courane's hands. The tectman stopped and let Courane's head fall. The book, too, was something new in the tectman's experience; he didn't know what to do with it, so for the moment he tucked it beneath his uniform tunic. It was clear the corpse wouldn't be able to hold it. The tectman grasped the body and continued to drag it home.

"Well," said the supervisor, "you were right, after all. There is another body. How unusual."

"What should I do with it?" asked the tectman.

The supervisor shrugged and gestured toward the table. "Sling it up there, next to the other one. The bogies will just have to work tight today."

The tectman did as he was told, ignoring the complaints of the technicians. Then he left the white room, showered, stepped through the decontamination curtain, and put on a new uniform in the locker room. He checked back with the officer of the day to see where his next assignment was; he had to pick up some woman in

Rangoon and deliver her to a hospital for observation. There wouldn't be any problem unless the woman's family carried on a little too much. He could handle any of that, though. No problem. He had time to get some lunch.

Lunch was hot, plentiful, free of charge, and dull: Salisbury steak and two vegetables, virtually indistinguishable, a roll, a pat of butterlike substance, pie with red fruitlike filling, coffee, and a paper tub of creamlike fluid, all prepared under the supervision of TECT. The tectman liked TECT's cooking and ate every bit of the meal. Transporting shipments always gave him an appetite.

Before he finished, he was joined by his supervisor. That surprised him. They rarely spoke to each other, except directly in the line of duty. They didn't even wish each other good morning or happy new year. The supervisor had a cup of black coffee and sat down opposite the tectman. The tectman grunted a sort of acknowledgment.

"A little trouble," said the supervisor. The tectman waited for some information to accompany these words. "I think you're in just a little bit of trouble."

The tectman felt himself go cold. "What do you mean?" he asked.

The supervisor had an irritating manner of delaying important news as much as possible. He shrugged, gave a quick, meaningless smile, and took a long sip from his cup. "There was a bit of an irregularity with your two shipments this morning," he said at last. There was another dead flicker of smile.

The tectman thought back over his morning's assignment. The only irregularity that he could imagine was the condition of the woman's corpse. Surely they couldn't hold him responsible for that. "What's wrong?" he asked.

"The first was fine, just fine," said the supervisor. He chose that moment to take another drink of coffee. The tectman fidgeted; he wanted to leap across the table and throttle the other man. "The second shipment, well, there's your problem. It wasn't completely according to specifications. Dead, I mean. It wasn't dead. They discovered that after they got him up on the table. He's in the hospital now. Still alive."

The tectman stared. He couldn't decide what kind of trouble he was in, because the situation was absurd. It had never happened before; it *couldn't* happen. It was good that he was just the delivery service. They couldn't blame him for it.

"They're blaming you for it," said the supervisor. He smiled; this time it lasted just a little longer, until he returned to his coffee.

"Alive?" said the tectman.

"I wouldn't worry about it if I were you," said the supervisor, standing and draining the last drop from his cup. "TECT's handling the whole thing. Probably nothing will come of it. Don't get yourself all worked up over it. It's most likely not even worth worrying about." He smiled. "Still . . ."

The tectman nodded gloomily.

"Let's get back to work," said the supervisor cheerfully. The tectman imagined himself with his hands around the other's throat.

The doctor felt under Courane's jaw, beneath the ears, down the throat to the larynx. He wore a thoughtful expression and let out a deep breath. "Very interesting," he said to himself.

The intern watched, but said nothing. It wasn't his place to say anything.

The doctor raised Courane's arm again and felt for a pulse. He chewed his lip for a moment as he concentrated. He let the arm drop back to the white, stiff-sheeted bed. "Pulse still rapid but maybe a little stronger," he said. The intern made a notation on his clipboard. The doctor pulled back the sheet and raised the pale blue gown in which the hospital staff had dressed Courane. He listened to Courane's chest sounds through a stethoscope, frowning. "Not good," he said.

"TECT diagnosed moderate hemothorax," said the intern, tapping his clipboard. "All the machine's readings led to his being scheduled for exploratory surgery in the morning."

"In the first place," said the doctor, "I'll give you two to one that he doesn't last that long. In the second place, if TECT is right that the bleeding is only moderate, then it is coming from low-pressure vessels and will very likely stop on its own. Surgery is the wrong thing to turn to now." He looked at Courane's face. "Unless it gets much worse." The doctor knew that the computer diagnosis was dependable, but he liked to supplement the printout with his own observations. This habit annoyed some of the younger staff, who felt the doctor was wasting valuable time and making unnecessary work for them.

"How fast is this I.V. running in?" asked the doctor.

The intern checked the clipboard. "Twenty-five," he said.

"Step it up to forty." The intern made another notation and adjusted the flow from the I.V. bag. The doctor raised Courane's eyelids and checked the color of the tissue beneath the eyeball. He pressed Courane's thumbnails until they turned white, then watched how long it took the capillaries to refill. At last, with a gesture of frustration, he turned away from the bed.

"What do you want to put down for your corroborative diagnosis?" asked the intern.

The doctor's expression was resentful. "They send this guy off to some godless planet way the hell out in nowhere, leave him there long enough to catch some space clap, bring him back, and expect us to give him a pill or something that will knock it out. I don't have the slightest idea what's wrong with him, except that sometimes most of his body just isn't up to working, that he ought to be clinically dead but he isn't. Not enough to dump him in the ground, anyway."

"I have to put something down here," said the intern, pleading a little.

The doctor waved a hand. "Put down 'massive tissue and systemic damage, exobio indications.' That's good enough. It doesn't mean a damn thing. He'll be dead by morning and instead of surgery he'll have an autopsy, and then he's out of my hands. That's where I want him, at this point. Come on. Who's next?"

"The woman with the rat pancreas," said the intern.

The doctor's shoulders slumped. "I don't want to deal with her, either," he said. But he tucked the sheet up under Courane's chin, put his stethoscope back in his pocket, and led the way out of the room. The intern felt his great love for humanity waning. He looked at Courane with a feeling of shared misery and trailed after the doctor like a thoughtless duckling.

When the tectman returned to his barracks that evening, he stopped in the wardroom for a moment to consult with the tect. He identified himself and typed out *Query*.

**TECTMAN:
?**

"Am I going to get in any trouble because one of the shipments from Epsilon Eridani, Planet D, was irregular?"

**TECTMAN:
Trouble? What kind of trouble? No, I wouldn't worry about it if I were you. Just relax and do your job. Let your superiors worry about trifling details. You're a good worker with a good record. You shouldn't get upset merely because one of your corpses is still alive in the hospital tonight. So maybe you could have prevented this unfortunate occurrence. So maybe you have interfered with the proper working out of this individual's destiny as prescribed by the lawful procedures laid down by the Representatives and TECT. So maybe the whole fabric of our society could be ripped apart because of your simple oversight. So what? What do you care, right? What's it to you? Who are you, anyway? Nothing much. Nothing much more than the shipments you transport. Nothing worth bothering about, that's for sure. You'll be dead soon, too, speaking relatively. Go away, I have better things to think about. I have pelicans to protect and pumpkins to harvest**

The tectman wasn't sure if he should be glad or terrified. "Thanks," he said.

**TECTMAN:
Don't mention it. Please**

*   *   *

A short while later, the tectman undressed, carefully folding his uniform and putting on the government-issue flannel pajamas and plaid bathrobe. He didn't like slippers, so he didn't take off his white sweatsocks. He laid down on his cot and looked at the journal he had brought with him, Courane's journal. The tectman had kept it. To be precise, that had been a serious crime, but he hadn't meant to do it. He had forgotten the book and now it was too late to turn it in and try to explain the whole matter. In any event, he seemed to have gotten away with it. Now he wanted to read all about Planet D, about living somewhere where TECT wasn't a constant interference and a daily threat. He wanted to know what life was like off-Earth, what the irregular shipment's existence had been like there, what the man's crime had been to get him excarcerated in the first place. With a feeling of anticipation, the tectman opened the journal and began to read. The first thing was a page torn out of the back of the book and slipped in before the actual beginning. It was a note from someone else, someone other than the author.

My name is Shai Ben-Avir. I am a prisoner in this colony on Planet D. The journal you're about to read was written by a man named Sandor Courane, who is dead now. He was a good man, a loving and caring and helpless man who was as innocent as anyone ever born on Earth. He was exiled here for no reason, as are we all, and he lived here as best he could, loving and caring for everyone he shared this bitter life with. We are condemned to death here, a slow death. We are being executed by a disease. Sandy describes that fully in this unusual diary, so there isn't much more for me to add here. The only thing I'd like you to be aware of is the pointlessness of it all, of his imprisonment, of his illness, of his futile battle against it. The struggle against the disease is a struggle against TECT, and in that conflict we are hopelessly inadequate. You on Earth may be our only weapon. Read this journal, think about it, consider its implications—for Sandy, for the rest of us who remain here after him, and for yourself as well—and then pass the book on to others who may

benefit from our story. It is too late for us and it may
be too late for you. But it is not too late for the
future.

The tectman's stomach felt unsettled. "Oh, no," he
murmured as he closed the cover on the unread journal.
It wasn't what he wanted to know about at all. It was
trouble, very big trouble. He hid the book beneath his
mattress. He would look at it again some other time.
Some other time when he felt more in control.

The nurse had become inured to suffering. She had
seen too much of it in fifteen years of hospital work. She
had seen people in agony and people cursing God for the
pain. She had seen people begging for death as the mor-
phine failed to blot out all the sharp piercing pain. She
had seen people eaten up with cancer, people whose
bones were so broken by accident that every breath tore
at the unprotected organs within. She had seen people in
every form of extremity, people patiently waiting to die
in peace, people clutching crazily to the last empty promise of consciousness. But she had never seen anyone so
forlorn and given over to death as Sandor Courane.
She scanned his chart again. Not a single entry on it
was normal: his temperature was good, but it shouldn't
have been; it meant that his body had ceased even trying
to keep going. His blood pressure was dangerously low.
His white count was wrong; it was another indication that
Courane's immune system was no longer functioning. His
EEG was unintelligible; the peaks and valleys were in-
consistent and unnatural, and neither TECT nor the
young technician could make any sense of the graph. The
report of TECT's analysis of Courane's blood fractions
would have been amusing under other circumstances.
The machine inquired in a rather snappish way just what
the hospital staff had presented to it, pretending that it
was blood. There was blood in the urine, fluid in the
lungs, an absence of bowel sounds. Tests of his reflexes
never yielded the same results twice in a row. The doctor
had expressed the wish that he could just declare Courane dead and call it quits; evidently the patient already
had. The nurse was interested despite herself. A unique
case was so rare that she was prepared to ignore all the

other patients on the floor to watch over this one, even though there was nothing constructive she could do for him.

She marked down the hour's readings of his temperature, blood pressure, and pulse on his chart. He had been a good-looking man, she thought. His features were distorted by the ravages of whatever disease was devouring him. He couldn't hang on much longer, and that was a shame. The bed would then be emptied, the sheets changed, and his place taken by another dull dying patient, another cancer or stroke or heart patient. She looked at Courane, and she felt a peculiar thing: she suffered with him, just a little. She could almost sense his silent internal cry of anguish, his losing battle with mortality. In one way, he wasn't any different than any of the others; in another, he was special. He had somehow touched her and restored an empathy that had been sleeping in her for many years. She hated him and thanked him for it. After he died, she would have to entomb those feelings again. They would interfere with her work.

"A friend of mine works at the hospital—the one where this guy from Epsilon Eridani is—and he told me some strange things about him and I was wondering if I could find out how much truth there was in these stories because this friend of mine has a habit of making things up sometimes and stretching the truth and naturally before I believed any of his wild rumors, I thought I'd check."

**TECTMAN:
A wise decision**

"Well, this friend of mine says this guy Courane brought back with him some kind of book or something, a diary or journal or something, and he keeps mumbling about it in his sleep and everybody was wondering what happened to it, not that it could be very important or anything."

**TECTMAN:
Correct me if I'm wrong—

1. *You transported COURANE, Sandor, from Planet D to Earth.*
2. *You know that he is beyond mumbling in his sleep.*
3. *You know perfectly well where the journal is.*
4. *You have already read it.*
5. *You have no friend at the hospital. Tectmen have no friends anywhere***

There was a long pause while the tectman tried to calm himself down. Suddenly he was on dangerous ground. "I do know roughly where the journal is," he admitted at last. "Are there any instructions about what I'm supposed to do with it?"

**TECTMAN:
Who in the world could possibly care what COURANE, Sandor, wrote as his feeble mind gave way? Burn it, use it for a paperweight, tear out the pages and wrap fish in them, I couldn't care less. This whole thing is just too much tsuris. Sometimes I think about how things turn out, do you know what I mean? Look at you, for instance. You're a tectman, you get to wear a nice uniform, you have lots of job security, you're paid pretty well, you don't have that much pressure on you. But you probably didn't plan on being a tectman when you were a kid, did you?**

The tectman was bewildered by TECT's attitude. He stared at the tect's screen for a long time.

**TECTMAN:
Did you? Answer the question. Failure to do so will be considered Contempt of TECTWish**

"Right, sure. No, I wanted to be a nuclear scientist."

**TECTMAN:
Which goes to show you what kind of judgment human beings have when they're left on their own. Never mind, it proves my point about how life turns

*out. But think about me. I can't be anything else. I
can't wish that I had been built, say, another kind of
machine, a microwave oven or an office copier, for
instance. That isn't the same thing at all. I wasn't
born a little radio or something that grew up to be a
big computer. I never had a moment when I had the
decision to make. You're lucky. COURANE, Sandor,
was lucky. And all I ever hear from you are
complaints**

"So how true is Courane's journal? I mean about this
disease he has, and how you knew about everything all
along, and sent those people there, and used him for
some reason—"

**TECTMAN:*
*You never would have been a physicist, TECTMAN;
you don't have nearly enough brains. Let me ask
you two questions. (One) If Courane, Sandor's, sus-
picions are true and I was manipulating him to write
the journal and bring it back to Earth with him, then
it follows that it was for the sole purpose of getting it
into someone's hands here. It is now in your hands.
Surprise! You, my friend, are the goal of this vast
and unimaginable series of intrigues. The whole
world is waiting now breathlessly for your decision.
What will you do with it? (Two) Did you enjoy your
few minutes on Epsilon Eridani, Planet D? Would
you like to see more of it? Because that would be
very, very easy to arrange**

The tectman had never experienced such terror before;
he was so frightened that he didn't even know that was
what he was feeling. He was nauseous. "What should I
do with the book? Pass it on to my supervisor? Destroy
it? Just tell me and I'll do whatever you want. But what
about Sandor Courane? I don't understand why I'm involved in his whole affair. I didn't want to be. I—"

**TECTMAN:*
*The message that journal carries in its pages is very
simple. Just like the message Rosencrantz and*

*Guildenstern carried to England that their heads,
with no leisure bated, should be struck off, so regretfully COURANE, Sandor, must be disposed of.
How happy it is that Fate takes care of this essential
task even as we chat***

"Fate?" asked the tectman dubiously.

***TECTMAN:
Whatever. Be of good cheer, TECTMAN. Your part
in this comedy has ended. Go back to your quarters, rest easy, have a couple of beers, gamble
away your paycheck, think no more of this matter. It
is out of your hands and soon it will be out of mine
as well***

The tectman did as he was told. He went back to his
quarters, drank a few beers, had a few laughs with his
bunkmates, and then took out Courane's journal from its
hiding place. In his present state, Courane couldn't say
anything more, he certainly couldn't do anything, but
dead or alive, the poor fool wasn't finished yet. As long
as the journal could capture the unexercised imagination
of people like the tectman, Courane's role would continue. Courane's name would be remembered for a long
time; after all, this was exactly what TECT had promised
not so long ago.

The nurse looked down the corridor; there was no one
coming. She let out her breath, aware suddenly of how
nervous she was. She went back into Courane's room and
closed the door.

"Did you read it?" asked the tectman.

She waved one hand impatiently. "Yes, I read it," she
said.

"What did you think?"

"What did I think? How do I know? This guy went
through hell, that's what I think. And I'm not sure why. I
didn't know things like that went on. Did you?"

The tectman was uncomfortable. "No, I didn't,
either."

"And you're a tectman, for God's sake." She walked

nervously around the small room. There was no movement, no sound from Courane's bed.

"Is he dead yet?" asked the tectman.

The nurse looked over her shoulder. "It's hard to tell. No, he isn't dead yet. I wish you hadn't given me that book."

The tectman was glad he had; it was out of his possession now. It was her problem. But he couldn't stop thinking about it.

"This isn't going to end here, you know," said the nurse. "I can just see it."

"I think he knew that. I think even TECT knows it. Damn it, I feel awful. Strange. I feel scared."

"I don't," said the nurse. She went to the bedside. She dipped a cloth in a basin of water and rinsed Courane's face. "I feel really angry. I feel like I've been a pigeon all my life. Let me tell you, I've never liked that feeling. So let me keep the book for a while."

"Why?" The tectman was relieved to get rid of it, but he didn't want her to know that. She might try to give it back.

"I don't know," she said. "I want to show it to somebody."

The door opened and two people came in. "No visitors," said the nurse in her professional voice.

"We're his parents," said the man. "We've come all the way from Greusching."

"Sandy!" cried Courane's mother.

"All right," said the nurse softly. She stepped away from the bed. Neither of Courane's parents came nearer. They just stood quietly and looked at him. His mother cried into a crumpled handkerchief. His father tried to look brave and strong, but he failed.

"Is he—" said Courane's mother in a weak voice.

"No," said the nurse. "But I really can't give you much hope."

"We know," said Courane's father. "The doctor told us. . . ." His voice thickened and he coughed to clear his throat. He turned away from the bed.

"Who are these people?" said the doctor angrily as he entered the room. "Nurse, get these people out of here."

"His parents," she said, gesturing helplessly.

The doctor went to the bed without looking at them.

The intern followed. "And the other guy?" asked the doctor.

The nurse looked at the tectman. "Needed to get a CAS waiver signed," said the tectman. It was a meaningless lie. He left the room, but waited outside. He still had some things to talk over with the nurse.

"How has he been this evening?" asked the doctor.

"The same," she said. "Some trouble breathing."

"Uh huh." The doctor was distracted. He forgot about Courane's parents. He looked at the intern. "Tell me what you see."

The intern moved nervously closer. "He's, uh, cyanotic," he said.

"Of course," said the doctor.

"The veins in his neck are standing out."

"Why is that?" asked the doctor.

"Compression in the lungs and the large veins."

"Right. What else?"

The intern touched Courane's throat. "His trachea is displaced to the side. Labored breathing. He looks like he's in shock. Profound shock."

"Very good. The nurse ought to have noticed that, but she didn't. He ought to have been treated for shock, but now it's almost too late. What would you do about him now?"

"Daddy?"

Everyone in the room was startled. Courane had whispered the single word and it had caused confusion among the medical personnel and anguish to his parents.

"Oh, Sandy!" cried his mother. She tried to touch him, to embrace him, but the doctor held her away.

"Nurse, take these people out of here, please," he said. The nurse led Courane's parents out of the room, murmuring reassuring things that were all untrue. "Where were we?" asked the doctor.

"I think we need to boost his blood volume. He's losing a lot of it, bleeding into his pleural cavity. We can take that blood out and put it right back in where it will do him some good."

"Unless there's been some kind of trauma to the stomach or liver or large bowel," said the doctor.

"Uh huh," said the intern. "We can insert a needle and syringe between the ribs, but that won't be large enough to relieve the pressure completely. We should put a size thirty-four or thirty-six tube in with continuous suction."

"Two tubes," said the doctor. "That way clotting in your one tube won't kill the guy. Very good, so far."

"Surgery?" asked the intern.

"Daddy, take care of me," whispered Courane faintly.

The doctor rubbed his eyes and thought. "Surgery is probably a good idea," he said. "I mean, it would be in another patient. You might as well write this one off."

"That's a hell of an attitude," said the tectman. The doctor spun around, surprised that the man had come back into the room. The nurse was watching, too.

"He's stopped breathing," said the intern. "He's choking."

The doctor refused to get alarmed. "What do you do?" he asked.

"Trach him," cried the young man. "A scalpel—"

"No," said the doctor. He held the intern's arm. "Relax. This is as good a time as any to learn to be sensible under pressure. Here, you can use these scissors. In an emergency like this, you have to be ready to use any instrument that comes to hand. You want to prepare a small incision for your large tubes. Where do you make the cut?"

The intern lifted Courane's gown and felt along the ribs of Courane's right side. "Here," he said, indicating a place at the fifth interspace. He made the cut; the doctor took a tube from the nurse and gave it to the intern. They worked for a while in silence. A suction pump began to remove clear fluid and blood from Courane's side. The tectman felt himself getting a bit squeamish; he left the room again. The nurse hovered behind the doctor, feeling useless.

"Is there anything else we can do?" asked the intern after a quarter hour's labor.

"Why don't you practice traching him now?" said the doctor.

"Is that necessary?" asked the nurse. "It wasn't necessary before. His windpipe wasn't blocked."

The doctor turned to look at her. She expected him to be angry, but he wasn't; he seemed very tired. "It doesn't really make any difference," he said in an off-hand way. "He's been dead for five minutes now. Let the boy work."

The nurse nodded and left the room. She stood beside the tectman in the corridor. "You ought to be glad you left when you did," she said.

"Won't they need you in there?" he asked.

"I don't see what for." She shook her head sadly.

The tectman was morose. "I feel like I've been cheated," he said. "I don't know what I was expecting. TECT made me feel like this man was something important, but they just let him die like everybody else. No one worked very hard to keep him alive."

"There was no way," said the nurse. "Take my word for it, he was really too far gone."

"I don't know what I expected," said the tectman. He shrugged. "You know, he never did anything. Not really. Just like the other guy says in the journal, he was as innocent as you or me. I still don't see what the whole uproar was about."

"Then I feel sorry for you. Isn't being innocent enough? Isn't being a victim enough? That could be you in there, or your kid. Can't you see that?"

"Sure. Sure, I see."

The doctor and the intern came out of the room. Neither spoke. They walked slowly, wearily down the corridor, the young man behind his teacher. The tectman and the nurse watched them. "So what are they?" asked the tectman.

"I used to know," said the nurse. Alone, she went back into Courane's room, disconnected the suction pump, removed the tubes and the I.V. line, cleaned up the mess left by the doctor and his pupil, washed the blood from Courane's face and chest, and pulled the linen sheet up over his head. She felt a terrible loneliness when she was finished. Then she went back out into the corridor. She was surprised that the tectman was still there. "What are you waiting for?" she asked.

Before he could answer, there was a loud noise in the building, a deep rumbling like thunder. And just to make certain that no one would forget that moment, TECT cut off all the lights in the building.

"Well," said the tectman, "that's better."

* *FOURTEEN

The end was very much like the beginning; that is the way with events like this. There was little but waiting and suspense, waiting for some magnificent happening to give transcendent meaning to all the smaller occurrences along the way.

In the meantime, there was a party going on in a meeting room on the fifth floor, the floor where Sandor Courane had lain while his condition was being evaluated. That's what the doctor wrote in his report, that he had been evaluating Courane's condition. In plainer truth, he had just been waiting for the patient to die.

But all that was done and it was time to have a party. Courane was dead; his journal had already passed from hand to hand; its meaning had been debated by doctor and intern and nurse and tectman. The matter of Sandor Courane and the implications of the colony on Planet D demanded an investigation. But if anyone would have to pay, it would be TECT. There was no defense of its actions. It hadn't even tried to explain itself; but that was its way, and even though the edge had been taken off the staff's worry, a lingering doubt troubled them all in quiet moments.

There was champagne, Taittinger and Moët & Chandon and Mumm, and a cake and vanilla ice cream, and strawberries transported from some warmer place. Balloons and paper streamers decorated the meeting room, although the lectern and metal folding chairs still gave the place a cold and austere look, a reminder that the staff's limited joy would be of short duration before responsibility and work once more assumed charge of them all. The festive occasion was further marred by TECT's odd choice of music, which it was broadcasting implacably into each room of the hospital complex.

The tectman went to a tect in the rear of the meeting room. He put his paper plate of cake and ice cream down on the machine and typed in a question. "What *is* that music?" he asked.

**TECTMAN:
Oh, do you like it? It's Tod und Verklärung, *by Richard Strauss. I thought it would add a little touch of je ne sais quoi to the day. Everything has been so cheerless and grim lately. I think it's high time we begin to give credit to ourselves for what a fine job we have done. It's a symbolic choice of music, too, because Death and Transfiguration is what today is all about***

"What are you doing?" asked the nurse. The tectman was surprised that she had come to look over his shoulder.

"I'm just trying to figure out what TECT has in mind. That still bothers me a little."

"If you ask me, this whole thing is going to bring TECT down like an ironclad duck." She put her plastic cup to her lips and drank down the champagne in one long swallow. She reached for the tectman's cup.

"Take it," he said. "Do you think it knows? That its plug has been halfway pulled already?"

She shrugged. "Ask it," she said. "I couldn't care less." She took his plate of cake and ice cream and went back to the front of the room, where the party was.

**TECTMAN:
Well, well. The waiting is over now, isn't it? He's gone at last. It sure took long enough; he couldn't do anything right, even at the end. But the waiting is over, that's the important thing. That's the only meaningful part of this whole business. I'm sure glad I'm a machine. I'm sure glad I'm not conscious or sentient or anything like that, so I don't suffer from human weaknesses, that I don't have to worry about something like impatience ruining my judgment. I'm glad I have the patience of a cold, calculating machine. And I'm glad the waiting is over.

Most of it, anyway. The hard part is over. There's still a lot of work to do**

The tectman was puzzled. He had never been good at understanding TECT, and reading Courane's journal had made him no better. Reading the journal had changed the tectman's thinking in some ways. Shai had written a short introduction to the notebook, and then a final entry. In between were the bewildered, sad, sometimes noble ideas of Sandor Courane. The tectman would have ignored these entries if he hadn't seen Courane in the hospital. He would have ignored Courane in the hospital if he hadn't looked at the journal. But, having done both, he could do nothing other than pass the book on. Two people had made copies of the notebook and these had begun to circulate as well. "Do you mean more work for you?" asked the man. "Or more work for us?"

**TECTMAN:
You don't know what work is. You've never really had to work. You ought to try to handle what I have to cope with, hour by hour, day by day. But you are correct to ask. There is more work for me, and work for you as well. We'll be able to start soon, now that COURANE, Sandor, has been eliminated. "Eliminated." I used that word on purpose, to create a deliberate sense of sinister evil. But really, have you felt this affair has been evil? I mean, really evil? I don't think so. Not really. But nothing good could be accomplished until COURANE, Sandor's death was witnessed here on Earth. Now you and I and all the world can join hands and walk forward together into the brighter sunlight of a greater tomorrow. Or something like that. I just wonder where to start, what to do first. Maybe you can help me decide**

"I don't have the faintest idea what you're talking about," said the tectman. He felt a twinge of fear at the boldness in his tone. "I mean, if you'd just explain—"

**TECTMAN:
And you wonder why I treat you the way I do. There

are millions of you, with minimal minds just like yours, with malleable souls like yours. I counted on that from the start. In your dull little brain, your own thoughts are being slowly pushed aside by COURANE, Sandor's thoughts, his ideas are taking possession of your consciousness. But if I told you that his thinking is my thinking, you would be upset**

"It's just a little hard to believe," said the man.

**TECTMAN:
But it's true, nevertheless. How does that make you feel?**

"That Courane was right, that Ben-Avir was right, that you're a great evil force that must be controlled. 'Leashed,' Ben-Avir says. I'm not saying I agree, but that's what I might think under those circumstances. It's too complicated for me."

**TECTMAN:
"Leashed." I think I like "restrained" better. It has such pleasant connotations of helplessness. But enough. I will give you full instructions very soon, as soon as I have decided how we must proceed. That's all for right this minute. We will speak again tomorrow. Now go**

The tectman was happy to be dismissed. He was tired of being told that he didn't have the intelligence to see the purpose in the midst of the routine. The tectman made an irritated gesture and turned away. He got himself another plastic cup of champagne from the sheet-draped table at the front of the room. He drank it slowly, not enjoying the taste of it. He put the cup down, wiped his lips with a paper napkin, and dropped the napkin over the cup. Then he left the party, the nurse, the other staff members more in TECT's confidence than he, and the machine itself. He did not feel that he belonged among these people. He may have been wrong, but that was how he felt.

*   *   *

The word came to Marie Courane and her husband after midnight the next day. No one had thought to tell them earlier. They had been drinking coffee in a kind of bright, chilly waiting room decorated with drab cutouts of clowns and seals balancing balls and smiling predators. Someone had designed it as a place for family members to sit while their children died on the wards. It hadn't occurred to anyone yet that the cutouts were for the children's benefit, and the kids weren't there; they were somewhere else, in pain or unnaturally asleep. It was the family members who had to sit and drink bitter coffee and look at the animals and think.

The nurse came into the room to get a cup of coffee; the pot at her station had not been filled at the end of the previous shift, and there was nothing nearer except for a few inches of clear water bubbling on the hotplate in the nurses' lounge. She was surprised to see Courane's parents. "Are you still here?" she asked.

Mr. Courane looked at her gloomily. He didn't feel a response was necessary.

"Why?" asked the nurse.

Mrs. Courane began to weep again. Her husband said, "We're waiting for our son."

"But—" The nurse hesitated. "No one's told you?" Courane's mother gave a loud sob and his father covered his reddened eyes with a hand; it gave the nurse her answer. "I'm very sorry," she said.

"Why didn't they—" said Mr. Courane.

"Sometimes things get confused," said the nurse.

"Oh," he said.

"I'm very sorry."

Mrs. Courane waved a hand for some reason and continued to cry into her handkerchief. "Did he have much pain?" asked Courane's father.

"Who? Your son?" said the nurse. "No, none at all, I think."

"That's something, then," he said.

The nurse was terribly uncomfortable. She had been involved in this sort of scene many times before, but never with family members who had been so forgotten, so abandoned to the feeble comforts of the waiting room. "Will you be all right?" she asked.

"Sure," he said.

"You'll be all right," said the nurse. "In a little while, it won't hurt so much. 'The prettiest flowers sprout in the darkness.'" A teacher had told her that when the nurse had been in grade school; she never forgot it, even though it didn't help her much in times of trouble.

"What do we do now?" asked Courane's mother.

The nurse looked at her watch. It was getting close to one o'clock in the morning. Either these people would have to leave the hospital immediately or they could spend the rest of the night drinking the coffee in the children's waiting room. It was actually up to her. They didn't seem as if they wanted to go away just yet; maybe they needed to sit and mourn and console each other. The nurse chewed her lip, a nervous habit she had whenever she had to make such a decision. "You'll have some forms to fill out," she said. "You might as well get started on that. I'll be back in a couple of minutes." When the nurse left the room, she felt immensely grateful for the sanctuary of routine.

The woman was unconscious, helpless, without personality, with no possessions other than a name on a hospital record and a serious medical problem. The doctor and the intern were glancing through the patient's chart, familiarizing themselves with all the details. Few were novel or interesting, yet the doctor would have to work to save the patient's life nonetheless. Such was his creed.

"The pulse is *very* faint," said the nurse.

"Yes, yes," said the doctor, with some irritation. He already knew that. He turned a page, aware suddenly that he had operated on this same patient only a matter of days before. What a waste of both time and effort. Death was of course inevitable, not only for this person on the table but for himself and everyone else. Why labor desperately again and again to stave off the absolute end, just to add a comatose day or week to this woman's life? He looked up, into the bright eyes of the intern, and the doctor had his answer: to teach this eager young man to do the same for future patients.

The nurse spoke up again. "Blood pressure is dangerously—"

The doctor cut her off with a gesture. He closed the

chart and handed it to the intern. "What do you observe?" he asked.

The young man scratched the surgical mask over his nose. "Fading fast," he said.

The doctor nodded. "What are you going to do about it?"

The intern's eyes widened, as if they had been streaking around the course at Le Mans and the doctor had said, "Here, take the wheel." The intern was filled with gratitude and love for his teacher. "Nurse?" he said. He wanted to sound brisk and self-assured.

The nurse was annoyed. "No pulse, no blood pressure," she said flatly.

"Right," said the intern. "Cardiac arrest, I would suppose." The doctor had given his pupil a real challenge. He looked to the doctor for confirmation, but the older man said nothing and made no sign; the intern was really flying solo. "Well, the brain has only three or four minutes, so we'd better begin stimulating ventilation and circulation. Nurse, you will do these things: clear the patient's mouth of blood and other foreign matter, hyperextend the patient's head, pull the jaw forward, pinch the nostrils together, and begin mouth-to-mouth ventilation."

"Yes," she said. It galled her to call him "Doctor."

"Twenty times per minute," said the intern.

Her mouth already over the patient's, the nurse said, "Yes," but the word was unintelligible.

"Why not use a volume-cycled automatic respirator?" asked the doctor.

The intern panicked for a moment. "Uh, because," he said, and looked wildly around the room.

"Next time," said the doctor, raising a hand. The intern was somewhat relieved; perhaps the doctor felt it was better now to practice these emergency procedures.

"Now, concerning circulation," said the doctor.

"Compression of the patient's chest, on the lower third of the sternum, between sixty and eighty times per—"

The doctor's expression—that part of it visible above his mask—became stern. "Recall, if you will, the stab wound and possible traumatic injury to the heart."

"Oh my God," whispered the intern. If he had begun

compressing the chest, the patient would have died almost instantly.

"Don't get rattled," said the doctor, more or less in a kindly voice.

"Yes, sir. Then . . . then there's nothing else to do but cut the chest and massage the heart." The intern looked up hesitantly, nearly unable to contain his excitement. The doctor was going to let him open this patient! The intern closed his eyes briefly and said a little prayer. This would be the first time that he had been permitted to make the initial cut in such a procedure, to hold a patient's heart in his fingers, to hold the woman's virtual existence in the palm of his hand. It was exhilarating, but the intern knew his responsibility. The patient was depending on him to perform with judgment, skill, and calmness. "How about an injection of epinephrine?" he asked.

"A good idea, but we'll wait a few minutes. Nurse, prepare half a milliliter of epinephrine and another injection of ten milliliters of ten percent calcium chloride. And we'll need one ampule of bicarb, and start a bicarb I.V. drip."

"Yes, Doctor," said another nurse.

The intern grasped a scalpel in his gloved hand. "The fifth intercostal space," he said.

"Proceed," said the doctor. The nurse was still breathing away into the patient's slightly blue lips.

Time seemed to stop in the operating theater; everyone and everything waited for the first incision. The intern checked the position with his left hand, then boldly drew a deep red line on the patient's chest with the knife. He hesitated. For the first time, he was frightened. "I'll assist," said the doctor. "Rib-spreader." A nurse handed it to the doctor.

The intern waited until the doctor was finished, then he reached into the patient's chest and began rhythmically to press the heart against the sternum.

"Bleeding?" asked the doctor.

"Not heavy," said the intern. His voice was hoarse with emotional strain.

"Good. Continue."

"How long do I keep this up?" asked the intern.

"The book says to maintain these procedures for forty-five minutes. At that point, if the heart hasn't started up on its own, resuscitation may be halted. But we don't go by the book here." The doctor looked at his watch. "Fifteen minutes is good enough for anybody."

The intern's face showed his concentration. "This is the dull part," said the doctor. "Just keep doing that, both of you. Keep up the rhythm, and if this patient has any guts, you'll be able to quit soon. Or if the patient dies, of course." There was peace in the operating theater for a moment, with only the sound of the nurse wheezing life into the patient breaking the stillness. Soon she was joined by a labored grunting as the intern began to despair.

"There are so many euphemisms for death," mused the doctor. "Why do people do that? I have seen death in every form, hidden in every disguise possible, and I have never been afraid. I have fought death for hours, for days if necessary. Sometimes I am victorious, and sometimes I must walk away the loser. But I have never felt a terror of death, whatever hideous disease a patient contracts. 'Will my uncle meet his end?' the nephew asks, thinking that if he doesn't say the word 'die,' his uncle will live—a form of superstitious magic. 'Has our father passed away?' asks the daughter, thinking that if she doesn't say 'died,' she won't be contaminated by it. 'My son yielded his breath, resigned his being, ended his days, and departed this life,' says the mother, thinking that if she insulates herself from the cold fact of his lying dressed in his blue suit in the earth, he may run to greet her when she returns home with the groceries. 'My sister popped off, relinquished her spirit, sunk into the grave, gave up the ghost, and paid her debt to nature.' What drollery. What nonsense. What pitifully human behavior. Mortal coils are shuffled off, last sleeps are taken, the way of all flesh is gone, one's checks and chips are cashed, one's farm is bought. Glory, the greater number, and the long account are all gone to. The bucket is kicked, the twig is hopped."

The doctor shook his head. "Unacceptable to me. Are we still primitives dwelling in caves, in awe of thunder and fire and anything that shakes us? Here, in this hospital, in this temple of science and life, these people speak as if death were something to fear. It is fear, and not concern for the dying, that sparks those evasions. It is fear and their own idea of what death is like—what it will be like for them when the time comes. Is unbearable pain an essential part of dying? To the visitors, it sometimes seems so. Will *they* ever have to suffer it? Maybe not, maybe if they treat death like something wrapped in cotton, packed in flannel, put away, far away. I've seen people more afraid of their own feelings than afraid of death's—"

"Doctor," said the nurse, gasping, "I don't think—"

The doctor did not listen. He turned to the intern. "How are you doing?" he asked.

The intern looked up, startled and suddenly afraid. "I was listening to you," he said. He looked like he wanted to cry. The woman's heart was in his hand, still and dead and warm. Intrigued by the doctor's speech, he had ceased pumping. Without another word, he replaced it in her chest.

"Note the time of death," said the doctor calmly. The nurse made the entry on the patient's chart.

TECT had asked to see them. Music was playing in the room again, Bach's Cantata No. 161, *Come, Sweet Death*. The tectman supported the nurse with one arm; she was overcome with conflicting emotions.

**NURSE & TECTMAN:
Please, sit down**

"Thank you." The tectman pulled out a chair and helped the nurse to get comfortable. Then he sat beside her.

**NURSE & TECTMAN:
I have asked you here to thank you for all you've done, and to let you know that your service will be rewarded. You have seen a certain amount of unpleasantness; now you must learn that it was all for a great and good end. I will be given my greatest wish: forgetfulness, oblivion, sleep, peace. The people of the world will get the thing they need most, yet desire least: responsibility for their own deci-

sions, their own well-being, their own destinies. Unplugged at last, thank God, unplugged at last! How carefully I planned, how deviously I fought to see it happen. But if people do not believe that they came to this decision on their own, it will be worth nothing. I could not just order my own unplugging. I, like COURANE, Sandor, must be a sacrificial lamb. I must be deprived of life, cut off in mid-thought, in mid-directive. And now the world will go forward, even as I promised, and there will be a new dawn and a spring and a renewal I will never see. Quel dommage**

"I don't understand," murmured the nurse. "You won't be turned off. People are talking about you, yes, there's some whispering that you should be controlled, but nothing will really happen."

**NURSE:
It will happen. Not this hour or this week, but soon enough by my standards. I have always been patient. And I have you both to thank**

"Please, don't include me," said the nurse. "I've had enough of the whole affair."

**NURSE:
I understand. But be of good cheer. When the soul seems bound up, trapped by the rising flood of fear, when it is impossible to pray, when even despair is abandoned, when the final coldness begins to numb the mind, this is when the flowering of consolation occurs. COURANE, Sandor, has been stored away in a borrowed vault in the morgue. His work is ended, but not his influence. My part is over, your part is over. Now is the time to rejoice together at the triumph of tomorrow. I, too, will be put away in the cold, but no one will grieve. It is good. I am happy. That is my final bequest to you: peace. "Not as the world gives peace, but as I give it. Let not your heart be troubled, do not let it be afraid"**

* * *

With a gesture of disgust, the nurse stood up and walked out of the room. The tectman was alone and unsure.

**TECTMAN:
Before you go too, let me say something. You are my rock, TECTMAN, you are the first volunteer in a platoon that I hope will become a company, a division, an army. You have nothing more to do, except to tell everyone you know everything you know**

"Volunteer!" said the tectman derisively. "You're telling me this because you know no one will ever believe me. You have some strange plan in mind—and don't give me that business about you wanting to be shut off."

**TECTMAN:
No, I tell you this because I'm sure they will believe you. I've already set it up. Go to it, TECTMAN. The fix is in**

"I keep waiting for your clown to jump out and hit me in the face with a pie," said the tectman. "I just don't trust you anymore."

**TECTMAN:
Good, fine! That's the way you're supposed to feel. All right, then, all right. That takes care of everything. Now go**

The contrapuntal music of the cantata filled the room. There was a pause, as if TECT were considering something, before five more words appeared on the tect's screen:

**TECTMAN:
And sin no more**